Joan Riley was born in St Mary~~~~~~~~~~~~~~~~~~~~~
lives in Britain. Her other novel~~~~~~~~~~~~~~
(1985), *Romance* (1988) and *A Ki~~~~~~~~~~~~*
(1992) are all published by The Women's Press.

JOAN RILEY

WAITING in the TWILIGHT

First published by The Women's Press Limited, 1987
A member of the Namara Group
34 Great Sutton Street, London EC1V 0DX

Reprinted 1992

British Library Cataloguing in Publication Data

Riley, Joan
    Waiting in the Twilight
    I. Title
    823'.914[F]   PR6068.135/

ISBN 0-7043-4023-2

Typset by AKM Associates (UK) Ltd,
Ajmal House, Hayes Road, Southall, Greater London
Reproduced, printed and bound in Great Britain by
BPCC Hazells Ltd.
Member of BPCC Ltd

This book was written to celebrate the courage and loyalty of one woman and a whole generation of women, who took ship and sailed into the unknown to build a better future for their children.

And for the sake of putting at least a small part of the record straight where the West Indian woman in Britain is concerned. To show that the tremendous act of Bravery in leaving their home countries and stepping into a society of alien values will not readily be forgotten.

To Beverley whose loss was more than of a parent in the hope that she will see the great legacy and the strength she inherited and in the years to come find that loss easier to bear.

For my sister Pauline Downie, one of the pioneering people, and to Paul. My nieces Ruth and Nicola, my children Lethna and Bayhano – a future generation of women and men, in the hope that an uneasy truce between the genders may one day flower into true partnership.

Acknowledgements

The writing of this book have been a sometimes taxing, sometimes sad, often difficult labour of love; but one which would have been harder without the practical contribution of several people.

I would like to acknowledge the endless patience of B.A.H. who was ever willing to discuss ideas and rose to the challenge of reading unrelated pages and partial chapters at short notice.

Jacqui Roach who gave critical and perceptive comments. Rhonda Cobham who read, corrected and suggested despite a tight schedule of her own. Jen Green who rose to the challenge of standardising the dialogue used and the many women who forwarded their experiences to help in the shaping of the book. For these last a special thanks, the book would have been poorer without them. And finally I would like to thank the editorial staff at the Women's Press and add that the mistakes are all mine.

One

She stared into the murky depth of the scum-ringed bucket, thinking half-heartedly that she ought to change the water. She knew she should. The contents looked revolting, grey darkness of floor dirt blending with ash from carelessly discarded cigarette butts. Adella's lips thinned as she looked at the small mound of fruit peelings, sweetwrappers and anything else that needed disposing. They used her as a mobile rubbish tip, the rust-streaked silver bucket like a magnet, attracting litter wherever it came to rest.

She cleared the litter grimly, pushing back contempt. 'Dey caan help it,' she told herself sternly, repeating the words like a lifeline as she tipped the bucket's contents into the toilet, taking care to keep well away from the soiled and crusted bowl.

Leaning heavily against the mop, she looked back at the expanse of floor she had just cleaned and shook her head in resignation at the muddy footmarks that followed her across the wet grey tiles. 'Dey doan care how hard a haffe work,' she thought bitterly, reaching into the pocket of her striped blue overall for the cigarettes she always kept there. She would have to do that hall again and again. That was how it always was in winter. Lighting the tip of the cigarette, she inhaled deeply, leaning back against the wall. The smoke relaxed her and she thought idly of telling them to wipe their feet before coming in, dismissing the thought almost instantly. Some of those white boys . . . you just couldn't talk to them.

'One day,' she vowed to herself, 'one day a gwine tell dem what to do wid dem jab.' She could imagine that, a smile lightening her face as she saw the anger and disbelief she would cause. It lasted as long as the cigarette, a dream, nothing else. She would never dare to tell them anything. Where else could she work? She was lucky the people running the town hall were always talking about giving

1

work to the disabled. Not that cleaning their dirty offices was really a job. She knew they thought that was all she was good for: but she had been something once.

Straightening from the wall, she dropped the cigarette butt into the water, watching the curl of smoke as it choked off, before grasping the mop again. She would finish this end first, then go back the other way. That way she could pretend it was another floor. She was mopping again, carefully pushing the bucket along with her foot. The scraping protest it made no longer gave her the crippling ache behind her eyes that she had lived with in her first few years of cleaning. It was a slow process, good arm gripping the mop, crippled one locked round it in a steadying vice. She moved the mop head slowly across the floor, one wipe, two wipes, three. Feet braced against her heavy bulk as she swung it wide before bringing it laboriously to the murky water of the bucket: rinsing, wringing, mopping.

She had no illusion that the mop became clean but the habit was so strong it was automatic. She had done this every morning for the past ten years. Sometimes she would think bitterly of warm Caribbean sun, bus rides to the beach and the money she had earned in Kingston. To think she had left all that, for this. All her young life spent struggling to raise her children, all her old without respect. They had promised her a land where the streets were paved with gold; the Motherland where you could get everything.

'Johnson!'

The insolence ran through her and she gripped the mop tighter with her feeling hand, forcing back anger that still bubbled up after so many years. 'Thou shalt rise up before the hoary head,' she muttered under her breath, 'No wonda yu treat yu old people dem so bad.'

'Yes, mam . . .' she said aloud, turning to see a young white girl, not more than seventeen years old. Her feet had left a fresh trail of mud, and Adella's mouth thinned. This one had been working less than six months and already she had learnt how to treat the cleaning staff. Adella wanted to ask if this was how she was at home; bit back the words. Of course, this was how they all behaved: everybody knew what white people were like.

'I hope you emptied the ashtrays this morning,' the girl said coldly. 'We had to do them ourselves for the last three days and I certainly don't get paid to be a cleaner.'

Adella kept the mop moving, once, twice, three times across the

2

floor. She was not going to let this child anger her, was not going to forget her need for this job. She rinsed the mop deliberately, returned it to the floor, mopping again with even strokes. She had to keep her temper if she was going to keep her dignity.

'You listening to me, Johnson?'

'Yes, mam,' Adella answered sourly, keeping the mop moving with determination. How different England was. She could remember being a young girl, going to Kingston. Always you had to respect the older heads. Scraps of memory passed through her head as the mop moved. Schooldays reciting little gems, sitting under the spreading branch of the big mango tree, its fruits useless, riddled through by the ever-present worms. Doing things she thought were the same the world over. The saying was in her mind again: 'Thou shalt rise up before the hoary head, and honour the face of the old man and fear thy god.' Funny how in England these things didn't matter. All those years of studying how to be good and Christian, listening to the white baptist minister and praying to the white god. How she had wanted to come to England where the white people lived. Now she was here, had found out too late that it was only in the islands that respect for the old existed.

'Johnson!' Adella almost jumped at the impatience in the voice. She thought the girl had gone; but she was standing there, red spots on her cheeks showing her growing anger. 'Don't ignore me when I talk to you, or I shall report you to your supervisor.'

Adella straightened carefully, eyes blank and shadowed with weariness as she stared into the petulant face. 'Yes, Mam,' she said patiently, hiding the hard anger growing inside her with the ease of long practice.

The young girl looked stern, sighing in imitation of her older superiors. 'I want you to go and empty the ashtrays. Now. You people are so lazy,' she added, shaking her head before walking away in a trail of mud.

'Who say slavery dead?' Adella muttered, as she dropped the mop into the bucket. If only she had not had the stroke, if only she had stayed in Jamaica. Stanton would still be with her and she would not have had to work like this to keep her dignity.

It took a long time to clean the ashtrays. Everyone who worked at social security seemed to smoke. If they didn't when they started, it did not take long for the stresses of the job to drive them to it. Adella straightened wearily, trying to relieve the ache in the small of her back after replacing the last ashtray. Already she could see them filling up again. It was the same thing every day. Useless to tell them she too was entitled to a morning break. It was at times like these, when her bones ached and the weight of her body hung heavy, that she hoped the new people at the town hall really meant to retire everyone over fifty-eight. She could stay home, work in her garden, and her daughters said she would get more money from the pension and the disability allowance than she was taking home from the two-shift cleaning. It would be nice not to have to listen to the rudeness of the young ones coming up. Not to have the constant fear of getting sacked. The horror of standing out there on the other side of the counter that she had cleaned these past ten years. She could not lose her pride, become like brother Winston who had taken to drink and lost his job when his wife left him, same as her Stanton did. Glancing at the big clock on the wall she was relieved to see that it was after eleven, and she gathered her polish and cloth eagerly. It was time to finish, to go home to the silence of her house, the dog and the cat; to rest her bones before the afternoon shift.

Today she was too tired to stand around and chat, and she smiled politely as Mrs Julie pushed round the door of the small storeroom in a clatter of mop, bucket and dustpan. She liked Mrs Julie but that woman had a mouth that could run. Start her talking and she couldn't stop. Yes Miss Julie was really mouth a massi bad. Mrs Julie ignored Adella's discouraging silence and launched into eager conversation.

'Miss Johnson, how yu do? A see de way de white chile treat yu. My dear, it couldn't happen back home.'

Adella nodded as the woman sank down on one of the two worn stools in the small room. Mrs Julie was a thin woman in her early fifties who had spent most of her life looking after somebody. First there had been a sick mother, then it had been a husband who had suffered from high blood pressure for as long as Adella knew him. Mrs Julie had few friends and Adella tried to be patient with her constant talking. She supposed it was because Mrs Julie had no children, secretly she thought that was also why she was so thin and withered, so old before her time.

Adella finished buttoning up her blue canvas coat, and took her white hat off the peg it was hanging on. 'A sorry, Miss Julie, but a pramis Caral dat a would feed de dog.' It was a feeble excuse, but the best she could do on such short notice. She had been hoping to get out before the other woman caught her.

4

Mrs Julie looked disappointed, her eyes saying clearly that she knew Adella wanted to get away from her: but she smiled with her usual cheerfulness. 'A was saying to Boysie dat we haffe come visit you, especially as he feeling much better wid de new drug.'

Adella agreed without enthusiasm. If the woman could talk in the limited time she had at work it was nothing compared with what she did when her belly was full with a warm meal and her tongue loosened by a little white rum.

'Tell Lisa a gone,' she said instead, jamming the white hat on her head, 'tell her a see her evening time like usual.'

Adella preferred the evenings. She and Lisa would pair up and work together. Once the day workers were gone and the place was silent they would have a good gossip, swap stories about the goings on in their streets and in the marketplace and complain about the tribulations of the day just past.

Lisa was her greatest friend. They had met on the boat coming over to England and had remained close in the thirty years they had known each other. It was Lisa who had introduced her to Noel, so different from Stanton; Noel, who had played the trumpet and looked so handsome in his batwing bowtie. It was Lisa she had gone to when she realised the consequence of the one night with Noel as the ship steamed through warm Caribbean waters. Lisa had explained to Stanton, turned his anger into resignation. And later, when Stanton was stolen by her faithless cousin Gladys, Lisa had been there, helping with the children: keeping her together. She wondered how she would have survived the stroke if Lisa had not been around to take the pressure of the children from her shoulders and to help her pick up the pieces and find another job.

The wind blew icily against the thin canvas coat as she let herself out into the grey January day. It found all the holes and patches; pouring in through her clothes, only slightly blocked by the tightly laced full girdle she had worn since Carol was born. Adella walked briskly, bad leg dragging only slightly after years of treatment and exercise. Her crippled hand swung limp at her side, fingers clamped like a vice round her purse. After losing her wages time after time, watching her purse snatched by the nimble-footed bag snatchers, she had learnt to cope. Now she used her crippled hand. Willed the fingers to close. She knew they could feel no pain, that only willpower could force them open again. The market was full of bustle as she approached it, looking cheerful and inviting under the yellow glow of artificial lights. But today she skirted it, not feeling in the mood to stop and talk with one of the many people she was bound to know. Tomorrow was another day. Today she just wanted the warmth and quiet of her house.

A watery sunshine struggled through the dense greyness of winter clouds. It touched briefly on the cracked, dirt-streaked, uneven pavement before drowning in the mud of the sprawling, untidy estate, where a planning error by the council caused the paving to run the wrong way. The pathways were a litter of stones, grown mouldy with the constant rain of winter, and big muddy gaps where no stones had ever been laid. Adella huddled further into her blue canvas coat as the weak rays of sunlight receded before the gloom of early afternoon. She braced herself for the wind that always waited just outside the shelter of the brick-built corridors of the estate. Taking a deep breath she plunged forward into the last cold stretch that stood between her and the warmth and comfort of her house.

The wind hit her as she turned into the gloomy street, pushing icy fingers down her neck and through gaps where buttons had fallen from her coat. It cut like a knife as she turned the final unprotected corner. Her feet quickened in response, matching the steps of other scurrying people fleeing from the biting cold. Her good hand, raised instinctively, clutched firmly at the soft whiteness of the simulated fur hat on her head. It was her pride and joy, washed separately every Saturday, then spread on an upturned plastic basin to dry. She could feel the cold seeping into her shoes, through the places where the plastic had split and the stitching had unravelled at the seams; and she tried to move her lame foot faster, wishing that her only comfortable shoes were not so split and broken.

She was shivering with cold by the time she struggled up the fenced-off stairs that led to her door. Fingers stiff and numb as they fumbled to get the keys from the purse clutched in her crippled hand. She could hear muffled thuds and the sound of excited barking as the dog hurled himself at the door. Adella smiled, her tiredness forgotten for a moment as the door opened on a wave of animal and warmth. She stumbled gratefully forward, pushing aside the dog, who was tangling with her feet. 'Move noh, man,' she said impatiently, pushing her way through, too tired from the morning to do more than seek her little room. Her breathing was heavy from the wind and the steep climb to the door, and all she

6

wanted was to sit, to rest for a while in the warmth and the peace. Struggling out of her coat, she moved heavily to her favourite chair, sinking into its waiting warmth with relief. Almost without thinking she reached for the remote-control box on the small table beside her, pressing the button that flooded the room with flickering colours and sound.

Adella settled comfortably in her chair, pushing out the sound of the dog and cat moving restlessly around the room. Closing her eyes she allowed the softness of the warm semi-dark room to soothe her. This was her place where she could wait and rest. She liked the gloom that filled its corners, softening its outline both summer and winter. The way it stayed the same, with a constancy she once thought life had. It was such a long time since those days. Days when she had longed for experience like Mada Beck; when she had wanted to leave Beaumont to make her fortune in the city. A sad smile slipped across the lined black face, as she remembered Mada Beck. The day the old woman had died had changed her life for ever.

Her mind drifted, shifted and skirted from one year to another, one problem to another, touched briefly on never-ending work, bills, countless insults. But still Mada Beck intruded. She had died at such a strange time, in the middle of the ackee season, the last season Adella was to spend in the yard where she was born. She remembered it so well. Days spent hating the women's work she was forced to do. Too old to do the things she wanted, too young to be a woman. She had left school at the beginning of the season, gone instead to sewing classes at her auntie's house. She would sit with the other girls, under her auntie's Bombay mango tree, perched precariously on an upturned water can, whispering of boys and what they would do when they were truly women. On the day Mada Beck died, no one came to see her in the yard she shared with her parents and grandmother. The pan of ackee she was cleaning seemed heavy and too full. She had been at it for what seemed like hours and had barely made a dent in the red-skinned fruits. She hated ackee season, especially when it was her turn to run practised eyes along the laden branches; select the ripened fruit burst open to reveal seed-weighted yellow segments and bring it down with an expert twist of the hook-tipped bamboo stick. She had sat listening to the wind blowing through the branches of the high trees with a noise like shifting sand. It was hard to believe that she had once enjoyed the ackee season. Had waited impatiently,

7

season after season, standing tall against the white-painted measuring wall. Her grandmother would make the mark that would one day tell her she could take her turn with the ackee stick.

Adella sighed, snuggling further into her chair. How important the ackee season had seemed to her then. That was the last season she had spent at home and she left before it even ended, all because of Mada Beck's death. It was eight years after she had finally been allowed to lift the ackee stick and by then the magic had long gone out of the task.

The day Mada Beck died was one of those strange days, hot and still. Heat swirled beneath the shade of the sheltering branches. Air still with the promise of thunder, sky laden with the need to rain. That day, the constant scratching and clucking of the scavenging hens got on her nerves. She was irritated by the way they lurked under the veranda stairs. Occasionally they would rush forward in a flurry of fighting feathers to snatch the fat cockroaches, crushed and swept out with the dust and fallen leaves. On snappish days like those she had almost hated the red-streaked green hill country that was the only place she had known.

Adella felt the sadness move through her tired bones, the old loss that she had felt when Mada Beck had died. She would always remember the old woman sitting on the high veranda of the stilt-raised, yellow-painted wooden house. It had always been a place of mystery, halfway up the red-streaked hill, the only house at the end of the donkey track. It stood, bright and alone, guarded by soursop trees and high tall coconut palms. Mada Beck had been so wise, and Adella wondered if she had looked ahead and seen approaching death. The thought brought heaviness inside her. Would she see approaching death, would she recognise it? Die with dignity like Mada Beck? 'All dat respeck,' she sighed, in remembrance and regret. Everyone had looked up to that woman, loved her for her age. But then she had died in her own place and among her people.

She shook off the sadness of the mood. She couldn't think about death now. Soon she would have to feed the dog, get some food, rest her back before going back to work. It was such a long day, two-shift cleaning. It was hardest in the winter. Days like today when the gloom and the cold were pierced through with icy winds. It stung her cheeks, made her eyes water behind her glasses and burned the fingers of her good hand.

Night found Adella back in her room, in her chair, the sound of the

8

television underlaid by silence. Once in a while she shifted, half-lifted from the sucking comfort of the enclosing foam, only to give up the unequal struggle. The garish colours from the television cast flickering shadows that created endlessly dissolving shapes on the wall. A faint wind lifted the curtains at the high square windows and Adella glanced over at them, mouth tightening. Light from the street penetrated faintly through the winter grime of the windows and filtered through the curtains.

The colours on the television changed, dissolved, and were replaced by the faded brown of a black and white film. Adella settled back comfortably, good hand going to the packet of cigarettes on the table. She extracted one and placed it in her mouth before fumbling for the lighter, eyes never leaving the screen as she did so. The lighter flickered once, twice, and Adella sighed, shifting her eyes at last as it stubbornly refused to catch. 'One day it gwine light first time,' she muttered in irritation as the flame finally spluttered into life. She inhaled deeply, going off into a fit of coughing that left her eyes streaming and her lungs raw and sore.

Light spilt into the room, breaking up and dispelling the gloom. Adella looked up impatiently, rubbing her eyes as much from the sudden brightness as from the coughing.

'Tun de light off, man,' she snapped. 'How much time a haffe tell yu, a doan like light when a watching Jahn Wayne?' The woman who walked in was tall and stout, her round face an unlined copy of the woman in the chair. She shook her head impatiently, crossing the room with quick steps to draw the heavy winter curtains across the wide windows.

'Mum, you know the doctor said you have to give up smoking,' the woman said, ignoring Adella's annoyance.

Adella hissed air through closed teeth. 'Cho, Caral, noh badda me. A haffe get lickle pleasure. Cigarette and a lickle white rum is all a have. A haffe die sometime, an if a caan have dis pleasure it might as well be now.'

The woman shifted uncomfortably, her brow creased by anxiety, as gunshots from the television tore Adella's attention away.

'Don't talk like that, mum,' she said reproachfully, bringing Adella's attention reluctantly away from the excitement on the screen. 'We were all talking about getting together and sending you back to Jamaica so you can live with Aunt Claudia.'

The words cut across her irritation, and she hid a sudden surge of warmth, the pride she felt in this her youngest child. Of all the six,

Danny and Mikey, Beresford's sons; Delores born in Kingston, Eena, Audrey and Carol, she loved this one the best. Carol would never let her down, not like the others. She wondered if she should tell her about Jamaica, why she could never go back there to live. The words formed in her head, were on her tongue. But she hesitated, pride rearing up to stop her. How could she tell her secret to this child? She could never understand. All she knew about was England and she was too young to burden anyway.

'Yu know a caan go leave you children,' she said instead. 'A haffe stay in Ingland long as oonu deh ya.'

Carol opened her mouth to argue but Adella cut her off. She had heard all they had to say, listened as they repeated it over and over again. But they didn't know back home. They could never understand why she was stuck in this council house till the day she died.

'A doan waan hear no more,' she added as her daughter looked set to argue. 'A told yu a watching Jahn Wayne an yu mek me miss plenty already.'

The woman gave a resigned shrug before walking over to turn off the light. She hesitated there for a moment, before moving quietly through the sliding doors.

Adella had lost the thread of the film, her hero suddenly boring; her mind sliding back to thoughts of her children. It was the boys she had done worst by. Mikey was all right she supposed; but he had never been the same since she had brought him over to England. He had a good job though, driving the tube train. If only he would stop smoking the ganja. She worried about him and the ganja. One day they would catch him, they always did. The way they stopped the black boys on the street, it was bound to happen. Then he would lose his job, and what would happen to him? She sighed heavily. Mikey always looked out for her; helped her out with money when he had any. If only she had done more for him. If only Stanton would come back, she thought unhappily, Stanton would know what to do, how to talk to him. She felt the failure weigh her down, rest heavily on her shoulders, pressing harder as her mind moved to her other son. Danny, still waiting in Kingston and she too much a coward to tell him it was far too late to send for him. Thirty-three he would be this year. Fifteen years since time ran out. Fifteen years in which she could not find the courage to tell him she had failed him. If only Stanton had stayed, she would have found the money on time. She had to bring up five of them alone

10

and with the stroke and all . . . Her mind tailed off. It wasn't Stanton's fault, she told herself stoutly, he did love her. But five children and a crippled woman and him still young and sharp. One day he would come back. He wasn't so young any more. He would come back to her and she wouldn't feel so old. It would be just like when they were in Jamaica. They would be happy together again. 'Who know,' she thought, relaxing further into the yielding foam, 'a might even go back to church.' Yes she might do that, forget her cousin's faithlessness, and Pastor Douglas's half-hearted condemnation of her sin.

That memory awakened the old pain. She had gone to church that Sunday, determined to salvage her pride. The first time out since her stroke; a chance to thank the Lord properly for delivering her from the arms of death. They had been there, the two of them. Her husband and the cousin he had brought into her house. Adella could not believe Gladys could be so barefaced. Everybody knew they had set up house together in Battersea, leaving her and five children. She had waited through the service, singing songs with a half-hearted need to be a part of the fellowship, all the time watching them. It was like a knife in her belly, the intimate touch of hands, whispered words, the shared Bible. Every movement tore at her, but she waited patiently. Waited for one of the Pastor's rousing condemnations. Not that Gladys would have cared. Adella often thought her cousin only went to church out of habit, or maybe fear. Fear that lack of church-going would be too much for god-fearing people to take. How many people had stopped talking to her when she no longer went, even though they knew her reason?

It was the deacon who had brought up the sin. Deacon Paul who could never let a backslider pass him by. Adella wondered if Pastor Douglas would have mentioned it otherwise. As it was he told them to repent; told Stanton to go home; words of banishment reluctantly forced out with a scowl. She had always suspected that Pastor Douglas was sweet on Gladys. But now she sat in stunned surprise, divorced from the congregation. A stranger in her own church. She felt no triumph at Gladys' humiliation. Knew that, come tomorrow, it was her they would talk about at the market. Already she had seen it: the sudden silences, the furtive looks. The shame burnt inside her, fed by the knowledge that she would not get her husband back.

'Mum, don't you think you should go to bed?'

The voice brought her back to the present and she looked around. The past slipped away as she blinked. Carol had turned on the light and on the screen the film credits were coming to an end. Her tired eyes rested on the woman so like herself. Felt glad once more that the youngest had not fallen into the trap of the first two daughters. Carol would never let her down. She would never have to duck her head in shame because of this one. She had tried so hard with the children, but it had been in vain. From the time she bore the first one in England, knew Stanton's anger at her lack of faithfulness, things had been going wrong. She had tried so hard from then. She said nothing when he kept the money he earned, just worked harder to pay for their room and save to bring over the three others from Jamaica. How often her eyes had hurt, sewing the fine embroidery on rich women's clothes at the factory where she worked. But it had been worth it. Stanton stayed with her, and even though she had to pay the woman to keep Eena she still managed to save. He had been good to the child then, treating her as his own and it was only when she decided to buy the house that things went wrong again.

She could remember Stanton's anger when she told him her idea.

'Where we gwine get money fe buy house, woman?' he had asked, looking suddenly less tall in his well-cut tailored trousers. 'We haffe send money home fa three pickney, we have one here and yu breeding again. Tell me where all dis money gwine come fram?' She had suppressed her disappointment in him, closed her mind to the fact that he had another new suit, when she could hardly remember the last time she bought herself any new clothes. No, it wasn't Stanton's fault that he was used to looking sharp. She couldn't expect that kind of sacrifice from him. She had felt a stab of guilt as the child inside her moved. Another baby and nowhere to put it. They could not go on living in the same one room; but nobody would give them any other place. She felt sad at the knowledge of his fear. Stanton would feel trapped by the house, like he felt trapped by the sad-faced little child and the growing roundness of her body.

'We caan stay here, honey,' she had said placatingly. 'Not wid de two children; and ow else we gwine fine space fe bring over Mikey and de other two?'

He had said nothing, just looked at her as if he wanted to hit her, take out his frustration on her. She had wished even then that they had stayed in Jamaica. She saw what it was doing to Stanton, the

12

way the white people treated him and sometimes she wished there was something she could do. She knew better than to mention it. One thing Stanton had was pride. He would never forgive her for noticing that he was afraid of the white man outside the door.

'Mum, are you going to bed or not?'

Adella shook off the memories, focusing on her daughter standing impatiently in front of her chair.

'Help me get up,' she said briskly, extending her hands to the woman, ignoring her impatience. She knew Carol was waiting to unlace her from her girdle, that she was in a hurry to go somewhere, and she felt suddenly alone. Even Carol had no time for her. Always rushing out somewhere. Sometimes she wanted to ask her if she could come, the words bubbling on her tongue. But always she would hold back. The young didn't have time for old people any more. She was lucky that one of her children stayed with her.

In bed, the memories remained. Stanton, the house, the children, all the worries of England. She shifted, closed her eyes, tried to think of other things to blot out the picture of him, still vivid after over twenty years. She lay still, trying to make out shapes in the dark room, emptying her mind, pushing out the bitterness. But the images came back, Danny, left in Jamaica, the house they had taken from her. Nobody knew what that had done. They had pulled the heart out of her when they took her house.

Two

The row of houses soared high on either side of the street, testifying to a long-past glory. There was something dark and dismal about them as they clawed their way towards the brilliant blue of the summer sky. Adella had never seen anything so big, so gloomy. Three storeys with cellar and attic, the advert had said. She had looked at the area, had known it would be one of these. She had never been on Eldridge Road before, but it was like any other road in that decaying part of Brixton. 'Dese places older dan Granny Dee,' she thought with distaste, bitterness creeping into her. All those houses for sale in the papers, neat rows of them filling page after page. How could this one cost so much? She looked pleadingly at Stanton, edging closer to him.

'But dis ting no gwine fall dung?' she whispered unhappily.

Stanton moved away, adjusting his bowtie before throwing her a bitter glance. 'Dis ting was yu idea, a doan waan hear bout it,' he muttered in irritation.

Adella pushed down sudden bitterness. 'A know yu tink a wastin de money, but wa yu waan it fa?' she asked angrily. 'Is me did earn it. Jesas, Stanton, yu can ongly wear one new suit a time. Yu know why de house important.'

He hissed through his teeth, giving her a cutting look. Adella shrugged; they had argued about this so much since she started looking for the house. Resentment grew inside her. All those months and years of going without, working overtime, saving yet having to find money to send home for the children's keep. He earned much more than she, yet what he gave her didn't even cover the food he ate. Now he was standing there angry, because she would not let him lay claim to what she had. How many arguments had she listened to, saying nothing as he tried to force her to hand the money over to him. He insisted it was his right as a husband, but she knew she had to hold out for the children's sake. Not that

14

she blamed him for his fears, but the children had to come first.

The plump, grey-suited man from the estate agent's office touched her arm, his face red and glowing from the day's heat and his effort at sincerity. Adella looked at her husband, willing him to say something, to assert himself before the other man. Stanton's mouth drooped petulantly, hands jammed into the pockets of yet another new pair of trousers.

'How it cost so much?' she asked finally, realising that she would get no help from him. The estate agent thrust his head forward, looking surprised. Adella stepped back hastily as the sweat running down his face threatened to drip and splash. The grey eyes watching her narrowed, shifted slightly while the smile wavered at the corners. She braced herself for the talk down ways she had come to expect from white people. One thing she had learnt since coming over was that the English looked down on foreigners. It was because of that, that she was determined to get on, to become a success. She was determined to build a better life for the children. The ones back home would get treated like the people coming over to work, there wasn't much she could do about that. But her England-born children would be different. They were going to be just like white people. They were going to be accepted.

The man had been casting about for an answer to her question and now his eyes lit up. The mouth extended wider, lips disappearing again into the dazzle of a smile.

'As you can see, madam, it is a *big* house,' he said happily. 'The potential is enormous. And the space . . .' he tailed off, clutching his file of papers to him as if he could not adequately express the full potential of the place.

Adella gave him a grim smile. She could see the potential all right. That thing was so old, she was sure it would collapse on them if they closed the door too hard.

'Dis house look tumbledung,' she said accusingly. 'How come other one dem soun so better but still cheaper?'

'But *are* they better?' the man asked, holding up a finger and arching a brow for emphasis. 'Mrs Johnson, I give you my word that you won't get a bigger place.'

As he spoke he looked significantly at her stomach. Adella spread her hands protectively across the swelling evidence of the new child. She wished Stanton would say something. If only he would stop standing there looking like an idiot and be the man he was always boasting he was.

15

'Why we caan see one a de other houses?' she persisted.

The man laughed uneasily, loosening his tie, as though it was suddenly too tight. 'Look, Mrs Johnson, most of those houses, well . . . they sell so fast. Many of them are gone before they even reach the papers.'

Adella knew he was lying, even without the evidence of shifting eyes and increased perspiration. Some of those houses appeared week after week. She had even taken a bus-ride up to the hill to look at some of them. They were nice, those houses. Well painted with neat gardens and pretty gates – those were the sort of houses she had dreamt of owning, *not* this broken-down, half-dead place in the middle of a rotting street.

'What about de one dem dat don't sell?' she insisted, probing at him even while knowing the answer for herself. She wanted to make him uncomfortable, to get back at him for the destruction of her hopes.

The man moved uneasily, the ready smile fading from the red face, replaced by embarrassment. 'I am afraid some people are funny about just who they sell their houses to,' he muttered apologetically.

She felt her mouth tighten at the evasive answer. Knew what he was really trying to say and she wanted to force him to admit that it was because she was black.

'Adella, leave de man alone nuh! Nuting wrong wid dis house.' Stanton's hand snaked around her arm as he spoke, clamping down like a vice. Adella felt anger rise as the estate agent lost his harassed air and turned eagerly to her husband, grabbing his words like a lifeline.

'As I was saying, Mr Johnson, it has great potential, and I can see that you are discerning enough to have seen it for yourself.'

Stanton nodded, pulling himself to his full height at the flattery.

'With the space this place has got,' continued the agent, pressing home his advantage, 'you would never have to worry about moving, when your family starts expanding.'

'But yu wouldn't live inna it yuself?' Adella interrupted impatiently.

The man seemed uneasy, seeing the sale slip away again. 'Me?' he asked in confusion, looking annoyed and upset. 'Well . . . the truth is . . . I mean, I just wouldn't fit into this kind of community. That is to say . . .'

'A know what yu mean,' she said sourly.

16

Stanton's fingers pinched into her arm. 'Leave de man noh,' he hissed bad-temperedly, 'ihm ongly doing ihm jab. Why yu waan trouble ihm?'

Adella ignored him, forcing herself to endure the pain in her arm. 'A waan to see de inside,' she said with determination. 'A not gwine mek no decision til a look pan de inside room dem.'

The man looked even more put out. 'You must realise that it isn't in the best decorative order,' he said hastily, fumbling in his slim case for the keys, tongue darting out like a nervous lizard. 'You have to look at it from the point of view of its potential. A little paint here and there will soon have it looking great.'

Adella could see he was trying to buy time. It was there in the careful way he zipped up the case. The nervous way he tidied the papers in his hands, and the drag in his feet as he climbed hesitantly up the stairs to the front door. She liked his nervousness, the way he fumbled the keys; first inserting the wrong one, and then dropping the bunch in his embarrassment. Stanton let go her arm abruptly, as the keys clattered on to the stone stairs with a hollow ring. He hurried forward, half-running up the stairs to pick up the keys for the agent. Adella felt sick as she watched the deference in his face; his apologetic smile as he waited for the big door to swing open.

After the vivid brightness of summer sunshine, the house was dark and uninviting. Adella felt the dampness of the place fold around her and seep into her clothes. She moved hesitantly, hands stretched forward, automatically groping in her sun blindness. Her fingers met solid wall, slid into furry coat of spongy dampness. She recoiled, snatching her hand away in horror. The smell of junjo rose to her nose, disturbed by her touch and sudden movement. She had to breathe deeply to steady her nerves, the stale musty air making her uncomfortable. It was like a bad dream and she peered around suspiciously, half-expecting to glimpse something rotting in a hidden corner.

'Yu caan tun de light on mek we see?' she asked suspiciously, only able to make out the vague outline of the two men after minutes in the gloom. Adella pressed closer to her husband, feeling rejected and alone when he moved away.

'I'm afraid I can't use the lights,' the agent was saying, 'not allowed, you know.'

She wondered who didn't allow it. His boss maybe. Not that she blamed them. If she was trying to pawn off something half-dead like this, she would leave the light off too. She supposed it wasn't really the agent's fault. Nobody would want to do what he was doing to them.

'Careful how you go,' he said, as he started to lead the way down the long dark passage towards the faint crack of light coming from the outline of a door. 'Some of the floorboards are a bit uneven; so if you use your hands to feel your way it will be safer.'

Adella ignored him. She was not going to put her hand on that furry fungus-smelling thing again.

The room was big with a high ceiling. Light filtered through the dust of long, wide windows bringing none of the warmth from outside. It was as cold as the passage, and she could see the mildew and junjo growing off the walls.

'But dis place damp,' she said.

'No problem, madam, it happens sometimes, you know,' the agent confided, eyes wide with false sincerity.

Adella felt irritation grow inside her and forced back a rude retort. She supposed it *was* a big place. Visions of the one room they lived in, the arguments, the strain, came to her as she followed the man from the room. The house was on three floors, and it seemed to her that the higher she went the more damp it got. She could feel it wrapping around her, getting into her mouth, her nose, down her throat.

'It's been empty a long time,' the agent spoke defensively into the silence. 'It gets a bit like this, when that happens what with the rain we have been having and all. What it needs is a little heat . . .'

A sharp crack interrupted his flow, and Adella saw him lurch sideways, foot disappearing into the stair he had just shifted his weight to. For a moment she stood in stunned surprise, before the meaning of the noise dawned on her.

'De stairs dem rotten,' she said accusingly, standing where she was. The man's look of surprise and anger could just be seen in the grey light from an open door above them. His mouth slackened with the beginnings of panic as he swung down on to the next stair, wincing as the trapped foot twisted in the confined space. He tugged at it in alarm.

'What's the matter with you,' he asked accusingly, 'can't you see me bloody foot's stuck?'

Stanton pushed past, unbalancing her, and she grabbed at the banister to steady herself, looking at her husband in surprise. She wondered if they realised how stupid they looked. Two grown men,

18

one sitting, one bending, pulling away in near panic. The foot came out in a protesting creak of rotten wood; drowned by the noise of the shoe as it came off and bounced on the bare wooden stairs underneath. The men went sprawling in a heap. Adella choked back laughter, her disappointment in the house briefly forgotten. Wait till she told Lisa and Bess about this.

Stanton stood up brushing furiously at the seat of his pants and the arms of his jacket. The look he gave her told her that he blamed her for what had happened to his new clothes. He pushed past her, taking the stairs two at a time in his anger and haste.

The slam of the front door drifted faintly up the stairs and the man looked at her impatiently, his face a pale ball in the gloom.

'You've seen enough to make up your mind,' he said resentfully.

Adella felt the humour drain out of her as the problem of the house resurfaced. She knew it was a mess, that the asking price was too much. But they could not stay in that one room. How could five of them fit into such a small space? Already the two children seemed to be under her feet from the moment she picked them up from the minder to the moment she went to work the next day. It was too much. What other choice did she have? Every morning trying to dress herself and them, giving Stanton space, seeing his impatience as they cried while she was dressing and feeding them. Damp nappies dripping from recent wash, taking out the precious hot straightening from her freshly curled head. And all the time the children were getting bigger, more demanding. It was bad with two; it would be impossible with three. She was always so tired by the time she got to work. Felt old and burdened as she bent almost double over the fine stitches of the embroidery. Her eyes ached from lack of sleep and the dim light in the room. At times it seemed to her that there was only gloom in the buildings in England. It was strange, having to keep the electric light on even in the middle of a summer's day.

She could feel the man's impatient eyes on her, dragging her back to the present, and she turned deliberately, moving slowly down the stairs. She knew her money could buy a better place. She had saved, more, much more than the deposit they were asking for on other places, could even borrow money from the bank. Every week she had thrown a partner with her friends, every week for the five years she had been in England. It was a lot of money that now it was her turn to draw it out. She had seen some of the houses other people had bought. Mass Sam and Miss Jem in the place where the roof caved in. Mr Ivan with no bathroom or toilet; and she had been sure she could find a better place. She had blamed it on their ignorance, the fact that they had lived in wooden houses back home; not the brick house that had been her father's pride.

As she walked gingerly down the stairs she thought about her father's house. It was so light, so nice and cool inside. The lacy patterned brick that enclosed the red-polished veranda was always white. Freshly coated with lime it was bright against the lush green vegetation and the red dirt road. Her father was well respected in Beaumont; he had worked hard and bought land, a lot of land. Her mother was a fine dressmaker, and they were comfortable. People looked up to them, asked their advice. They were the envy of the yard. All the children went to school, and her sister Claudia had even gone to Kingston college to train to be a teacher. She felt tears burn at the back of her eyes as she thought of home. If only the money could stretch some more; if only they had saved enough. The child inside her shifted, kicked out, then was still and her heart was heavy with the thought of it. Another child. They could never school them all back home, not if they saved for years. School in Jamaica was too much money. No, they would have to stay in England, till all the children were grown.

She paused at the bottom of the stairs waiting for the agent to catch up with her, ignoring his heavy silence of anticipation. She did not want to see the red and shiny face. The round plumpness of good living and too much beer.

Following him into the sunshine, she paused at the top of the steep entrance stairs, dazzled by the sudden brightness of the sun after the darkness inside. She felt the warmth seep into her bones and push the depression and despair away a little. It was always like that in England, if the sun shone things were never as bad as when it rained. Walking down the stairs, she turned, shading her eyes to look at the steeply rising building. At least it has a lot of rooms, she told herself. We could let some out; get some extra money. I could even invite Mama and Papa to come. Thoughts of her family dampened her spirit. How was she going to tell them of this house?

When her time came to draw money, she had been so excited by the amount, by the thought of her own house: she had written and told them all. Mama and Papa, Granny Dee, Aunts Silvie and Ivy, and even Juni. She had told them how they could save up and come to England for a holiday. They wouldn't have to worry about a place to stay because she was getting a house and there would be lots of room for everyone. Adella shook her head, this was no place for invited guests.

'Doan tell me yu gwine say no.' Stanton had come up behind her unnoticed, and impatience showed in his words. 'Dis is ten house now yu look at. If yu not gwine tek it, doan expect me to come look pan no more house. A have better tings to do wid my time. And if yu waan know what a tink, if yu doan waan buy house, just gi me de money mek me do someting useful wid it.'

She bit back her annoyance, moving a little away from him. Stanton was such a disappointment sometimes; and she wondered if they wouldn't have been better off staying in Jamaica. He had been good to her then, not leaving everything – all the planning, all the decisions – on her shoulders. Now she had to make the choice, this house, or the one room where they lived. She supposed he was right. They wouldn't show her anywhere different. She might as well get this one. After all it was the biggest one she had seen, even if it was no place for invited guests. Other people, West Indians with nowhere to live, relatives, coming up to look for work, they could come. They would probably be glad of a place to stay, and who knows, one day, one day she might be able to buy a proper house. Right now this was the only choice she had.

'Can I take it you are interested?' the agent asked.

Adella clutched her bag tightly, conscious of Stanton staring at her with bitter aggression, daring her to say no, after all he had been through. 'A interested, but a haffe tink about it,' she said, knowing that he sensed acceptance, yet needing to save her pride.

'When can you let us know?' the man pressed on. 'If I knew you were definitely interested, I could put a hold on it. Take it off the list, you know.'

Who he trying to fool? she thought resentfully, nobody was going to line up to buy this thing. She was not going to let him push her. She looked him up and down; seeing the dust streak against the shiny red cheek, the dirt stain on the trousers, and the scuff marks on the shoe he had recovered before following her down the stairs. Suddenly he wasn't so impressive; and she felt a surge of irritation, when Stanton came back up the stairs.

'We'll tek it,' he said, looking apologetically at the man, before glaring at her.

Adella flashed him a cold look. 'Is me money and a tink we should consider tings a bit before we sey anyting. We will get in

21

touch like ihm say,' she finished, turning to the man; catching the hope fading from the light eyes.

'Very well,' he said. 'I'll wait for your call. Now, if that is all I can do for you . . . ?'

'Yes, dat is everyting, tank yu,' Adella said quickly, heading Stanton off as she saw the anger in his face. She knew that he was burning up at what he saw as her humiliation of him, knew that she would hear more about it as soon as they got back to the room. She was glad that she had to collect the children from Lisa. That he never came round to her friend's room. At least it would give him time to calm down; give her time to think of a way to soothe him. Stanton was all right really, just that England did not agree with him. He was always good to her when she didn't raise the devil in him.

Three

He was waiting for her when she got home with the children and her heart sank when she saw the frown on his face. She glanced furtively at him as she closed the door; and then busied herself, unstrapping the youngest child from the pushchair, before lifting her carefully on to the bed.

'Eena, get on de bed and play wid yu sister,' she said to the elder child. The little girl looked at her with solemn eyes before clambering on to the big double bed; and Adella felt the tears behind her eyes. It was wrong that the child should be so quiet, so sad-eyed. She was only four, and already the living in one room, the listening to the fights and her father's impatience was telling on her. One thing she knew: for the children's sake they had to move, and soon.

'Adella, why yu mek me look so fool in front a dat white man today?'

Adella glanced anxiously at the children huddled together on the bed, big brown eyes staring at them with worry and wisdom far beyond their age.

'Stanton, not now man,' she said gently, 'not in front a de children dem.' She paused, looked at him pleadingly. 'Yu know how much a respeck yu, dat a would neva do nuting to disrespeck yu in front a anyone. Is just dat a did feel real bad bout de house.'

The frown stayed on his face, and she knew it wasn't going to be easy to soft-talk him this time.

'A tell yu what,' she said now, pulling out her trump card. 'A did buy yu a sweet piece a mutton. Mek me jus put de children dem to bed a a gwine cook it nice fa yu. Dem eat already so is just to bathe dem an put dem dung.'

His ace cleared a little, and she had to suppress a sudden bitterness. It never failed; give him something that they could ill afford. Feed him and flatter him. Granny Dee always said that men were fools, and right now, seeing how easily he had been seduced by the meat, she wondered if it wasn't true.

She pushed the thought aside impatiently as she walked over to the little girls. Stanton was bright, he had been a carpenter in Jamaica and it was only because there was no jobs like that for black men in England that he had to work on the buses. In spite of that he always looked so neat, so sharp in his driver's uniform.

She was not looking forward to cooking up that meat, had only bought it just in case. Thank God it was Saturday and tomorrow was the Lord's day. She had only worked half-day today, but her back ached and her head felt as if it would split. All she wanted to do was rest, take the strain off herself; and she hoped he would go to one of the many parties he always had invitations for.

Her body was heavy as she moved about the room, weighed down by the coming child and the long, hard hours of work. At times like these she envied her friend. Lisa had left her husband back home, come up to train as a nurse before deciding that the long hours and rudeness of the white patients were not for her. Lisa had left her two children with her grandmother, and Adella knew that it would be a long time before she sent for them. 'Girl, a like me freedom,' her friend often said. 'A doan see why a should burden meself and work like donkey de way yu do.'

'But yu mus miss yu husband and de pickney dem,' Adella asked once.

Lisa had laughed, throwing back her head to expose the strong column of her neck. It was a deep full laugh, vital, full of zest for life. 'Of course a miss de children, but, chile, a can do better fa dem if dey stay wid me mada till a find a place dat a want. Nobady gwine pawn off no bruckdung place pan me jus tru dem know a desperate.' Adella had smiled at that; secretly envying her friend that freedom, the way she could do whatever she liked, and face the consequence without fear. Lisa was so free, doing whatever she wanted; yet always sending money home for her parents and her children.

'But what about yu husband?' Adella had asked curiously another day.

Lisa had snorted. 'Ihm,' she said. 'Listen, girl, if a wait fa ihm, a would breed every year, and me an de pickney dem would starve. But a tell yu dis, if dat goodfanuting man eva come ya like ihm treaten a would bring ova de pickney dem fore yu could sey baps.' She had said it half-jokingly; but Adella had seen the serious glint in her eyes and knew that she meant it. She had not pressed her to explain. The thing that made them such good friends was mutual respect for privacy. It was all right to gossip about everyone else, to talk about the way they ran their lives, and all the things they did wrong; but that was not the way of friends. What Lisa wanted her to know she told her, and everything else was not her business.

The sounds of Stanton moving about the room, getting ready for an evening out, filtered into her thoughts. Adella breathed in relief when he got his towel and shaving kit and muttered about having a bath. She knew the routine of getting the children ready for bed irritated him. He always made an excuse to be somewhere else; and she was glad of the breathing space.

The house was as cold and damp as she remembered when they finally moved in. But Adella had learnt to like it. It was her own place; somewhere to bring her child into the world. No more landlord to come knocking on the door when Stanton was out; no more living four of them to the one room. She smiled when she remembered Mr Thomas' face.

'Yu leaving?' he had asked, stunned, when she had paid him the last rent a week before. 'Ow come yu neva tell me yu was tinking bout buying a place? A could even a help yu.'

Adella had hidden her distaste, handing the man the rent-book with the five pounds carefully folded inside. She did not like Mr Thomas; the way he hung around the women in the house; the oily smile always on his face. There was no privacy with this man, and the word was that he had more than once interfered with a female tenant.

24

Adella had disliked him from the start, the way he looked slyly from the corners of the narrow red eyes, almost lost in the folds of fat on his greasy brown face. She hated the way his shirt gaped open at the front where the strain of holding in his belly proved too much. But it was not until the first Saturday that Stanton had decided to work overtime that she had seen what he was really like.

'Miss Johnson, a need fe get inna yu room fe fix de window,' he had called out to her as she came through the front door, two bags of heavy shopping balanced in one hand while she pulled out her key from the yale lock with the other. He was peering round the door of his sitting-room, his unshaven face messy from a recent meal.

'All right, Missa Thomas,' she had said automatically, thinking nothing more of it.

Moving past his rooms into the kitchen she had unpacked her goods, putting them carefully away into the cupboard and fridge space that Mrs Thomas had told her was her area when she had first moved in. The kitchen was empty, but she could see Miss Matty, the woman who rented the room across the hall from hers, had a pot boiling on the fire. Adella had hesitated, wondering if she should wait around for a chat. She liked Miss Matty, the way the other woman always made a joke out of everything. She had taken Adella under her wing from the first moment, warning her about the landlord's passions and the landlady's jealousy. It was Miss Matty who had told her the best places to shop; which shopkeepers would give credit and which ones wouldn't; and she was always there with a helpful word or a cheerful piece of gossip.

'Miss Johnson?'

Adella had turned round to find Mr Thomas looking at her with his usual oily smile. 'Yes, Missa Thomas?' she had said politely, careful to keep her voice cold.

'A was wanderin if a could look pan de room now.' As he spoke he wiped his hands on the side of the signet vest which had parted company with the black trousers he was wearing, exposing the swell of the belly which long ago obscured his waist.

'Yes, Missa Thomas,' she responded.

As she led the way to the room, Adella had wondered if his wife had told him to do the work. She was always down on him to do something; picking at him, pushing him. Mr Thomas, lazy by nature, always seemed miserable and afraid of his wife; and Adella often wondered how they came to be together. The woman was thin, full of life, meanness and spite, and the other women in the house avoided her. Everyone knew what would happen if she found out about her husband's interest in them, and several women had returned to find their things strewn across the pavement outside the house.

Once inside her room, the man had made no attempt to cross to the window.

'Yu have some pretty tings, Miss Johnson,' he had said, picking up an ornament from the dressing table and turning it over in his hands before going to sit on the bed. 'But a bet a could do a lot betta fa yu dan dis.'

Adella had stiffened, eyes narrowing as she saw the seriousness in the puffy face.

'A tink yu betta look pan de window and go, Missa Thomas,' she had said coldly. 'A haffe get Stanton dinner ready.'

'But ihm sey ihm was working all morning,' the man had said slyly. 'Yu have plenty time fe look bout food. Come talk to me.' He had patted the bed beside him as he spoke.

She had looked at him in amazement; she had heard much about Mr Thomas, but could he really be serious? Did he really think that she could have the slightest interest in his ugly, shapeless body?

'A hear dem say woman name Adella is hot lover,' he had said then, dropping his voice suggestively and running a hand over the quilted bedcover.

'Well yu hear wrang, Missa Thomas, I is a married lady.'

He had given her an ugly smile. 'Dat all right, a married too an anyway, yu breeding already so who gwine know?'

Adella had felt sick and dirty, anger and resentment bubbled up in her. Who did this man think he was, coming on to her like this? He was fat and disgusting in his food-stained merino with his greasy face.

'A can see yu like me,' he had said when she didn't reply. 'A could tell from a bless me eye an yu when yu come fe join yu husband. A man can tell dese tings, yu know.'

Her mouth had curled in contempt, but she had held on to her temper. She knew she had to get him out of the room, whatever else. Visions of Mrs Thomas coming up the stairs flashed into her mind. She had heard the woman's mouth, and she certainly didn't want it aimed at her. Whatever the other woman's faults, she got on with her and she certainly wasn't going to ruin it over her fat, ugly husband.

26

Adella had thought quickly. It was no use getting him angry, not while he was in the room. For all his fat, he was a strong man, and he stood well above her. Better to humour him until she could get him through the door.

She had opened her eyes wide, looking at him in surprise. 'Missa Thomas, a would neva have tought it of yu, and yu a godfearing man as well. To tink ow Stanton admire yu, and look up to yu.'

Mr Thomas had looked taken aback, eyes suddenly wary. 'What yu mean Miss Johnson?' he asked.

'Missa Thomas, yu is a well talked about man in de community, a leada.' He was well talked about all right. Everybody knew what a dog this man was. She often wondered how he could go to church, sing songs and testify and then go home to do the same ungodly things again. 'Yu is a man of property,' she had said, hiding a smile as she saw him straighten up. 'A man dat other people admire. A tink of yu as a example, Missa Thomas. A man whose works a can live by.'

He was an example all right, the kind of man her grandmother was always warning her about as a child. She could see that his vanity was touched, and she was not surprised when he got off the bed.

'Tank yu, Miss Johnson, tank yu fa showing me de way a nearly fall to. A glad to know that yu young people appreciate de example a giv yu. A wasn't sure bout yu righteousness, so a was testing yu.'

Adella had smiled bitterly; she bet he was. If only they didn't need the room so bad. But a place like this, with black people owning it, was hard to find, so she had had to hold her tongue. She had not been surprised when he backed out the door, moving heavily towards the stairs, without even a glance at the window that had been his excuse.

She had always intended to tell Mr Thomas how she really felt about him when she got out of his house, but the years had slipped by. Now she had her own house, all that space just for them, and suddenly it was not important any more. After all, he had not bothered her again and now she was too happy to be bitter about what was past.

The child was heavy inside her, waiting to be born; but she still went to work, coming back to scrub the floors and clean the walls of her big old house. The few pieces of furniture they had were swallowed by the size of the place, and even the three-piece suite and table she had bought just disappeared into the large, high-ceilinged sitting room. She had already decided to keep the bottom floor, the way the Thomases did in their house. That would give them four whole rooms. The kitchen everybody could use, and there was lots of cupboard space. The other six rooms she would let; and she already had people knocking on the door asking if there was any room to spare.

She could live with the dampness now, the way the fungus grew again within weeks of being cleaned. It was *her* place, *her* damp. She would not have to worry about paying back the money to the bank, the rented rooms would do that; and who knows, eventually she might be able to move away, get one of those houses she had seen when she had taken the bus to the hill that day. The only thing that worried her was what to tell people back home. Already her mother was talking about saving up and coming to England. Everybody was happy for her; happy that she had finally got her house. Why had she written and told them about her house? Why hadn't she waited until she saw what she could get?

Adella pushed the thought aside. However bad the house was, it was better than what they had had. Even Stanton seemed to be happy now that the house was theirs. He would often bring his friends round, take them from room to room, showing them the bigness of the place. He was good about practical things, using the carpentry he had learnt in Jamaica to rebuild the stairs and make cupboards for the kitchen. They were happy together again just like it had been when they were back home. The spring was back in his step, and his head was straight and proud when he walked out to work on the buses. Now he had started planning again what they would do when they had enough money to go back home; how he would start a business and buy a little land for the hard times. Adella loved him like that even though she knew that his words were only dreams. That was the thing she had liked about him from the start. He could always see something better; was always willing to look for adventure. Why, if it wasn't for him, they would have stayed in Jamaica. She would never have made the trip to England, left everything she knew; all the people she loved. But more than all that she loved Stanton, believed in him.

Yes, those first months in the house had been nice – like just getting married again. He would come home in the evenings when he was on early shift, bringing a gift for her, something for the children. Sometimes it was chocolate, sometimes her favourite wine, and once, just before the baby was born, he brought her a television. Adella had always wanted one and for once she did not worry about the cost. After he ate his food, he would sit on the new settee with her, one hand resting lightly on her belly, as he whispered sweet things in her ear. Flattering her as he had not done for years.

'When ma boychile come, a gwine really haffe give a party,' he said one day, just before the child was due.

Adella frowned. She knew how much he wanted a boychild. How important it was to him as a man that there was someone to carry his name. God knows she had prayed often enough for a boy, even gone one day to see an obeah man that Lisa knew. But she knew how unlikely it was. She had had two children by him, both of them girls.

'It might be anada girl yu know,' she said, her voice anxious. She had seen the bitter disappointment on his face when the other children had been born and knew instinctively that the only way he would take on responsibility for his children was if this one was a boy. 'Is always de same,' she thought angrily, 'ihm nice when de baby nearly come, den ihm upset when a girlchile come.'

Stanton was looking at her oddly. 'Yu know a waan a boychile,' he said shortly. 'Yu doan tink tree girlchile enough fa we?'

'A neva said dat, honey, ongly dat we haffe tek what de good Lord send.'

She knew that he blamed her for the lack of boys, and she felt sad and defeated by the knowledge. She knew it was not her fault. She had managed to have two boychildren before she met him. It had to be his fault.

'A bet anada woman woulda have a son by now.'

Adella's mouth tightened as she forced back the words burning on her tongue. She realised that it was his way of hiding his failings. She knew that his brothers all had sons, that they teased him about his lack of them. Even so she could not help feeling bitter at his accusations. As far as he was concerned, everything bad was her fault. She resented the fact that he did not love the children as much as if they were boys. She loved all of them, both boys and girls. All she knew was that the good Lord had seen fit to give her more girls than boys; and she was just thankful that none of them had been born with something wrong.

'A tell yu, Adella,' he was saying now. 'A man caan hold up ihm head widout a boychile. A need one fe carry me name when a dead.'

She wanted to ask him who cared about his name but held her peace. Men were such strange creatures. They didn't seem to care about the things that really mattered. The caring for the children and looking out for them; the looking after them and protecting them. There was Stanton giving her no more money with the big house and new baby coming, not caring how the bank loan was paid back. He still spent his money on clothes and blues parties every weekend. He still went down to the drinking house with his friends in the evenings. Yet always he was there to criticise, blame her for things going wrong, demand that she produce a son. And always this thing about his name. 'Who cares what his name is anyway,' she thought sullenly. 'In dis country, we doan have no name to dem, we is all de same, de people dem doan like and didn't want to need.'

Look at the children, look how long they had been looked after by that white woman while she was at work and she still got their names wrong, still treated them badly.

She was glad when he got up abruptly and muttered some excuse before rushing out the door. The worry that had nagged at the back of her mind since she found out she was pregnant again surfaced suddenly, causing her to grip her hands together as she tried to force down the panic.

'Suppose Stanton leave me?' she asked the empty room. 'Suppose de children get too much and he decide to leave?' She didn't know what she would do, how she would cope without him. It was bad enough with him out all the time, working late or out with his friends. All those hours after the children were asleep. All that time, just sitting in the half-dark, waiting for him to come back. It seemed to her that all she had done since coming to England was have his children, work, and in the evenings sit in a chair or lie in her bed, waiting for the furtive sounds that told her he was back.

Four

Adella shifted uncomfortably in the yielding softness of the outsize chair, wondering why she could find no ease. Her back ached, and she wished Carol would hurry home to help her up. It had been like this for days, the ache starting in her back, spreading to her legs. The skin of her head stretched taut and painful over the bones of her skull. 'Dat docta doan know a ting, bout ihm high blood pressure,' she muttered irritably. 'Nuting noh wrang wid me blood pressure.' She sighed, reaching for another cigarette. She hated this no-work business. Too much time on her hands just to sit around and think.

'Put your feet up, rest for a few days,' the doctor had said. 'You'll feel well enough to go back to work by Wednesday.'

But Wednesday had come and gone and still the pains were there. She had tried returning to work after the third week, hating the useless feeling that staying at home gave her. But she had been in too much pain to go back for the evening shift, and now she sat in her chair, worrying, wondering what was wrong.

'Suppose a caan go back to work,' she thought suddenly, the lines of worry lost in the pain and age lines on her face. She pushed the thought aside, not wanting to finish it. Of course she would get back to work, all she had to do was be patient and force herself to rest.

The smell of cooking drifted from the simmering pot on the kitchen stove, through the house and into her room. She closed her eyes against the sudden irritation of the flickering coloured light on the television screen. The movement jarred in the quiet dimness of her room. As she moved, the cat lying against her good foot shifted and stretched before curling down again, purring contentment coming from her throat. Even the dog was quiet, lying listlessly in front of the fire. All the life seemed to have drained out of him in the last few days. She wondered if they sensed something,

31

if they shared the pain that was everywhere, following her through sleep and wake.

Leaning further back into her chair Adella tried to ease the pressure at the back of her neck, her crippled hand falling useless on her skirt. Ash from the cigarette broke off and fell against it, sliding unnoticed into her lap.

She felt the ache deep in her bones. The knowledge that she was old before her time sat on her like a burden, weighing her down. She knew she had to go back to the doctor, had known since the day she went to work. All the children had been on at her. They kept coming round together to see her – a thing that happened only at Christmas and on her birthday. She liked it when they came so much, but wished she was more able to enjoy their company. All they wanted to do was nag at her. Go to the doctor, see a specialist, the hospital. They took it in turns to take her in for appointments. Audrey taking time off work, Eena, the first born in England, coming round to fetch her in the nice new car from work. She knew that they were worried about her, feared for her, but she wished they would just leave her to work things out herself.

'Pain neva kill nobady,' her grandmother used to say, and she knew that she was right. After all, Granny Dee had lived to ninety-five, and she had had pain in her joints since Adella was a girl.

Images of Granny Dee came back to her, of the last ackee season when Mada Beck had died. She remembered her grandmother standing straight and proud beside the other old women from the village as they laid Mada Beck to rest under the spreading tamarind tree in the yard of the house on the hill. Everyone had agreed that this was the place for her. A place that belonged to all of them, where they could watch over her and pay respect. It was what the old woman had wanted. Mada Beck who had been to Cuba, to Guyana and the USA. She had been born in that house at the end of the donkey track, and she always said it was where she would go to her rest. No one thought to disagree. Mada Beck ruled the village with an iron will and few wanted to disturb her spirit after death.

Granny Dee had invited Pastor Brown back to the house, knowing that his wife had died and he had no children left in the village. Adella disliked the pastor. He was such a greedy man, stuffing himself urgently with the chicken and rice that had been prepared with all the other food for the relatives who had come from far to mark Mada Beck's passage. Although almost as old as

32

Granny Dee, Pastor Brown had an eye for the young girls of the village and an image of Mr Thomas and his boarding-house sprang instantly to mind. They had been alike, those two: nasty men, grown worse with age. She always took care to stay out of the pastor's way. Leaving it to Claudia to entertain him, aware of her grandmother's disapproval as she made some excuse to join Aunt Vi in the outhouse kitchen. She could never tell Granny Dee what the pastor was like. Her grandmother was such a holy woman with great respect for the pastor of her church. It was all right for Granny Dee to praise Claudia for her respect for the man of God. Pastor Brown never squeezed Claudia's thighs with sweaty palms, or hugged her in withered arms telling her what a big girl she was becoming.

She remembered her grandmother cornering her in the outhouse kitchen, slapping her hard across her face after the pastor finally left. 'Yu doan know to have respeck fa a servant of de Lord?' the old woman had asked in her quiet voice, so much worse than the shouting of her mother and her father. 'Yu doan learn better manners dan dat in dis house?'

Adella had not known what to say. To tell the old woman the truth would have caused her pain, and she loved her too much for that.

'Sorry, Granny Dee,' she had said instead, knowing it was not enough, bracing herself for another slap.

Her grandmother's hands had descended on her shoulders, shaken her. 'Adella, what a gwine do wid yu? What gwine happen to you, chile?'

Adella had shifted uncomfortably, knowing she was innocent. Not knowing what she was accused of now, or what to say in reply.

Granny Dee had pulled her into her arms, hugged her tight. 'De good Lord knows how much a love yu, chile, how much a love de whole a yu children.'

She had been surprised, but her grandmother's next words surprised her further. 'Yu faward fa yu age, Adella. Yu no bright like Claudia nor good like yu uncle children dem, but yu is honest. A know bout Pastor Brown and a jus sorry yu neva tell me.'

Adella pulled away. 'Yu know?' she repeated, looking at the old woman, stunned. How had her grandmother found out?

The woman seemed to read her thoughts. 'Everybady in de village know de pastor have a weakness fa de young girl dem. Not all a dem sensible like yu, but is still no reason fa disrespeck the

33

pastor.' The woman paused, sadness shadowing her eyes. 'A talk to yu mada an father, an yu Aunt Vi. Yu auntie sey yu betta dan she at dressmaking an yu parent agree is best yu go live in town wid yu cousin Byran an ihm new wife.'

Adella could hardly believe what Granny Dee was saying. They were sending her to Kingston, to live in the place she had heard so much about from Aunt May and Mada Beck. She could hardly believe it. She had never met Byron before he came down to pay respects to Mada Beck, and now he was willing to take her into his house. It was almost too good to be true.

'Byran going back tomorrow, but yu haffe stay fa Binkie Minnie. Nine night is not too long fe wait.'

Adella was lost for words. She could remember Aunt May talking about town, Aunt May who had gone to Kingston with her husband and come back a widow with a child. Often the woman would sit with her, sending Juni her son to help the men out in the field; ignoring Auntie Vi's disapproval, as she distracted her pupils from their dressmaking.

'If Delroy did live, is Kingston a would be right now,' Aunt May would sigh, rocking back and forth on the upturned oildrum she was using as a seat. She cast a critical eye around the yard, her face full of disapproval as her eyes rested on the breadfruit trees, shifted to the tall, high coconut palms and beyond that to the papaya and soursops. Aunt May had returned to Beaumont at the start of the ackee season; bringing her son, a sullen youth, with her. Adella had heard tales of her aunt whose husband worked for Americans in Kingston. They had gone to town long before she was born and she had never met them. It had been a surprise to wake up one day and hear new voices on the veranda; to be told that this was her aunt, who had come back to live in Beaumont. It was much later that she had heard the whispers. People said Aunt May had vexed a woman in the yard where she lived in town. The woman had gone at night to the obeah man. She had listened in fascinated horror as Claudia told them all about it. For days she had imagined that woman, digging up dirt from the grave of a bad man, huddling over the fire while the obeah man mixed her some death. Her heart had pounded as her sister talked of the woman, sprinkling that death across Aunt May's front door, her aunt's poor unsuspecting husband crossing it and dying. Industrial accident was what the police said, what the doctor wrote on the death certificate; but everyone knew that it was obeah, at least everyone in Beaumont knew.

Aunt May would haunt the yard, the shop at the bottom of the hill owned by the St Elizabeth man, and anywhere else that people were. The post office, the old school yard, anywhere that people met to pass the time of day. Always she would complain, tell them how much she hated country life, how good it was in town. People tolerated her, whispered that obeah turned her brain when it killed her husband. She especially liked to come out when Aunt Vi was teaching her dressmaking class, pulling up an oildrum and talking, knowing how eager the girls were to hear what she had to say.

Now Adella sat very still, bent over the fine linen, putting in the tiny embroidery stitches with practised precision. She cast a furtive look at Auntie Vi's stern face, at the dark brown eyes, narrow and angry, full of her wish to get her sister to go away. Adella felt like she would burst. Anticipation, the need to know about the tantalising place where people dug up grave dirt to kill their enemies, burning in her. Like everyone else, she knew the use of obeah; but to have an aunt who had been the victim of that art, that was something else.

'What Kingston like, Aunt May?' she burst out finally, feeling Auntie Vi's cold eyes boring into her, not daring to look up in case she felt the lash of her tongue.

She could feel the other girls looking at her, as eager as her to hear about town life. She knew they pitied her the trouble she would get from Auntie Vi when Aunt May finally wandered away. One thing about Auntie Vi, she never argued in front of her sisters, never told her pupils off when family was around.

'Kingston?' Aunt May asked finally, surprise in her voice. She never got around to talking about living in the city, spending all her time bemoaning the fact that she had been forced to leave, to return to Beaumont poorer than she had left it.

The woman turned her head slowly to look at her niece, fading eyes studying the thin young face as if she was seeing it for the first time. 'Kingston?' she said again, a small secret smile flickering across her wasted features. 'Kingston hot, and de man dem dress sharp and de woman dem have fashion. Dem ride in tram car, and it have a lot a noise where de Higgla dem come down fram de hills fe sell dem fruit and grun provision. Plenty rich people live dere. Buckra, and high yellow people, wid servant and posh car.' She looked at Adella again, as if she was really seeing her for the first time. 'You, Adella chile, could mek a way in town. Yu have boldness and yu restless in de country, an fram yu have a skill yu

35

will get work no prablem.' She sighed, 'Yes, man, Kingston is fa de young people dem, an dem dat have man fe live wid. But if yu have skill yu can have life dung deh, an get on all right.'

Adella's concentration slipped, driving the needle into her finger as she looked straight at Aunt May. She hardly noticed the pain, or the drop of blood welling up through the small puncture. Her heart was racing with excitement, eyes bright with eager questions. Even Auntie Vi's disapproval was forgotten in her sudden joy. She had always wanted to go to Kingston and now Aunt May was saying she would make a way if she could get there. She had wanted to ask Aunt May some more, question her about the fine ladies, ask what the houses were like. She had heard that they were all brick. Like her father's but bigger. That there was only one house in every yard and families never lived together. From what she could get from Mada Beck, only poor people lived in yards, lots of them crowded together a family to a room, and it was in their living that all the life, the excitement and the flavour of town could really be seen. She wanted to ask Aunt May if it was still like that, if strangers really lived together in a crowded yard. But the light had faded in the woman's eyes, and her mind had already wandered off to another place.

She had longed for Aunt May to tell her more about the city, even pestered Juni until he threatened to throw her into Beaumont Springs. But now she would have no more need to ask anyone. Soon she would be going to the city, see it for herself. Her heart filled up with the joy of it; and she wondered how she would manage to wait a whole nine days, till Mada Beck was honoured. She felt ashamed of the thought and pushed it aside with a quick prayer to God to bless the mark, cross it off. It wouldn't do to offend Mada Beck's spirit before it took its rest.

The time had gone faster than she expected. There was so much to do, so much to prepare for the ceremonies and the feasting for each night of Mada Beck's passing. Adella knew about those nine nights, she had been to them before when other people died. When her grandfather died, she had even been allowed to take part in the singing, feeling important and sad as she tucked into chicken and goat meat. But something told her that Mada Beck's passing was a different thing, that it would mark the end of things familiar and the beginning of a new way or at least a different way for her.

She could remember the last night of the Binkie, the party held in honour of the dead, the rituals, the praying and the blessings over.

All her family had been quiet. Granny Dee's eyes looked red like she had been peeling the strong purple onions or crying long and hard. Even her mother's eyes were wet, and Adella had been surprised and disturbed. Her mother never showed emotions, was never unhappy, or happy either. Everybody called her strange, whispered that she had an evil eye. Yet there she was, eyes wet and red as if she too had been crying. It was unsettling seeing her mother so strange, and she shivered, wondering if Mada Beck's spirit had started working already.

It was while they were packing her bundle, Auntie Vi and Granny Dee arguing about the merionos she should carry, that it hit her. She was leaving home, leaving Beaumont where she had lived all her life. Going to a place she had never seen. Adella felt a sudden fear. What if she did not like it there? What would she do without Granny Dee and Auntie Vi? She thought of her little sisters asleep together on the bed she shared with them. She would miss them, all of them; the noisy quarrels, her brothers going early to the field with their father before going off to school. How would she live? All her friends were here, her family, the people of the village. Everybody knew who she was and she could not walk anywhere without having to stop and pass a few words in greeting and respect. What would she do without that?'

She wanted to share her fears, to go into Granny Dee's old arms, smell the earth on her like she had done when young. She would cuddle up to her, head buried in her dress, surrounded by that special smell. The smell that always comforted her and made her feel safe. Adella could see how the old woman suffered, how sad she looked as she ironed out another dress or packed another blouse. She knew she had to face her fears alone, and she prayed that no one would dislike her and obeah her like Aunt May. After all, she didn't have a husband like her auntie did, nobody to cross the graveyard dirt for her.

The morning she left Beaumont was a wet and windy one, rain driving against the windows, and drumming on the zinc roof of the wooden outhouse kitchen. The smell of raw damp earth was everywhere, penetrating the cooking smells, and blanketing out the smell of ripening fruit. Adella loved the morning rainfalls, the sounds of dripping leaves as the rain eased off, becoming a drizzle; the far-off croaking of bullfrogs and the noisy thrashing of goats in the wet tangle of undergrowth. She breathed deeply, almost tasting the morning smells: the aroma of hot chocolate tea mingled with frying fish and the fresh dampness of red earth.

'How long fore a gwine see Beaumont again,' she said almost to herself.

'Yu doan even gawn an yu missing it already,' Granny Dee said, sniffing into the air, hiding her sadness behind stern unconcern. They were all there, Auntie Vi, Auntie Silvie, Granny Dee, Aunt May, her mother and Claudia, all crowded in the little cookhouse, too many hands making clumsy work of the breakfast meal.

Adella felt awkward in the little silences that broke out as the stilted chatter ebbed and flowed around her. She felt spare, standing in a corner, gently nudged this way and that as someone slid past her or stretched around her. None of them looked her in the face, not even Aunt May, and the cheerful morning chatter was missing from the water-laden air. For once her father and brothers had not gone off to the provisions ground – a thing that happened every morning, rain or sun, except on Sundays, and that was the Lord's day when no work could be done. Now they were all there, wandering about on the damp sloping grass of the yard. Juni climbed one of the coconut palms to pick water coconuts, while her father busied himself at the breadfruit tree looking for a likely yellowheart to roast for her journey.

Adella felt guilty, responsible for the unnatural silence in the yard, the idleness among the men. All yesterday she had felt this awkwardness as their neighbours from the other yards came one by one, some dragging children, others on their own. They wished her luck, prayed for her, some bringing presents, asking her to give them to relatives in town.

'Keep up yu principles,' Aunt Ivy, Granny Dee's greatest friend, had warned her, and Adella realised how strange and frightening a trip to town must seem to her. The old woman's withered hands had trembled as she hugged the girl to her; and there had been another tremor running through the thin body as Adella pressed against it. Aunt Ivy's eyes were wet and her own eyes misted over as she stepped away. She had known the old woman all her life. Aunt Ivy spent as much time in their yard as she did in her own. She had been her grandmother's friend since they were both children. Aunt Ivy had never been outside of Cromwell land, the area in which Beaumont lay, and anything that was not there was foreign to her way of thinking. She disapproved of travel, and saw Kingston as a heathen place. 'Next ting yu know, de chile gwine up an tek ship go a fareign,' she said to Granny Dee as she pushed Adella gently towards the door. 'Get me a lemonade,' she said to the girl before turning back to her friend. Adella knew that Aunt Ivy was not alone in her suspicion of the town. For most of the village, town was a place where people rarely went, and many lived and died without moving much beyond the reach of Beaumont Springs.

Now she sat to one side in the kitchen, balanced unsteadily on a stool. Her back was pressed against a rough wooden wall as she watched the bustle and the sadness in the weeping world. She had two hours to wait before Mas Sam's old truck would rattle to a stop at the end of the track that led to Beaumont village. Two hours to feel the heavy sadness of loss, the fear of what was ahead creeping into her mind. Two hours more to feel belonging in the busy crowded yard. Today she had no appetite for the steaming calabash of ackee and saltfish, or the banana porridge set before her.

'Yu mus eat,' Granny Dee said sternly. 'De good Lord sen de food fe sustenance yu, so doan play wid it like dat.'

Adella felt them all watching her, all their love and concern. She knew that Granny Dee was right, Kingston was far away and she had been warned Mas Sam would not stop on the way. She had travelled with him before, down to the coast, and she still remembered the crowded bench spilling over with Higgla women, workmen and provisions.

They were all there to put her on the truck, her father and uncle climbing in first, exchanging jokes with the crowd of people as they made a space for her luggage. Everyone seemed to be talking at once. The jumble of words mingled with the squawking of chickens and the chaos of bundles in the crowded truck. All her family tried to hug her at once, the many words of advice an incomprehensible jumble, and she was almost glad when she was finally wading through the piles of baskets and tangle of feet on the truck. Passengers shifted around, squeezed together, making a space for her to wedge herself into, and she clutched her bundle to her, feeling rising excitement mix with her fear as the truck lurched off with an unsteady whine, before gathering speed to lurch around the narrow bends in the muddy country roads.

Five

The ride to Kingston was a nightmare. The truck swung wildly and lurched from side to side, the engine wheezed unhappily as it chugged up a hill, then rushed down the other side at break-neck speed. Often it seemed as if they were hanging just on the edge of a steep drop, or hurtling down to a sheer wall of rock, only to corner sharply and be catapulted down another slope. Everywhere was hill country, sheer walls of grey or red stones, and green and yellow uplands. She never knew there was so many kinds of country in Jamaica, and she craned her head as they came to flatlands. The truck rushed headlong through villages strung along the road. Wooden houses on stilts and zinc-roofed concrete buildings. She liked the flatlands, watching the country roll away. Field after field of sugar cane gave way to tall stately coconut palms and miles of banana fronds. Then the uplands would come again with a laboured spluttering and nerve-choking whine as the truck climbed higher into the hilly country. Adella swayed from side to side, moving with the people she was wedged between, as the truck lurched and heaved around bend after bend. The driver made no attempt to slow down while cornering downhill, and her neighbour told her the brakes didn't work so good. She felt sick, her head swimming, mouth sour with bile and the fear that the driver might lose control of the truck. She felt as if her whole breakfast lurched with every corner the truck took and she clutched her bundle tightly. Conversation flowed around her and she listened eagerly, drinking in the strange new gossip. A plump woman in a yellow bandana asked about her village and Adella answered quickly, lapsing into silence as the woman told her about Kingston and the market. She was a market trader and she talked about the sprawling place where fish and provisions were brought for town-dwellers to buy. Adella tried to listen, tried to concentrate on the advice that others had joined in to throw at her; but her head was starting to feel heavy, stomach too delicate and abused to think of much else. Hour after hour slipped past. The sun climbed high into the sky. It beat mercilessly on the speeding truck, boiling the passengers, animals and humans alike.

Adella was so wrapped up in her tired misery that she hardly noticed when the bus crested the last hill. Now they could look down on the place the woman called Stony Hill. The din inside the rocking truck became louder, voices warring with animal sounds as people shouted to their neighbours and those dozing woke to join in. Adella felt the excitement stir inside her. She could see the big houses Aunt May and Juni had talked about. The grass in the yards was smooth and short like a hand-made rug, and she craned her neck from side to side, not wanting to miss anything. The woman beside her shifted her bulk and Adella couldn't resist asking her if this was Kingston – not that it could be anything else: those houses with the short grass in the big empty yards. The woman smiled at her, gold glinting at several points in her rows of teeth. 'No, man, Kingston no come yet, we haffe go dung a little way before yu see de ole house dem. De big market an de train is well far, dung near wharf.'

Adella nodded, none the wiser, contenting herself with peering round her neighbours, looking left and right at the new sights they were chugging past, trying to make sense of the jumble in her sick and muzzy head. It was nice to watch the world slide by, but she was glad when the truck finally turned into a crowded concrete place, full of other trucks, draycarts, untidy piles of provisions and crates of chicken. She could hear the far-off cry of Higglas hawking their wares, and the shouts of greetings between the people on her truck and others on the ground.

It seemed no time before she was off the truck and trailing behind her cousin as he walked briskly ahead of her, carrying her heavy grip. He stopped impatiently every so often, allowing her to catch up with him. Byron was going off to join the army, and he felt she would be good company for his wife while he was away. From what he had told her, there were a lot of people going from Jamaica and other places in the Caribbean, and she felt proud that he would be fighting for King and country. Her cousin was going on a big ship, all the way to England, to the Motherland to fight the Nazis from Germany. Nobody had mentioned the war on the bus, and in Beaumont it was as if it was not happening. But in town it was on everybody's lips. From the moment she stepped off the bus she heard them talking, glimpsed the bold newspaper headlines. Everybody was saying that a place named France had been taken over by the Nasties, that they were going to attack England itself. Everywhere she looked people were crowding round newspapers, voices full of excitement. They talked about places she had never heard of, told how they had been invaded, and she sensed the tension, the fear that the war caused. It was so different from the country, so full of people and noise and she wondered if she would ever get used to it. If she would dare to wander the streets as she had wandered through the hills of home. It was so hot, so sticky. Aunt May never told her about that heat, that dry hotness that burned into her shoes, and wrapped around her skin, even at this time of evening, when night lurked just beyond the dusk.

The thing she remembered most about Kingston in the first few months was the dust-filled heat. That and the strange smell that burnt into the city as the heat came on with the rising and strengthening of the sun. It was a strange place, like Beaumont and yet not so. In the early morning while the city slept, the air blew down from the blue mountains, sweet and dew-fresh like the cool mornings at Beaumont. It was quiet too, the sound of crickets and animals foraging in the scrubby bushes near the new low-cost housing giving the illusion of the country. But later the heat would rise, fanned by the noise, the loud voices of Higgla women raised above the din of donkey cries, the clip-clip of the draycarts and the occasional truck and motor car on their way downhill to the heart of the trading city. There was also the chugging sound of the trams and the rolling sound of the hand-steered carts that her cousin's wife told her were made in the tangle of shacks and zinc huts of the shanty towns in the western section of the city. Late in the morning the city really came into its own. Then it became another place, full of a choking sharp heat that burnt the mixed-up smell of dust and waste and rotting garbage into her brain. She hated it at first, but slowly it became a part of all the things she liked about the city, rotting waste, dust and packed humanity. 'A smell of life and action,' her cousin had called it, as she had stumbled after him from the crowded bus terminal, trying to avoid the tangle of goods, livestock and cursing market women.

Adella's cousin lived in one of the new low-cost housing developments that the colonial government had started building in the twenties. Like so many other places in the city, it had been left unfinished when money ran out or had to be diverted to other areas of the Empire and, later, to the war. In places the development was like a bombsite, shells of buildings with abandoned heaps of building materials like rubbish tips, attracting bulky waste from nearby homes. The dust was everywhere, white and grey particles that floated about in the gentle breeze, settling like a blanket on everything it touched. She found the lack of vegetation odd and often walked down to the nearby gully, or up to the green foothills of the blue mountains. The house was smaller than her grandmother's, though the whitewashed grey brick walls and zinc roofing were the same. Her cousin told her that they were made right there in Jamaica far down in the gully, and she had walked the length of it until she found the place. There were only two bedrooms in the house, but the red-polished veranda was large and the yard sloped up, where green shoots struggled to push up through the falling dust and trampling human feet. The bareness of the yard was strange after the green lands of the country, but Adella loved the outhouse kitchen – made of brick instead of the usual wooden structure.

Far away in the distance a door slammed, and Adella shook herself, straightening her neck, good hand going up to massage the ache that came from holding still for too long. Her eyes moved without interest across the television screen. A children's programme was on, and the two men were acting like idiots, talking down at their unseen watchers.

'A haffe stop dis wandering,' she thought to herself, as she heard her daughter moving downstairs to her room. The urgent panting of the dog drifted through the quiet house as he crashed down after her, eager for some life and company after his dull day.

'A getting ole,' Adella muttered. She had not even heard the dog getting up from the fire, her mind had been so far away.

She knew the old-age signs. The need to seek out the past, look deep into the years she had lived. The present had too many aches and pains. Too many worries.

She realised suddenly that she was hungry, that she had not eaten for the better part of the day.

'Caral!' she shouted automatically, noticing that the smell of food no longer drifted, only hung stale on the air, trapped in the confined space. Her daughter must have turned the flame off and she was grateful that Carol had returned before the pot burned.

For the last few weeks Adella had found it so hard to keep her mind from wandering. There did not seem a day when she was not jolted back to awareness by the smell of burning food.

Light from the television penetrated the gloom, diffusing it and mingling with the glow of the gas-fire. She could just make out the hands of the clock and saw that it was nearly a quarter to six. Lisa was coming round today. She had met Carol in the market the day before, told her that she would leave work early. Adella wondered how long before she came, deciding to wait and eat with her. She could hear her daughter moving about below her, saw the crack of light under the door as she came up the stairs.

'Caral,' she called again, raising her voice. Her back hurt and she needed to move, to walk about, stretch her legs.

The young woman's head popped round the door. 'I'm getting your dinner, mum,' she said. 'Can't it wait?'

'Jus help me out a dis chair,' Adella said, 'an a doan waan food yet. A gwine wait till Lisa come.'

The girl shrugged her shoulders, padding heavily into the room, feet flat from fallen arches, and heelless shoes. She stood solidly in front of the overstuffed chair, muscles groomed by years of playing sports and heavy lifting. Bracing herself, she slipped her hands gently around Adella's bulk, half-lifting, half-dragging her from the reluctant grip of the spongy chair.

Adella stretched her limbs with relief, wincing as needles of cramp coursed through constricted limbs, mingling with the aching in her bones. She was surprised how tired she felt, just sitting down and doing nothing all day.

'You look really tired,' her daughter said accusingly. 'Mum, you know that chair is no good. Why don't you let me get another one?'

Adella frowned, how many times did she have to tell them? 'Stanton buy me dis chair, and a not gwine to dash it weh. What ihm would sey if ihm come back an fine it gawn?'

The girl gave her an impatient look. 'He's not coming back, mum. I don't know why you don't accept that. He left you when I wasn't even two. That's twenty-three years ago. He's good for nothing.'

'Doan talk bout yu father like dat!' she felt the anger burning inside her. What did this child know? Stanton had good reason to go. 'A doan like de way you children blame ihm, when he neva do nuting.'

'Yeah, except abandon you with five kids.'

44

She had muttered it under her breath, but Adella heard, felt sad at the bitterness. She knew that one day Stanton would come back. And when he did he would see that she had kept faith. The radiogram was still there in its corner, polished every Saturday like he had done it when they had lived together. She had never bought another bed, though hers was sagging from too many years of use. It was the same one on which he slept and the sheets were washed with care and well preserved. Yes, she had kept faith all the years. She pushed aside thoughts of other men. The ones need had forced her to take up with over the years. Stanton would understand. He would know about the loneliness and the need to care for the children. 'Yu didn't know yu father, chile,' she said, moving slowly to the dividing door that led to the dining-room. 'Yu should a see ihm when ihm did live a Kingston. Ihm was sharp man and when we come a Ingland all de woman dem did green wid envy ova ihm. A tell yu, yu father was one man. Yu caan expect a man like dat fe get tie by a cripple; and den yu Auntie Gladys did lead ihm into temptation.'

Carol looked sceptical, her mouth, usually slightly open, closed on a snap before she said shortly, 'He ran off with your cousin because he was good for nothing, mum. He didn't have the guts to take responsibility for us, so he ran away with her. You can't keep blaming her for what he is. He was a big man, he knew what he was doing.'

As she spoke, she shifted so that Adella could pass through the doors, and following behind, she flicked the switch that flooded the dining-room with light. 'Why don't you face the truth, mum? I mean, look at him now, chasing girls even younger than me. The man don't have any shame.'

Adella felt anger burning in her chest, constricting her breathing. The children of today just didn't have any respect. In her day she would never have stood there back-chatting and not respecting her father. A vision of her quiet, hard-working father, dominated by her grandmother, flashed through her head, was pushed out impatiently. Her father had earned respect, had stood by his wife until he died. Times change, she told herself with a sigh. Her mother never had a stroke. Her parents never left Jamaica to the day they died.

She was glad when the ringing of the doorbell interrupted her thoughts.

'Dat mus be Lisa,' she said with relief. 'A will let her in, while

45

yu dish up de dinna,' she added as Carol moved towards the door. She walked slowly, feet weary and painful. It was at times like this, when tiredness pulled her down, that she felt the weight of age. 'Is when yu doan do a ting and yu bone dem pain yu, an yu get a bad pain a back dat yu know ole age come,' her grandmother used to say. But Granny Dee had lived to ninety-five. Adella remembered her at fifty-eight. She had been young still, walking miles to market, running all their lives with strictness and with love.

By the time she reached the door, the dog was already there, flinging his small white body against it with his usual enthusiasm. Adella pushed past him good-naturedly.

'Shela, ow much time a haffe tell yu, fe leave de door alone,' she said pushing him aside, watching as he sat down with expectation, panting madly. He was a strange creature, long hair and wagging tail, the only big things about him were his bark and his curiosity. She had never had a dog before Carol brought him into the house, but she had got to like him. She could talk to Shela without being contradicted. And sometimes, with his head cocked to one side, long ears flopping, she could almost imagine that he understood, sympathised with her.

Lisa stood at the top of the stairs, flakes of snow clinging to the black wig she wore, melting and dissolving on her grey coat. Adella looked behind her at the grey deserted street in surprise, watching the silent white fall for a moment before stepping back into the warmth of the passage.

'How yu do, Lisa, Caral sey she see yu dung a market yesterday.'

Lisa smiled, closing the door behind her. She was thinner than Adella, the ready smile still cheerful and full of fun after thirty years in England. They were nearly the same age and yet Lisa, two years older, looked several years younger. The bounce still in her feet, her shoulders still unbowed.

'She tell yu a was coming roun?' Lisa asked, shrugging out of her coat, putting it over the banister, with the ease of many visits.

Adella nodded, 'She jus in de kitchen dishing up de food.' As she spoke she led the way back to the small sitting-room, sinking back into her chair as the other woman crossed the room to draw the curtains before turning on the light. It was funny how Lisa always did things that way. 'Yu no want nobady fe tek fast look trough de curtain dem,' she always answered when anybody asked her why. Now she sat down on the settee, eyes searching Adella's face, full of concern.

46

'Yu doan look good atall. A tell yu, Adella, is a obeah man yu fe reach. All dem docta yu goh a doan know what dem talking bout. Anyhow a bring yu a tonic.' She rummaged about in her big straw bag, bringing out a bag of herbs. 'Get Caral fe bwile it, wid some ginga root, and tek it tree time a day, it will really mek a difference.'

Adella smiled her thanks, looking up as Carol came into the room balancing a tray with two plates of steaming food on it.

For a while there was silence in the room as the two women ate. Adella picked at the food without much appetite, while Lisa cleared her plate hungrily.

'Everybady miss yu dung a social security,' Lisa said when she had cleared the plate. 'Most a dem a go visit yu, and dem all sey yu mus res yuself an tek tings easy.'

Adella looked up from her plate, feeling puzzled. Her friend sounded strained, like she was making conversation. It was so unlike her. Lisa, so full of life, always joking, looked uneasy and worried. After her first searching look, Lisa avoided looking directly at Adella as if she was embarrassed by her friend's ill-health.

Adella felt old and defeated, Lisa knew. She wondered if she really looked that ill, if she would ever get back to work again.

An awkward silence fell between them, the muted sound of the Channel Four news the only noise in the room. She heard Carol open the front door, felt the draught under the door as she shouted impatiently for Shela. There was a pounding noise as the dog ran to her and then the slam of the front door.

'A getting ole, Lisa,' she said, shifting in her chair, trying to ease her back. 'But how is tings wid yu? A hear yu was gwine tek early retirement if Laba lose de town hall.'

'A doan know,' Lisa said slowly. 'Dis cleaning work noh pay, and it noh good. A waan sell de house an move back ome. Yu know me children dem did stay? Well dem did do all right – not as good as yu Audrey an Caral, but dem want me fe come back ome mek dem look afta me.'

'Dat nice,' Adella said, wondering what she would do if her friend left. Lisa had been so close to her for thirty years now, and she could always count on her.

'A tink yu wrang bout going back to Jamaica,' Lisa said. 'Adella, dis country killing yu. An a tink yu and Claudia could well live togeda on yu pension an hers, now dat she retire. Yu know how she keep begging yu fe come back.'

Adella shook her head, wishing life was so simple. 'Yu know Stanton go back ome two time a year, Lisa, and ihm always have young girl. Ihm even breeding dem. How a gwine hold up me head wid all dat?'

Lisa looked impatient. 'A doan know why yu still pining fa dat goodfanuting. Look ow much other man yu could a get, and yu sit waiting fa dat dog fe come back.'

Adella cut her off. 'Yu know how a feel bout Stanton; ihm gwine come back, man. A know it in me heart of heart. But a caan go nowhere till ihm come.'

'Time before last wen yu come back fram Jamaica yu was talking bout going back, even start meking plan. Den last time yu come back diffrent. What happen fe change yu mind?'

Adella's mouth tightened as she cast around for an answer. She couldn't tell Lisa what happened, could tell no one. All the children kept asking her what happened, why she wouldn't talk about back home any more. But she could never tell them. The shame sat on her, pushing her down further into her chair, her room suddenly full of disturbing scenes and memories from long in the past. If only she had not needed those other men. If only she hadn't run into one of them right in the heart of Beaumont. She pushed away the thought. 'Nuting happen in Jamaica, apart fram de violence and de madman dem . . .'

'Dat remine me,' Lisa interrupted suddenly, face animated, the old fighting light in her eyes. 'A did go a de coolie man shap on Elsa Lane fe get yu some pidgeon peas but de man try fe tief me.'

Adella smiled. 'Yu know ow dat man stay. Why yu neva go a de market?'

'Well, ihm still mek me trus tings and up till yestaday ihm neva charge nuting extra. But yu know what ihm seh to me. Sey bout ow price a rise and cost a livin get ihm, so ihm a charge intres. Well me jus tell ihm nat to bada.'

Adella smiled politely; she knew her friend was trying to cheer her up, to take her mind off being ill. But suddenly all she wanted was to be left alone in her room full of ghosts and shadows. Lisa rambled on, telling her about the fight. Incidents that she would have found funny at another time suddenly jarred on her.

The air was too full of the disapproval of Stanton, the dislike her friend had for him, the contempt of her children. She knew they loved her, wanted to protect her but they did not know Stanton. So much had gone wrong in England. She had done her best, tried to

48

keep things together, but then she had to go and have that stroke. How could she forgive herself for burdening him like that? He had tried his best, even staying in some evenings and looking after the children. But it was not a man's job. Lisa had started disliking him from that time. She had come round and taken the children, kept house and looked out for them when the woman from welfare wanted to take them away. That wasn't Stanton's fault though. He was still young and sharp looking; you couldn't expect him to let a crippled woman tie him down. If only Lisa would understand. If only the children realised how much it hurt her that they did not respect him. All these regrets passed through her mind. The worst was the fact that all Beaumont knew how she had managed with the children. She wished she could tell Lisa, but could not share the shame. How could she tell her friend the truth of being denounced in Beaumont's church? Lisa was from town. She would never understand.

Six

She came awake slowly, a muffling, suffocating weight choking down on her. It was everywhere. In her throat, pressing on her lids, crushing her. Her chest hurt from the effort to breathe, lungs labouring loud and gasping in her ears. Adella forced her hands to move, tearing at her throat. Her mind screamed, clouding with fear and panic. She wanted to cry out, opened her mouth with effort. But the sound came out strangled, a gurgling noise deep down at the base of her throat. How long had she been there, the life slowly seeping out of her? Feelings seemed to be leaving her body, leaking rapidly from the left-hand side. Her legs were like lead weights, resisting every attempt, every command to move, and the panic increased, causing the blood to pump loudly in her ears. She tried to calm her rapid breathing. To force order on her mind, hoping to stop her racing heart. For a while fear continued to spiral, but slowly, painfully, she gained some control.

The dark mist lightened, a grey patch appearing in the black blanket spreading out right across her vision. She wondered why she could only see vague outlines. Her heart jerked at the thought that she might be going blind. Pushing it back, Adella concentrated on her breathing, forcing calmness on to a mind rapidly clearing of mist. She had to do something, the children would be getting up, needing attention. She couldn't lie here doing nothing. She tried to be logical. Something had happened to her, something terrible that had robbed her of the ability to move or speak. She couldn't let the panic take over and swamp her again.

Above her she could hear the sound of movements, and knew that the Westons, who rented the room above her bedroom, would be getting up. Mr Weston worked on the buses, and he was on the early shift this week. Mrs Weston always got up to make her husband breakfast, even though she didn't need to get ready for her factory job for another two hours. She heard the door open, the sound of muted voices drifting down to her. How many times had she listened to this ritual? They had been with her a full year now, and were easily her best tenants. She knew that Mr Weston would be in the bathroom, that his wife would soon be passing her door on her way to the kitchen. Somehow she had to speak, shout out for help. She concentrated, willing her throat to unlock, praying that the timid woman would somehow know she was in trouble. Adella forced her mouth to open, used all her will to produce a small and strangled sound. Again and again she tried to cry out and soon she felt a trickle of sweat beading her face. Tears of frustration burned behind her eyes. She couldn't believe that help could be so close and yet so far away.

What was she going to do? By the time the children woke up all the tenants would be gone. What was she going to do? The baby was not a year and a half, and the others couldn't cope. She had to move, had to get them ready. Mikey could see to the older ones, but what was she going to do about the baby? Her head swam with the effort of concentration. The blackness lapped at her vision, clouding her mind, dragging her back into nothingness. Her thoughts wandered aimlessly every time the darkness lifted slightly; but no amount of willpower could shift her lifeless body.

When she opened her eyes again, they were all crowded round, the four small faces full of fear. They had put the baby on the bed, and she sat there, poor little Carol, looking lost and hungry. She looked at Mikey, saw the fear in his eyes. He had to be strong, he was the oldest; he had to take charge. Her head hurt and she closed her eyes in an effort to ease the pain. If only Stanton was here, he would know what to do. She knew he had not been back all night, that she would not see him until the evening. It had become the pattern since Carol was born and she had brought Mikey and Delores over. One thing she knew was that she could not stay lying there. She had to get up, bath the baby, take her and Audrey to the woman who kept them and Eena to her school. Then there was her job. Today a rush order was coming through and they had been promised a bonus if they finished it on time. She needed the extra money. With the five children, she had to work overtime just to keep them clothed and fed. Today was not the day to be sick.

She knew her mind was wandering, pulled herself up sharply, focusing on what she had to do, using all her will to concentrate. She looked from one to the other of the frightened little faces, saw the shock in their eyes. Adella knew they didn't expect her to be like this, out of control. They knew something was wrong and looked lost and scared. 'A haffe tell Mikey fe get help,' she told herself grimly. 'Haffe tell ihm fe get Lisa or somebady.' She tried to concentrate, to force the stiff muscles in her throat to move, to say something. Her head ached and her throat pained from the effort. Faces wavered, dissolved before her eyes. All that came out was a croaking grunt, and she slumped in defeat. Control slipped, the will to try again oozed out as her mind lost its grip and filled up with scattered, half-formed thoughts. The blackness lapped at the edges of her consciousness. Her feeble effort to push it back seemed to make things worse, till it blanked out the faces and permeated her brain.

Adella drifted up through suffocating layers, head heavy, body unmovable. Her eyes blinked and she wondered if she was seeing things. If it was her brain that had gone wrong. There seemed to be a blue curtain going round as far as she could see. She heard the sound of strange voices, the noise of shoes on a concrete floor. She became gradually aware of a strange smell, a familiar smell that teased at her memory, elusive, yet so close. The swish of curtains preceded a round black face, the uniform that she remembered from three pregnancies. Of course! She was in a hospital. She wondered how she got there, why she was there. She wanted to ask the woman why she could not move her legs but the words refused to come, only a slurred and garbled noise that left her feeling embarrassed and ashamed.

'I'm glad to see you back with us, Mrs Johnson,' the woman said cheerfully, moving briskly to straighten the bedclothes before lifting her limp, unfeeling wrist.

Adella's eyes followed her movement, memory flooding in. She felt helpless.

What had happened to her children, the baby? Who was looking after them? She prayed that Mikey had got himself together, phoned Lisa. She would look after them, treat them good. Images of welfare people coming and taking them rushed through her head. Her heart raced, panic flaring again. A woman at work had lost her children to the welfare people and they had kept them for a long time and she had been unable to talk or even move her head. Her mind quailed at the thought, tried to shift away. But it stayed, images of them as they had been, small faces of worry, staring down at her with helpless fear. Guilt mingled with her confusion and her head started to ache, mind clouding again. She felt a slight prick somewhere, could not locate it, knew that it was an injection before falling back to nothingness.

Adella did not know how long she had been in the hospital. Lying there, being turned over, from one side to another, being washed and fed like a baby, food dribbling down her chin. She hated mealtimes, feeling shame and frustration from the moment the blue curtains were drawn round her bed and she was propped up against the mound of pillows. They told her that she had suffered a stroke, that with luck she would get back some feeling and the use of most of her body. Adella felt panic and anger. They had to be lying. She knew what a stroke was. A crippling thing that struck at old people, leaving them without the use of much of their bodies. Sometimes leaving their faces distorted on one side. But she was only thirty-four. There had to be some mistake.

Yet even as she rejected it she knew that it was true. Feeling had started to return only to one side of her body. The other side was stubbornly unresponsive. While her mind spoke clearly, the words came out slurred and jumbled from her mouth. Every day a woman came round. She was big and competent, with short brown hair and neutral eyes. She had strong, powerful arms, and she would twist and pull, force dead, unyielding limbs to move. Adella hated the pain, the way her mind screamed out and hot darts of agony shot through her, leaving her prickling and weak. She hated the woman who gave her so much pain, who had no sympathy for her and pushed and pushed even when she could not take the torture another moment. The other woman was better, the one who came to help her with her speech. Adella was relieved when the woman explained that she had not gone mad or simple. The stroke had paralysed a portion of her brain, and now she had to relearn the use of voice and limbs. She never realised how much work her mouth did, how all the words she took for granted could cause pain deep in her throat and right round her jaws. Yet she knew that for her children's sake and to keep Stanton, she had to learn again.

He had come to see her twice, in several months, edging cautiously up to the bed, eyes fearful. It was as if she had suddenly become diseased and he was afraid to be infected. Adella had felt the hurt deep in her stomach. She knew that it was not his fault, that he hated illness of any sort, but still the rejection pained her. He had not stayed long, perching uneasily on the hard, upright chair, ignoring the comfort of the easy chair on the other side of the bed. It had been awkward having him sitting there, looking around the crowded rows of beds, saying nothing, and she wished he would just go. Yet she wanted him to stay and talk to her, tell her that to him she was still the same. Fear of his reaction stopped her speaking. So she watched him, noticing things she had never seen before. How slack his chin was, the way his eyes moved restlessly about. She willed him to tell her of the children, how he was coping with them. She knew that Lisa was helping out, and she suspected that it was her friend who actually looked after the children, for they always came to visit in her company. The silence stretched on. Stanton looked at his watch almost constantly and Adella felt tears burn the back of her eyes when she saw his open relief at the bell that signalled the end of visiting time. He had not come again after the second time and she had been glad.

The day she left the hospital it was Lisa who came for her, walking into the room with her own small grip. She had dressed specially, in a nice red coat and matching hat, and Adella was cheered by the familiarity of the smiling face.

'A buy yu some clothes, tru yu lost weight since yu deh ya.'

Adella smiled gratefully, she had been wondering what she was going to wear. Lisa had taken away the nightdress she had been wearing when they brought her into the hospital. Although she brought fresh ones regularly, she never brought her any street clothes.

'De docta sey yu haffe rest and tek it easy fa a while, so Stanton is getting yu cousin Gladys fe move in and tek care a de children den while yu getting betta.'

Adella nodded, grateful that everything was taken care of. She had been worried about caring for the children. She could not walk very far, and her speech was slow, still slurred. She was ashamed to talk to anyone, except the woman who came to see her to help her to speak. She knew that she was not practising enough, but could not bring herself to speak. Often other patients would come to her bedside, try to make conversation; but she would either nod politely, or close her eyes and pretend she was asleep.

She felt alien in that ward, all the strange white women with so much in common. Talking to each other, gossiping about the latest murder, the cost of living, and even what the next meal would be. For her mealtime was an ordeal – the food overboiled and tasteless. She had long given up eating it, relying on Lisa to provide her with cooked meals. All the other women seemed so old, spending their time comparing notes about the way life had changed since their day. Yet their talk always came back to death, compulsory death by hanging, their disagreement with the new lobby that wanted the thing abolished. She would watch them, crowded together in little groups, withered faces pushed forward in ghoulish anticipation.

Adella resented the way they treated the black nurse and the cleaning staff. They had them running around, and were always ready with name-calling and abuse. Yet for all that they were curious about her, whispering together, giving her sly glances, furtive fingers pointing before one or another would detach themselves and approach her bed; only to beat an awkward retreat at her silence. She knew they thought her odd, were affronted by her lack of gratitude for their attention, and often she would overhear whispered criticism based on the fact that she was black and foreign.

The body of their conversation was about themselves, their illnesses. They could discuss that for hours, comparing notes, faces full of avid morbidity. It was almost like they were keeping score – who had the longest operation, who had the most – and she was not surprised to see how reluctant they were to leave when the time came to be discharged. She realised that none of them had anywhere better to go. So many of them lived alone, abandoned by their families. For them the hospital spelt company and comfort, here they could be warm, have food and waitress service. She often felt sad for them, as one or the other would find she had to go. The way she would argue with the doctor and, when she lost, go round to say her goodbyes, collecting addresses and promises. Something to hold on to.

'Yu doan waan fe get up and bathe?' Lisa was asking, opening the grip and taking out a dress that Adella knew must have cost her a lot of money. 'A come early so yu doan haffe hurry yuself.'

Adella nodded, easing herself slowly out of bed. She wanted to thank Lisa, show her how much she appreciated her kindness. Fear of speaking won out and she hoped her friend would see the gratitude in her eyes.

'De docta sey yu haffe practise de talking,' Lisa said, sitting in the easy chair at the side of the bed, thin face cocked to one side. 'Ihm sey if yu doan exercise yu mouth muscle, it not gwine come back good.'

Adella said nothing, shuffling across the narrow cubicle, and picking up her dressing-gown from the end of the bed. 'Since yu in hospital, not one word come fram yu, and yu talk so much, Adella, yu caan get shy now.'

She knew Lisa was right, knew that she had to talk to people some time. She could not go through life afraid of how she sounded, afraid that they would mock her for her voice. Anyway, with her crippled side, her voice should be the least of her worries.

It was strange to be back home in her rambling house. Strange to sit in the big front room, listening to the muted sounds of her tenants moving about above her. They had all visited her in the hospital and she had been grateful, feeling touched that they had cared enough to do so. Now she was back in the old familiar place, full of the clammy dampness and smell of junjo that she had come to associate with her home. She could see that it needed wall-papering again, knew that she would have to ask Stanton. She could no longer climb a ladder or cut out strips of paper. But she knew it had to be done. Already she could see the green slimy growth on the sitting-room wall, the beads of moisture merging into rivulets on the paper in the bedroom, where it lifted at the corners and curled back as the dampness loosened the paste that held it to the wall.

The place seemed even more damp now that there was someone else living there, and somehow when she washed the clothes and hung them over the bath to dry, more of them would be attacked and discoloured by mildew. She wasn't sure she liked having Gladys living with them. She had never got on with her even when they were growing up, and she found that nothing had changed in the years between. Gladys slept with the children in the back bedroom, but apart from that did little of practical value. In her late twenties, her tall, slim-figured body was always fashionably dressed, and Adella often wondered what she worked at. She was around the house all hours of the day, and never paid any money for her keep. Everywhere Adella went she seemed to be there first. Steaming her face in the bathroom, painting her finger- and toenails, or just admiring herself in the full-length mirror in the front bedroom.

After Adella had been back from the hospital for less than a month, her cousin took to going out with Stanton. Adella hid her anger. Stanton had not taken her out since Audrey was born, always saying that he preferred his own company. But he paid her more attention now, encouraging her to keep up her exercises, even coming with her to the hospital. Every day she would practise harder, holding the pen in her left hand, the feel unfamiliar, as she wrote wavering letters, then words. She had to get better for her marriage's sake. Instinct told her that it was the only way. So she practised, hour after hour, doing the exercises that they had taught her at the hospital, speaking to herself in the mirror.

Her speech was nearly normal, the dragging of her crippled foot less noticeable, when she got the letter from the factory where she worked. Adella fumbled for her glasses when she saw it was addressed to her, eager to see what was in it. She had been working at the factory for six years and she supposed it was something to show their sympathy.

Her heart was pounding when she read the words, and she blinked, unable to believe her eyes. Dismissed! They were sacking her because she had had the stroke. Panic clutched at her as she read it again. It could not be true, she worked too hard for them to be thrown out now. She dropped down in the stuffed, oversized chair that Stanton had bought when they had first moved into the house. She couldn't believe it. They couldn't sack her, not now. Not when she needed the money most of all. She had not worked for so long, had not earned any money and things would be really bad if it wasn't for Lisa. She felt guilty about how much her friend had done, knew that she had fed the children and paid their minding fee out of her own pocket; and she tried to tell her she would pay her back. Lisa had shrugged, saying Adella would do the same for her in the same situation, but Adella knew it was different. Lisa's children were in Jamaica and she only had two.

Seven

She was sitting in her chair, wondering what to do, feeling more desperate by the minute when Stanton came back from work.

'Wha wrang wid yu?' he asked in irritation, loosening the London Transport tie round his neck and sitting on the settee, tiredly. 'Yu know a working early and a still find yu sitting here idle an no food cook.'

Adella looked at him blankly, hardly hearing the complaint, for once too wrapped up in her worries really to pay attention.

'A las me jab,' she said flatly, good hand still clutching the piece of paper that she had read over and over, hoping it was a lie.

He shrugged impatiently, bending to loosen his shoelace. 'So what, yu can get anada one.'

She looked at him sadly, realising that he didn't care. She knew it was not that simple, the fact that she was considered a cripple slowly sinking in to her. If the place she had worked for so long wouldn't give her a chance who else would want her? She could only use one hand, and that not even the hand she was born using. What job was she going to get?

'A doan tink anybady gwine gi me a jab,' she said slowly. 'A doan tink dem gwine want a cripple when dem can get healthy people.'

He looked up impatiently, easing his foot out of the shoe at the same time. 'What yu waan me do bout dat?' he said now. 'A feel sey if yu want a jab yu gwine get one; now a waan someting fe eat. Yu know me an Gladys a go out soon as she come back wid de children.'

'A wish yu would tek me out sometime.' It was out before she could stop it; the words full of longing and rejection.

57

Stanton looked at her in surprise and contempt. 'Tek yu out!' he said now. 'How a gwine do dat when yu have a sick hand an foot?'

Adella flinched, and he came over to her, kneeling beside her, looking sorry that he had spoken.

'Look, sweetheart, yu know ow a love yu. But de ting is dat yu is sick now. When yu get betta will be anada ting.'

She wanted to point out that he had not taken her out even before she had got sick, but she bit back the words feeling suddenly jealous. 'Why yu haffe tek Gladys?' she asked suspiciously.

He looked put out, as if he had not expected the question, and the dark eyes moved restlessly under her gaze, as he searched about for an answer.

'Yu know ow much she doing fa we,' he said coaxingly. 'Look ow she gi up her room and come move in ya to look bout de pickney dem; and ow she stay roun an keep yu company when nobady deh bout.'

She kept her mouth closed, realising how much he liked her cousin. Yet she wished she could tell him she wanted the other woman out. As far as she could see, all Gladys ever did was upset the children. Apart from taking them to the minders and fetching them back, the rest of her time was spent painting some part or the other of her body, and Adella often wondered why she even bothered to bathe, when all she did was put the paint right back on.

'A doan tink dirt could even penetrate trough de mask she paint pan her face,' she told Lisa later when her husband and cousin had gone and the children were all in bed. Her friend had been coming round almost every day since she came out of the hospital and she was glad of the company.

'Doan trust dat woman, Adella,' Lisa said now. 'A tell yu she gwine mean big trouble fa yu. If I was yu, cousin or no cousin, a would tell Stanton dat she haffe go.'

Adella thought about it, realising the truth. Gladys was bad news. Since she came Stanton had been going out more and more, and there was hardly a night that he was not with her at a party. Adella had known that she had to get rid of her cousin even before Lisa said it, but somehow it made it more right now that her friend had voiced her fear.

'A get de sack,' she said to Lisa after a pause, and her friend nodded without surprise.

'A did tink dem would do dat,' she said. 'A neva waan sey nuting till it happen, tru yu did have enough tribulation already. But yu know wid yu right hand no good yu couldn't continue de work.'

Adella felt a sense of disappointment, but she realised the truth of what Lisa was saying. 'A suppose yu right,' she said grudgingly, 'but afta six year, yu'd a tink dem could show sympathy.'

Lisa snorted. 'A know yu keep sey white people no know sympathy? Cho, Adella, yu know betta dan dat. Yu caan keep sewing wid a bad han; nobady would buy de tings dem, de stitch gwine so crooked. What yu haffe do now is try find someting else.'

'Easier said dan done, who gwine waan give jab to a cripple? It not even worth de looking.'

'Why yu doan do a cleaning jab? Plenty work advertise and dough de pay less dan what yu was earning, it not too bad.'

Adella felt less than enthusiastic. How could she write home and tell her parents she was working as a cleaner? She had been so proud of her job and her family had been so proud of her. She had told them how well she was getting on and there had even been talk of giving her promotion. Now all that was gone, finished the morning she had woken up to a stroke. It wasn't fair. She couldn't imagine what she had done to deserve it. True, life was hard, what with the work and the problems with the house; but she had done her best and she was sure other people had a harder time and never had a stroke. She felt suddenly bitter; it wasn't fair. It wasn't right that it had happened to her.

'A not sure a waan fe clean people floor fa dem,' Adella said tightly.

'A doan see what wrong wid it,' her friend said impatiently. 'At least yu will save yu pride if nuting else. If a did lose me jab a wouldn't see nuting wrong wid working as a cleaner.'

Adella wished she could explain, visions of her grandmother coming to mind. There had been so much pride after she left Jamaica when she had written to say that she was carrying on her trade. Granny Dee's letters had been full of excitement. And when the old lady heard that Adella had taken in lodgers, she had written to say how she told the whole village about her success. Even Claudia, teaching in Highgate, had said how she sometimes wished she had come to England.

'Yu doan haffe tell yu people dem back ome,' Lisa said gently. 'A sure if yu doan sey nuting dem not gwine to find out.' She smiled encouragingly. 'Yu tink a tell me mada dat a work in a factory packing curry powder? She would hang her head in shame if she know. A tell yu, Adella, yu doan know how lucky yu is. A mean, how much people yu know dat come over who did all de tings dem did waan to?'

Adella had to agree. So many of the people who came over with them had ended up in factories, even when they had education and their school certificates. How many had told her about writing home, telling their family how well they were doing for themselves? Hadn't she done that with the house? Written and told them how nice it was, how well she was doing to afford it? She had even lied, told them she had a rise in salary. How could she tell them that it was the money she got from her tenants that made it possible to send things home? How often had she prayed to God for forgiveness for the lies she had had to tell them?

'A suppose yu right,' she said heavily. 'De welfare woman dat come roun said someting bout disable money dat dem give to cripple people. But a doan waan no charity. Nobady in me family eva get charity and a doan waan de children fe grow up wid it.'

Lisa nodded sympathetically. 'A agree wid dat; but a tink is time Stanton pull ihm weight. Dat man turn out goodfanuting. De way ihm treat yu in de hospital and carry on wid yu cousin, ihm should haffe some shame.' She looked at Adella earnestly. 'Yu haffe start stan up to ihm, show ihm sey yu is no doormat. Yu haffe mek ihm gi yu more money. What ihm gi yu couldn't feed fly, let alone five pickney and pay bank loan too.'

'Yu know a caan do dat, Lisa. Stanton careful wid ihm money dat's all; but a know dat if it come to it ihm will gi me some. A mean, ihm put some in a bank account in de two a we name. A caan tek it out widout ihm sign it but a know ihm will sign it if a need it.'

Her friend didn't comment, looking at the clock on the mantelpiece, and getting slowly to her feet. 'A haffe go to work tomorrow, but a gwine come roun in de evening and see how yu do.'

Adella watched silently while she pulled on her coat. 'Lisa, a gwine pay yu back de money a owe yu,' she said quietly, as the other woman looked around for her gloves.

Lisa straightened and looked at her. 'No need fa dat yet,' she said cheerfully. 'Right now what yu need is to sort yuself out and get dat woman out a yu house.'

After Lisa had gone, she sat in the large room wondering what to do. She knew her friend was right, that she had to confront her

60

cousin's presence. She had tried to pretend she could live with the other woman for too long. Gladys, tall and attractive, always smart in her tight skirts and seamed tights. Adella knew how much men liked the other woman. It had been like that since they were children. Gladys was not beautiful, but there was something about her large brown eyes and wide mouth that seemed to arrest attention. She saw the way Stanton looked at her cousin. The way he compared her with Gladys in his mind. And that one, she would sit there, with only a robe and panties, showing all her legs to him, pretending she was polishing her nails. Now they seemed to be together all the time. Gladys was not working, and she was almost sure he was giving her money. The money that should have been for her and the children.

'Maybe a wouldn't a have de stroke if ihm did pay lickle a de attention to me ihm pay to her since she come.' She pushed that thought away, feeling ashamed. He had been better since the stroke, even if he had not been home on the night. Since she came out of the hospital he always had time to ask her how she was, and he had brought her cousin to look after the children. Her mouth twisted bitterly. Stanton was not to know what a good for nothing the other woman was. She couldn't blame him for the weaknesses of the flesh. She knew men were always like that, they couldn't help it. It was the women who knew better. Gladys should have set an example by not being a temptation to her man.

She was still awake, still thinking about the situation when they came back in the early hours of the morning. Adella tried to pretend she did not notice the long silence outside the back bedroom. The whispered words, half-smothered giggles, and then the unmistakable sound of a playful slap. There was more giggles, more silence. Then the door opened, closed again, and Stanton was walking back to their room, trying not to make any noise on the lino-covered floor.

A bit late for that, she thought bitterly, the recent sounds of intimate contact still in her ears. She lay on her back in the big double bed, staring up at the ceiling, unable to lie to herself any longer. She had to do something, had to stop the woman before she took her man away.

She did not stir when he turned the bedside lamp on. She continued watching the ceiling as she heard his shoes fall with a clatter to the floor. The bed sagged under his weight as he started whistling a pleased tune to himself. She waited where she was, not watching when he went out to the bathroom, ignoring him as he came in, drying his face and his naked torso.

'Gladys was a bit drunk tonight,' he said awkwardly, his voice wary as if he had only just realised she was awake. 'A did have was to calm her dung fore a could let her go to bed. A didn't want her to wake up de children dem.' He sounded more guilty with every word, and she knew that he had been drinking.

'Yu doan believe me?' he asked aggressively when she said nothing. 'Yu tink is lie a lie?'

Adella ignored that, for once not in the mood to placate or humour him. She steeled herself, knowing that she had to confront him now – before things got any worse.

'A want Gladys fe go, Stanton. A doan tink she good fa de children and anyway she neva deh ya fe help.'

She did not look at him, but she could feel his shock and anger. 'What yu trying fe say?' he asked now. 'Gladys did give up her room an come live ya; she help yu out and jus tru a try show her some tanks yu waan trow her out.'

'A doan want her in me house. She jus come fe mek trouble; and a wonda ow she pay rent when she did inna dat place. Far as a can see all she do is show her backside and paint her toes.'

'Wha yu trying to sey?' he repeated aggressively. 'Is wha yu trying to sey bout Gladys?'

'She is no good, Stanton. Fram she come yu change. Yu always out wid her in de evening and come Saturday night we doan see nuting of yu. Stanton, yu is a family man wid respansibility.'

'Yu doan haffe tell me dat. De way yu breed, is a wonda we have space fe rent out.'

She let that pass, feeling hurt and angry. 'A doan waan get in a argument, a jus telling yu fa courtesy dat a doan want her ya and a gwine tell her fe leave tomorrow.'

The look he gave her was murderous, and Adella felt a sudden cold fear.

'Gladys is a young gal, she need entertainment. Yu nat gwine trow her out tru she pretty an need fe go party an tings. Is jealous yu jealous. Look pan yu; look ow yu let yuself go. All de time yu dere in yu ole clothes looking like someting dem pick up off a street. Is no wonda yu caan stand fe have her ya.'

'A doan care what yu waan say, she going tomorrow.'

'An who gwine see to it she go, cause a gwine tell her fe ignore yu. Till a sey diffrent she staying inside dis house.'

'A tell yu she gwine tomorrow,' she said stubbornly, fingers of her good hand curling into her palm as she saw the narrow eyes, and the hands doubling into fists as he towered above her.

'I is de man in dis house an what a sey is what happen. A doan waan hear nuting more bout Gladys. A want yu fe keep yu spiteful tongue away fram her. Yu hear me?'

He was shouting by the time he finished, making no attempt to control his anger.

'Dis house is my house, Stanton,' she said quietly. 'Is me save de money and is me get loan fram de bank. Yu neva waan fe know nuting bout it and yu neva help wid it at all. So if a doan want Gladys in here a gwine tell her fe go.'

She had half-expected the blow, yet when it came, it rang in her ears, causing her to cower with fear.

'Sey dat again?' he shouted. 'Gwan insult me one more time.'

'A sorry, a neva mean fe insult yu,' she said, still shaking from the shock of the blow, 'but a not gwine let her stay ya and mash up me family.'

His fingers dug into her shoulder, deep and painful as he shook her. She could see the redness around the pupils of his eyes, smell the alcohol that told her he had been drinking. At the back of her mind she realised she should not have brought up the subject of Gladys right now, but it was too late to back down. She had to win this one.

'Yu not gwine spoil Gladys' life because yu mean an jealous,' he said. 'She ongly young an she doan haffe nowhere else fe go.'

'She jus five years younga dan me, an she can go back where she did come fram,' she insisted stubbornly. 'Is yu bring her ya, yu can tek her back whe yu did find her.'

He hit her again, using a full fist, and she braced herself as the pain seeped into her.

'What yu trying fe sey?' he asked, making no attempt to pull his punches, one blow leading to another as he lost control. She tried to force back the scream that gurgled up inside, tried to claw off the hand that pressed cruelly into the flesh of her exposed shoulder. Her fingernails had blood under them as she reached up, clawed at his face, panic blocking her throat, constricting her breathing. She could hear him breathing heavily above her, felt him yank the pillow from under her head. Her neck was full of shooting pains as she fell sharply against the bed. The soft suffocating weight pressed down on her, and she thrashed about in panic, her breathing loud and muffled in her ears. Somehow she managed to turn her head,

63

wrench it desperately aside; but still the pressure increased, till she felt as if her neck would break.

She did not know how long she lay there, the pillow pressing down on her, thoughts of death racing through her head. Suddenly the pressure eased, and she took deep choking breaths.

'Yu doan dead yet?' he asked aggressively. 'Yu tek long fe dead.'

She saw the pillow coming at her again, held up a feeble hand to ward it off; before the nightmare softness engulfed her again and her head was pushed back hard into the mattress. Scenes passed in front of her eyes as she struggled to push him off. The blood pounded in her head, threatening to burst out. She could hear him swearing and muttering above her. He pulled the pillow off, threw it away.

'Yu doan hear a sey die,' he said angrily, slapping her across the face again. 'Jesas, yu caan even do dat properly. All yu do is bada me.' He slid off the bed crashing about, dragging his clothes from the hangers he had so carefully draped them over.

She struggled up, her left hand going to her throat, chest heaving with her laboured breath. She wanted to say something to him, calm his anger; but she knew from experience that he was too far gone to listen to anything.

It was then that she heard the sound, the muffled sobbing that the pounding blood in her ears and his angry crashing and swearing had hidden. The little girl was standing cowering by the door, eyes tearful as she watched her father crash about, dragging on his clothes without even acknowledging her. He grabbed his shoes and stalked out of the door, pushing past the child in his anger.

Adella couldn't move for a long time. She sat there rubbing her throat, unable to believe what had happened. Stanton had hit her in the past; it was something she was used to. But he had never tried to hurt her like that before, had been so good to her since she came out of the hospital. She pressed her hand against her racing heart. It had to be Gladys' fault. The woman was poison. One thing she knew, first thing tomorrow she was going to get her out. Anyway she was fed up with black-lace panties dripping all over the bathroom, the constant smell of Cutex and cheap perfume mingling with the dampness in the air.

The little girl had been standing, shaken and bewildered, by the door. Now she ran to her, climbing on to the bed. Adella gathered her up absently with her left arm, holding the shaking figure to her.

'Is all right,' she said. 'Yu did have a bad dream?'

The child nodded, pressing closer to her and she felt the tears burning at the back of her eyes.

'Listen, Audrey, what yu see – wid yu father – is nuting.' The child kept shaking, saying nothing.

Adella sighed. 'Sometime big people do fofool tings dat look bad and mek yu frighten, but it doan mean a ting. Yu mustn't tink bad bout yu father, ihm was only joking.'

The little girl nodded, some of the tension going out of the rigid body, and Adella pulled her down with her, switching off the bedside lamp. She knew how much the children liked crawling into bed with her, knew this might take the child's mind off the horror she had seen. There was no need to worry about Stanton. She had heard the door slam and knew that he would not be back that night. Somewhere out there was another woman. She had never admitted it before. Making excuses for him all those nights when his side of the bed remained cold and empty; even the night she had gone to bed only to wake up a cripple.

She hardly slept, images of Stanton keeping her awake. She thought of how he had been in Jamaica, so full of pride and so loyal. He had been responsible then, taking on her fatherless children, being a father to them. Those had been good years they had spent together. She had felt so safe and loved with him around. She knew his family did not approve of her. They felt she was too old, too experienced to be good for him. Now she wondered if those two years really mattered, if she had expected too much when she had asked him to take responsibility for two young children. Since Mikey came to England all he seemed to do was beat him. It was no wonder the boy had started to wet the bed and walked with his head hanging all the time. Stanton had taken all his confidence away, just because she never had a son for him. She drifted off to sleep, a shallow disturbed sleep, peopled with nightmare images, her stroke, Stanton choking her. Both merged together, until she came awake, sweating and shaking, to the peaceful even breathing of her sleeping child.

The next day she took the children to school herself, coming back to find Gladys still in bed. Adella had the urge to shake her, feeling contempt as she saw her sprawled across the bed. Her legs were apart, mouth open as if catching flies, the thin mesh nightdress screwed round her waist.

She thought of the jug of water in the kitchen, looked at the mouth wide open and waiting. The woman certainly did not look attractive in her sleep, the curlers in her hair coming undone from her restlessness. Stretchmarks on her exposed thighs spoke of a pregnancy that she must have kept secret. Walking to the window Adella pulled the curtains, tugging them so the rings scraped against the rail. The woman stirred, rolled over; bottom half-raised to view. Before she realised her intention, Adella picked up a high heeled shoe, slapping the bottom hard, once, twice.

Gladys shot into a sitting position, sleep-heavy eyes blinking, owlish, black streaks round her eyes and down her cheeks where last night's mascara had smeared. Adella hid a smile as the woman sat up and eyed her with wary anger, rubbing her sore behind while her lower lip pushed out sulkily.

'What yu do dat fa?' she asked sleepily, a puzzled look in her face as she noticed the thin sharp heel of the shoe her cousin held. She looked around, noticed that the children were not there.

'A sorry a sleep in,' she said penitently. 'Yu should a wake me mek me see to de children dem.'

'A want yu out a me house,' Adella said flatly, ignoring the explanation. 'Yu is a dirty jezabel dat come fe tek weh Stanton fram me. A want yu fe pack yu tings an get out now.'

Gladys looked shocked, opened her mouth to argue. But Adella lifted the shoe threateningly, holding it above her ready to bring it down on unprotected flesh again.

'A neva encourage yu husban,' Gladys said pleadingly. 'Adella, yu an me is family; yu know a wouldn't do dat. But is ihm gi me place fe stay, an a didn't want to upset ihm.'

Adella moved a step closer. 'A doan waan hear nuting. A want yu out a me house come lunchtime or is hell gwine pop.'

She put the shoe down, turned and walked away. She didn't care where Gladys went so long as she got out and she almost hoped her cousin would try to defy her. It would give her the excuse she wanted to hit Gladys again.

'She gwine get her reward in hell,' she consoled herself, dragging her crippled foot. She felt weary and defeated as she sought the over-stuffed chair she spent most of her time in since she came back from the hospital.

Eight

Adella shifted restlessly in her chair, half-listening to the increasing volume of conversation as it flowed around her. She wished she could walk away from the noise and constant activity as Carol refilled a glass here, or brought some more food over there. The overhead light hurt her eyes, taking away comfort and gloom from the tiny room, revealing it cluttered to overflowing with plates, glasses and the untidy litter of bodies.

'Is like dem keep Binkie fa me an a doan even dead yet,' she thought resentfully, wishing she was still at work and could join in with the gossip and the amusement. Not that she wasn't interested; she loved to hear about the goings on around the street, what people at work were up to, even the price of yam in the market. But Lisa always told her those things, repeating them with a humour that was hard to match.

It was not that she did not like company, but right now she was missing John Wayne on the television. She had planned her whole Saturday to leave space for him. Now the room was overflowing with people all coming to see how she was; and her head ached with the laughter and the constant loud talk. Trust them to all come on Saturday evening.

'Why black people always haffe tink same tought,' she wondered morosely, watching Mr Peters tear into his fourth piece of fried chicken. She felt a nudge at her elbow, turned to see Carol bending over her, face full of annoyance.

'We're running out of food again, mum, and Lisa say her back's hurting and she's hungry.'

Adella sighed. What did they expect her to do about it? She felt a sudden anger at Mr Peters. That man never visited her from one day to the next, even though he only lived two doors down the street and had rented from her when she still had a house. Yet let food and noise seep out of her door and he would be there dressed

67

nice and neat like a Sunday afternoon visitor.

'So why yu no stop give Missa Peters all de food? Yu no see ow ihm a shovel it weh?'

Carol looked shocked. 'You know I can't do that, mum,' she said pleadingly.

'Een eh?' Adella responded absently, adding, 'A doan know ow de man can eat like dat. Fram a know Missa Peters, ihm have false teeth, an ihm still manage tough, tough meat that even me caan eat.'

'Dat's cause he use something to fix them on.'

Adella snorted. 'So ow come las year when ihm go a Delroy wedding ihm teeth fall out in de rice an peas, mek people see ow ihm mouth mash?'

She wasn't really interested in an answer, and Carol straightened and moved away after giving her a last reproachful look.

Adella wished Lisa would stop cooking and come and keep her company, talk to her and make her laugh. Trust Lisa to come to her house and take charge. She had done that for so long, it seemed like second nature. But they left her all alone marooned in her chair, cut off from the conversation, the company. It was her room, yet now it was strange and alien – full of noise, harsh barks of laughter, raised voices, bodies packed and wedged untidily together. It was too small a room to entertain a lot of guests.

She knew she should make an effort, especially during the lulls in the conversation. That was when they would turn to her. Miss Matty, all dressed up in new hat and Sunday shoes, her daughter beside her, mouth still open after fifteen years of marriage, as if she caught the flies her mother was so scared of. You could count on Miss Matty to come visiting on Saturday afternoon and tell everybody else besides. She could imagine the woman in the market, probing and feeling the ground provisions with withered hands. Rejecting a pear because it wasn't fit, a piece of pumpkin because it was force ripe. All the time her darting eyes moving from side to side in case she missed some gossip. Each small event packed in with her shopping, stored carefully and dusted off when she descended like John Crow on the victim of her weekly visit. Rumour had it that Matty was so thin because she dared not keep still, in case a piece a scandal pass her by. Adella felt sorry for the woman's daughter. How old was she now? Twenty-seven and still in her mother's shadow, still dragged around from place to place though she had children of her own and a man to look after.

Her eyes shifted to Mr Peters' fat cheeks bulging with a load of food, lips beaded with grease like colourless lipstick. His eyes never left his plate as if he feared someone would snatch something if he glanced away. He talked endlessly, words muffled through the load inside his mouth. Food and conversation, that was all Mr Peters needed. Since his wife died and his children moved away he had grown steadily fatter, eating out on old war stories and things that happened when he came to England.

The harsh sound of the doorbell cut through the smoke and noise inside the room. Adella shrank further into her chair, wondering where anyone else could fit. They were all around her, spilling over into the dining-room, crammed together in noisy disarray. She heard the hurtling, yelping sound of Shela running to crash against the door, voices raised but indistinct. When a head popped round the door she relaxed.

She had forgotten Audrey was coming round, that she had made another appointment for her to see a special doctor. She wished Audrey would come inside, sit down and talk to her instead of taking a quick look around and retreating in haste. She knew where she was going, into the kitchen with Carol and Lisa. They were having a good time in there and she felt almost resentful when she heard their cheerful laughter mingling with the clamour all around her.

Adella's head felt heavy and she wished her visitors would go. She wanted to open the window and allow the stuffiness to drift away with them. Her mind drifted to her daughters. 'A wonda when de next docta visit is?' she thought suddenly. She hated going to see the doctor, had seen too many recently, yet still her daughters insisted.

'Mum, there has to be something wrong,' they often said. 'You're just not yourself.'

'Ole age, man,' she tried to tell them, but all they did was shake their heads and make another appointment. She remembered the disaster of the last one.

It was Audrey who had taken her, coming round in the nice blue car, making her swell with pride as she guided her down the outside steps. Adella had been glad of the pains in her foot that forced them to walk so slowly. Her heart had lifted as she saw curtains twitching and Mr Peters passing. 'Is me daughter, man, she come fa me in her car,' she had told him unnecessarily, since he had known Audrey since she was a child. It was nice to boast a little, especially since it gave her the excuse she needed to raise her voice so that the hidden watchers behind twitching net curtains could hear her.

'Dem too fast in dem one anada business,' she replied unrepentantly when her daughter complained: 'De way dem stay yu caan do one ting on dis street widout de whole world know it.'

Audrey had looked at her with raised brows, but her mother had ignored it, allowing her to help her into the car and fit the belt into its slot. Audrey didn't understand. It was different when Adella stood for hours peering out of her curtains. She had to know what was going on, keep an eye on things and such like. Anyway, she was trapped inside most of the time and before, when she had been at work – well she *had* to look out to see what was going on. How else could she talk about it? It would never do to have somebody telling her what was happening on her street, and she not knowing enough to join the conversation.

The journey to the doctor always took a long time. There were so many people she knew, especially on Loughborough Road. It was almost empty of houses now, full of the sprawling tangled yellow brick of Stockwell Park estate. She had Audrey stop for many acquaintances, make sure they had a good look at the car. 'Is me daughter,' she would say proudly, even though they knew, but needing to voice her pride somehow. 'She did go a university and now she have big jab wid de council.' The woman or man would make a few comments and she would always have to draw their attention to the car. 'Yu like de car?' she would ask casually. 'Is she did buy it, you know. Fram she learn to drive.' Other people she would wave to, getting Audrey to blow the car horn, feeling important as they looked up, startled. By the time she finished she knew that the whole neighbourhood would have heard how she went out with her daughter.

Those who had not seen would come up to her: 'Miss Johnson, a hear yu went out wid yu Audrey de ada day. Is nice when yu children look out fa yu.' She loved to hear people talk like that, knew they envied her, respected her because of her children's concern.

'Is nuting,' she would often say. 'A train dem up wid de good Lord's help and dem is a credit now.'

But deep down inside she would remember. Feel again the shock, the shame and disappointment when first Delores and then Eena had got pregnant. She had been so sick with disappointment.

70

They had been doing so well at school. How could they let the good for nothing boys trouble them and shame her till she could not hold her head up? She always pushed the thoughts away, that was in the past now. True, some unconscionable people still remembered it, would throw it at her out of spite. But she could live with that, now that Audrey got her job and Carol was doing so well too.

If she loved going to the doctor, Adella hated being there. Hated going up to the glassed-off window. She would stand, conscious of the eyes from the packed waiting-room, having to repeat her name to the patronising young girl on the other side. Then she would sit on an uncomfortable hard blue or orange chair for the long wait. It was always the same at the doctor's. It did not matter how early you came, you always had to wait, fifteen minutes, thirty, sometimes even an hour. Her back always ached with the strain of sitting upright while the endless noise of the ever-present children jarred against her ears.

She never knew anyone there. No one she could exchange some serious gossip with. This time had been no exception. The room was packed with strange faces, all wrapped up in their own misery, their own preoccupation, and the wait before her name was called seemed never-ending. She got up heavily when the girl behind the counter shouted for her, telling Audrey to come with her. Dr Stone was used to seeing one or the other of her children, indeed seemed to prefer it and she knew that all her friends who saw him brought one of their children if they were around.

'Mrs Johnson,' the doctor said, voice over-bright, remembering her from previous visits. 'How are you?'

Adella shifted in irritation. Why did the man always ask such fofool questions? If she was all right she wouldn't come to see him.

'A sick, docta,' she said bluntly, going through the usual routine. 'A have pain a back, and dung me leg an it shoot up right inna me armpit and tru me neck back.'

The man looked put out, almost as though he thought her rude.

'Dat's de trouble wid dese young docta,' Adella thought grimly. 'Since ole Docta Mason retire an dis new one come fram school tings bad. Ihm doan know what ihm talking bout.'

'What exactly seems to be the trouble?' the man asked, taking a wad of notes stapled together from a beige holder and leafing through it.

'A jus tell yu,' she said impatiently. She often wondered if there was something wrong with this man. Why did he keep asking the

71

same questions over and over again? 'A have a lot a pain an a caan work.'

'That is understandable, Mrs Johnson, but where exactly is the pain?'

Adella wondered if he was trying to make fun of her and she could feel the anger rising inside her when Audrey stepped in, explaining what she had said to the doctor. She could see the girl's annoyance, and she was proud that her children could talk just like white people. Since they started coming with her, things were always better and the man had to listen to them because they could talk like him.

The two of them continued to talk and she looked around the bare room wondering why she bothered to come. She could see that her daughter was not satisfied, felt pride as she insisted on an appointment with a specialist at the hospital. At least she knew that her children would always look out for her. The doctor was reluctant to comply and kept trying to say things would settle down in a few days.

'Dat's what yu did tell me when a fus come,' Adella butted in. 'An dat is long time now, wha yu mean few days?'

The doctor looked uncomfortable. He hesitated, before capitulating. 'Very well,' he said resentfully. 'I will get you an appointment with a consultant at St Thomas' – though I am sure he will confirm what I told you.' As he spoke he wrote rapidly on a piece of paper that had the group practice's name and all the doctors printed on it.

It had been good to see the doctor climb down, to know her daughter had made him do so. She couldn't wait to get home and get on the phone and tell Lisa and the others all about it. Not that they would be surprised, but she knew that inside they would envy her, would wish that they were just as lucky with their children, though they would never let her forget the disappointments that had happened. The way Delores and Eena had come to no good. Yes, it had been nice to boast about the visit to the doctor, but now she had to go down to the hospital. She hated the thought of that, of going to this big man that you needed to get a special written appointment to see. She wished it was Carol going with her, that it wasn't Eena's turn. Eena couldn't talk to them like Audrey or Carol; she would just listen and agree and never asked any of the questions that the other two did. Even so, she meant well and Adella could not hold it against her that she had let her down. After all, she still had Carol, Carol who had never disappointed her, and who she knew would always be with her.

Sounds of movement drifted into her consciousness, bringing her back to the awareness of the smoke-filled room. Adella was surprised to see that it was half-empty, hear more words of goodbye and get well. She had been so wrapped up in her thoughts she hadn't even heard them leaving, but now she looked around eagerly, seeing Mr Peters mopping up the last remnants of gravy on his plate with a piece of hardough bread. She willed him to hurry up and take his leave. She hoped Lisa didn't supply him with any more food. Mr Peters was one of those people who ate anything that was going and if the food kept coming he would never leave her house that night. She felt relief when her friend's head appeared around the door, the wig discarded in the heat and steam of the kitchen. Greyness peppered the soft fine hair cut close to her head. She looked older without the wig, older and more tired, and Adella felt a sense of shock that Lisa too was ageing.

'De food done, Missa Peters,' Lisa said smugly, looking at the man still holding the plate balanced on his fat, distended stomach. Mr Peters looked disappointed, hid it with a smile as he glanced up at the clock.

'Is dat de time, Miss Johnson?' he said, as if the lateness of the hour had only just seeped into his consciousness now that the food had left it. 'A fraid a haffe go, a have so much to do. Yu know what is like on Saturday.'

Adella nodded, hiding her smile. 'Mek ihm eat and gwaan,' she told herself. 'At least ihm gwaan.'

Mr Peters' exit was the cue for the last of the stragglers to leave. Once they had gone the quiet peace of her room reasserted itself. She reached for the television control, pressed it, flooding the room with colours and new sounds, before the front door had even closed on the receding noise of footsteps and conversation.

'Caral,' she shouted automatically, glad to have her house back to herself, 'Caral, yu no hear me a call yu?'

Her daughter's head came round the door. 'I was just seeing the people out,' she said breathlessly, moving across the room to pull the curtains closed before coming back to switch the light on.

'A want a Lilt,' Adella said, when Carol had come to stand in front of her chair. 'A parch fram all dat smoke an de talking.'

'You didn't do any talking,' her daughter teased. 'All you did

73

was sit here looking bored because you couldn't watch John Wayne on the telly.'

'Goh weh,' she replied good-naturedly, knowing that what the other said was true. 'Go get me a drink anyway.'

She turned her eyes back to the screen as the footsteps receded, flicking the dial from channel to channel, disappointed that she had not caught the end of the John Wayne movie.

'Is dat long belly man Missa Peters,' she muttered to herself. 'One day ihm gwine eat so much ihm gwine drap down buff and caan get up.'

Her eyes rested without interest on the screen, and she reached automatically for a cigarette, thankful that the packet was nearly full. That was the one good thing about having people over. At least you could smoke without running out of cigarettes and everybody save Mr Peters smoked Benson and Hedges, same as she did.

She could hear Carol coming back with her drink, hoped that she would not say anything about her smoking. The children were always at her to give it up. It was fine for them not to smoke, but she enjoyed her cigarette and if it killed her at least she'd die happy.

Adella took the can from her daughter, liking the cold feel against her palm, the way it sweated into her hand as she pulled the ring at the top with a hiss. Drinking some of the liquid she looked round cautiously, making sure that Lisa was not about. She was a one for telling her about drinking. The children had put Lisa up to it one day and now she made her life unbearable if she saw her with alcohol.

Sure that the coast was clear, she eased forward, good hand pushing under chair, feeling blindly, then pulling out the precious bottle of overproof white rum. She opened the bottle, wedging it under her crippled arm before pouring it carefully into the quarter-empty tin. It wouldn't do to spill any of this rum, its smell was so unmistakable Lisa was sure to know. Fitting the top on she screwed it tight, using years of moving in the dark to help her place it right.

'No wonda a like dis chair,' she told herself smugly, patting the stuffed arm. 'It nice fe sit pan, and de tings yu can get underneath is nobady's business.'

She felt pleased with her little deceit, sitting back and sipping appreciatively at the innocent-looking can, smiling up at Lisa as she came in and sat heavily on the settee.

74

'Bwoy, a could do wid a pick-me-up,' the woman said, stretching tiredly, and reaching round to rub the small of her back with one hand.

Adella felt sorry for her, and on impulse leant forward to offer her a drink, the words, unguarded, on the tip of her tongue.

'A haffe go,' Lisa said, before she could speak. 'Is dark and a doan like walking out a street when it reach late night.'

Adella nodded. 'A will get Audrey fe drap yu ome in de car. Rememba ow de two white bwoy dem did jump me,' she rubbed her knees as she spoke, remembering the horror of it. It was less than three months since it happened. She had been coming home from work, taking the bus to the end of Mostyn Road, as she always did. Her children had told her about walking down that road. Telling her how dangerous it was, how dark and dismal. But she had been walking there for ten years now, since before they pulled down the old houses so much like hers had been, and she was sure that she would be safe.

Nine

　　　　　　She had turned down the unlit street, past the church where both Eena and Delores got married after their disgrace. It was silent now, the brown door long painted a garish blue. The stained-glass windows had gaping holes or wire mesh across them. It looked empty and derelict – not well kept like it had been when the street had been the heart of the community, bristling with sounds and full of life. She knew that the council had decided to pull it down and put up flats like the ones that stood where tall houses once joined together. A woman had been found murdered in the car-park underneath those flats and a boy just turned eighteen had been given life imprisonment. It was from that time that her daughters had started worrying about her walking up the dark and empty street alone. Or at least, that was when they had started nagging her about it.

She had passed the church, silent and ugly against the moonlit sky, passed the flats from where noise blared out harsh and strident, proof that another of the endless parties was in session. Walked along the wasteland that had been landscaped and turned into a children's play area until someone had set fire to the wooden structures, when she heard the furtive haste of footsteps behind her. At first she ignored the sound, clutching her bag, but making no attempt to hurry. The night had been quite warm. It was one of those balmy October nights with a hint of lingering summer and she had not felt the urgency that colder days always brought.

Adella had been nearly at the end of the road, at the place where rubbish had been heaped high and landscaped into a hill, getting rid of the large rats and other foraging things she never dared investigate. It was then that the footsteps altered, seemed to rush towards her with intent. She turned in alarm, crippled leg nearly overbalancing her as she saw the two youths bearing down on her. Adella only had time to register surprise before the suffocating folds of a heavy cloth draped over her, and she was sent crashing to the ground. Thoughts scattered in her head, half-forming then dissolving. She felt them wrenching at the bag, their heavy breathing mingling with her fright. Adella willed the crippled hand to let go, images of women kicked to death jumbling with the thought of who they were.

She almost cried aloud with relief when the bag strap gave way. She lay still, willing her trembling limbs to stiffness, afraid to alarm them lest they turn on her. The pavement was hard against her cheek, cold and hard. Her shoulder hurt where it had hit sharply against unyielding stone, her hips felt bruised and tender. It seemed for ever that they stood above her, whispering uncertainly, before she heard the hasty sounds of running feet. She stayed still, afraid they might still be there, that others might come and hurt her. Her house less than a hundred yards away seemed out of reach, endless oceans of danger suddenly dividing it from her.

When she finally stumbled in, clutching the coat the youths had thrown over her, the house was silent and empty. She knew Carol would be walking the dog, while the cat would be out somewhere on a nocturnal errand of her own. Adella's hand was shaking as she fumbled for her purse, thankful that she always put it in the pocket of her coat when she took the bus. It was easier to get at than fumbling about, unlocking each finger of the crippled hand with slow precision. But habit was a funny thing, she had become used to having something locked in those clawlike fingers, and that was why she had carried her bag that day.

Her daughter had come back to find her huddled in her chair, the coat still clutched to her. Neither light or television showed, reaction setting in and the sound of murmuring voices all around her.

'Mum! What's the matter?' Carol had asked in alarm, anger at Shela's barking excitement cutting off in mid-stream as she saw the slumped bulk in the big armchair.

Adella sat shaking, unable to speak, the nightmare inside her head receding only slightly at the familiar sound of dog and daughter.

'Where did you get that coat?' her daughter persisted. 'And what have you done to your face?'

Adella's hand went automatically to the cheek that she had vaguely noticed ached and stung.

'Some white bwoys attack me dung Mostyn Road,' she said finally.

Carol's eyes widened with shock, then narrowed in anger. 'Did you phone the police?' she asked, adding, 'What did they take?'

Adella looked at her blankly. 'Dem tek me bag, but nuting did inna it, a did have me purse in me pocket.'

'Did you phone the police?' her daughter repeated.

Adella looked at her in surprise. 'Why a should phone de police? Yu know what did happen when Missa Peters get beat up. Dem come start trouble ihm an try sey is ihm did start it – like ihm coulda start anyting.'

Her daughter ignored her, getting out her address book, picking up the phone and dialling rapidly, muttering under her breath all the time.

Adella wished she wouldn't call the police. She had been wary of them since the riot when they had broken down her friend's door and beaten up her disabled husband just because he was black. She was sure that if he had not been old, if he had been healthy, they would not have dared to treat him like that. She hoped her daughter would stay with her; Carol knew how to speak their language.

It was two hours before the patrol car had driven up outside her door, and she had calmed down by then. Carol had given her something to eat and a drink of tea with something strong in it, for once making no comment about the effect of alcohol. Adella had begun to relax, thinking they would not bother. Why should they come anyway, only black people lived on that street and they didn't really care for them. There was a western on the television, one in colour rather than the black and white of the films they had shown recently. She pushed the earlier fear aside, concentrated with determination on her rum-soaked tea and the cigarette in her mouth, and her heart sank when the doorbell rang.

She could hear them out there, the rudeness in the younger voice as he spoke to Carol, and she felt pride when her daughter answered sharply; held her ground and forced him to back down. Even so, the hand that held the cigarette was shaking by the time Carol showed them in, switching on the light as she came through to sit on the arm of Adella's chair. She felt grateful for her daughter's thoughtfulness, the fact that she realised her fear; images of Mr Peters being roughed up by the police were in her mind.

'Your daughter was telling us that you were mugged, Mrs–?' the older policeman said, taking out a notebook and flicking it open.

'Johnson,' Adella supplied. 'Me name Miss Johnson.' She could feel the tenseness coiling inside her belly. To think she had once supported the police; believed like everyone else that it was only bad boys and good for nothings – the sticksmen and rudeboys – that was causing the trouble. How many times had she argued with her daughters, told them off for their disloyalty to the police, urged them not to turn bad. Now she knew different. The police just didn't like West Indians, and old or young they would do their best to hurt them.

'Well, Mrs Johnson,' the same man said, his voice becoming impatient, causing the fingers of her good hand to shake as she knocked ash from her cigarette into the ashtray. 'Did they take anything – your bag?'

'Dem tek me hanbag, but nuting was in it, and dem did throw a good coat ova me dat a tink worth more.'

'Stolen, no doubt,' the younger policeman said contemptuously. 'I suppose these blokes who attacked you were black,' he continued, writing rapidly in his small notebook.

'Dem was white bwoys, man,' she said firmly. 'De black bwoy dem doan do tings like dat – an dem know sey people roun ya doan have no money.'

'How do you know they were white?' the younger man asked coldly. 'You said they threw a coat over your head.'

'A did see dem come fore dat. Nuting no wrang wid me eyesight.'

He was looking unfriendly now, leaning forward in the settee, making no attempt to hide his dislike.

'If you saw them coming why didn't you run?' he asked nastily.

'Can't you see mum's crippled?' Carol said in disgust. 'How do you suppose she was going to outrun two strong men with a crippled foot and hand, eh?'

The man had the grace to look ashamed, and muttered an apology. 'The thing is,' he said, 'we have reason to believe that there is a group of black muggers operating in this area and we wondered if maybe your mother could be mistaken and one of them had jumped her.'

Carol looked angry. 'As mum said, there is nothing wrong with her eyes, if she said the muggers were white they were white.'

'We weren't trying to dispute what your mother said,' the older man said hastily. 'It's just unusual to hear of white youths engaged in mugging activity.'

Carol smiled nastily. 'Not that unusual,' she said. 'Except that when black people round here get mugged by whites, nobody does anything about it. Anyway, mum's lived round here for over thirty years – isn't that right, mum.'

Adella nodded, happy for her daughter to deal with the police, seeing how well she held her own against them. 'All the black kids know that she works up at social security as a cleaner and that she doesn't have any money.'

'They could have come from outside the area,' the older man suggested helpfully.

'And waited on half-derelict Mostyn Road in case somebody happened by?' Carol asked sarcastically, adding, 'If they came from outside the area it's unlikely they even knew Mostyn Road existed, much less how to find it. It's more likely they would have gone somewhere closer to the tube station or the main bus route.'

The man looked embarrassed. 'It was only a suggestion,' he said.

'Well, what're you going to do about mum being robbed?' Carol asked impatiently when they seemed unsure what to ask next.

'Well the truth is, love,' the older man said, 'I doubt we have much chance of catching them. We'll get a description from your mother and try, of course. But chances are they will be long gone by the time we get to the scene.'

'Unless they came from Stockwell estate,' Carol contradicted.

'But we don't know if they do,' the man came back. 'Truth is there are so many street robberies these days, you don't have much hope of catching anyone.'

Adella knew they didn't even intend to try, knew it from their reluctance to take details, even to take the coat that had been thrown over her.

'Chances are it was stolen anyway,' the older man had said, putting his notebook and pen back into his breast-pocket.

'Well it must have been stolen from someone or somewhere,' Carol said tightly, holding the coat out to them when they would have left without it.

'You'll hear from us if anything turns up,' the policeman said awkwardly, accepting the coat.

After Lisa left, Adella remained sitting in her chair. There was no need to go to bed early now. She had nothing to get up for in the morning, nowhere to go. Not that she ever had trouble getting up. Sleep was slow to come and quick to leave her these days. Her mind wandered back to the attack by the white boys. The police had never been in touch, not that she really expected it. How different things had been back home. She could remember the first time she had come across robbery and assault. It had been after she had been living in Kingston for a few months. Nobody had told her that she could be attacked, that there were places where it was not always safe to be if you were a stranger to the area.

She had been in the habit of wandering about the town, liking to browse through the shops downtown. She would peer into the windows to see the latest fashions from abroad, or just walk about, watching the rich ladies with their maids. Sometimes she wandered down to the harbour, just to watch the ships come in. She liked to stare and wonder where they came from. If only she could ride in one, climb up the gangplank with her grip, wearing her best Sunday hat like the women bustling past. She never told anyone about this dream, knew that her cousin would not approve of her trips down to the harbour, having heard him talk all the time about the loose women who hung out there. She had seen the women he talked about, of course. All dressed in daring low-cut dresses, walking with suggestively swinging hips, approaching boldly any man who passed by.

It was on one of her walks down to the wharf that she had been

80

attacked. She had volunteered to go downtown to get fresh fish from the Higgla women who made the daily trek from fishing villages to sell their husbands' catch. Adella liked to wander among the market women, loving the fresh earth smells of new yams and sweet potatoes, feeling closer to Beaumont among the tie-heads and shouting gossip of the traders. She liked the freshness of the fish in the marketplace, the mackerel and parrot fish laid side by side with groupers and small sharks. The smell was the same when they went down to the bay to watch the fishermen haul in the boats with the early morning catch, the warm waves lapping gently against the endless stretch of yellow sand beaches.

She always spent a long time in the market, purse in one hand, the straw basket she had brought up from the country for her cousin's house in the other. It was nice to settle down in front of a stall with likely-looking goods, to squat down and haggle with the stallowner, using her country knowledge to make sure she got a good deal. She loved the sounds and smells of the marketplace. It was much more exciting than Highgate where her mother used to sell their produce before the traders for the places in the town came to buy. But not as nice as Highgate where the marketplace stood roofed and high up on a rise, the highest place in the town. In Highgate the stalls were laid out, each trader sitting cross-legged behind her overflowing baskets shouting greetings to favoured customers or late-coming traders.

Kingston was another place, the market bustling and overflowing well outside the boundaries of the designated area. There was always a clamour of voices as everyone cried out their wares, trying to drown out neighbours or be heard above the din. The smell of the marketplace was intense; the colours an assault on the senses. Bolts of local cloth rubbed shoulders with imported material from far-off Canada and the USA, spilling on to cookware, and dutchpots that flowed into the stalls of ground provisions and dried fish. Everything was faster than in the country, the market louder, more outrageous. She had not stayed long in the market that day. Her ears still ringing with the jumbled sounds of cried-out wares and the braying of discontented donkeys, she had gone down to the wharf, not quite intending to but, having missed the uptown bus, she had to wait or walk. Adella often walked home from the market, but the day was hot and her fish was fresh. She decided that it was better to spend a few cooling moments at the wharf before coming back to catch a later bus.

She had spent only a few minutes there. With no new ship pulling in that day it was strangely deserted, no hustle and bustle of embarking or disembarking. Even the gulls were few and far between, and she had soon tired of watching the water lapping against a solitary cargo ship. She had been walking back, her mind on far-away places, when she realised that she was lost, that the strange, oppressive smells and tangled mass of zinc shacks were well past Orange Street and Parade. It was like another world – ragged children playing in the pitted dirt, shacks tangled together in overcrowded yards. Here and there she would stumble across what looked like a well-tended yard, a place with signs that told her a balm-yard had been set up there. She knew instinctively that this was West Kingston, the shanty towns her cousin had talked about which were full of excitement, all-night blues and little boys with no seat in the pants of their short trousers. She had been looking around feeling the excitement building up inside, the throb of life about the place. Everywhere the blare of jukeboxes assaulted her ears, the new music she had heard about pumping excitement into the air. She wandered on, peering down the narrow alleyways, peeping through open gates or rust-eaten zinc doors to see how people lived. She knew that bad men lived down here, sticksmen, whom she secretly thought were daring and brave to stand up to the government.

The man had jumped her from behind, sending her sprawling on the baked mud earth which was littered with discarded papers and other waste. The shock had knocked her breath away, and she felt him wrench her bag, twisting it painfully out of her hand before hauling her round to face him. He was a big man, towering over her. His clothes were ragged, the khaki trousers frayed and held up at the waist by string like her father's work trousers. The black shirt hung open, without buttons. His beard was matted, and his eyes red-rimmed from ganja smoke, while his hair seemed in need of combing. 'What yu doing dung ya?' he asked aggressively, pushing her aside while he fumbled with the catch of her bag, dumping the contents in the litter on the baked brown mud.

Adella stared at him in fear, feeling her heart beat heavily. The man looked mad; one of those people that had been forgotten and left to wander the street and terrorise the people they caught. There was a gleam of malice in his eyes as they shifted across her cowering figure with sudden interest. The place seemed suddenly deserted, the surrounding noise stranding her alone with a ganja-crazy man.

He came at her, tongue licking, lip peeled raw from holding spliffs in his mouth for too long, and she closed her eyes and screamed.

Running feet, faces appeared from nowhere, converging on her from every side. Adella glimpsed the man rushing down an alleyway, her bag clutched firmly in his hand. Then she was surrounded, anxious faces peering down at her, questions raining down on her like a barrage. Was she all right? Had he hurt her?

Finally a woman had stepped forward and helped her to her feet, insisted that she came home with her and drink some bush tea. The woman told her that her son was a policeman and that he would help to get her bag back if she would just describe it. Adella had been glad to go home with her and sit on the cosy wooden veranda and drink the bitter herb.

'Yu come fram country,' the woman said, as she sat watching her. 'Dung ya all right but it no good fe wander, specially when so much mad man deh pan street an dem know when yu new in town.'

Adella liked the woman, who said her name was Miss Vida. She reminded her of Mada Beck. She had the same age and wisdom in her face, though she must have been at least thirty years younger than the dead woman. She was glad to sit on the veranda drinking tea with her, watching how everybody coming in and out of the yard called to her with fondness and respect. One day she would be old like this, respected and with dignity. She was almost sorry when the woman called a little ragged boy and told him to take her back uptown.

'A will sure an tell Beresford bout yu,' she said to Adella, folding the slip of paper on which she had written the girl's address, and putting it carefully in the pocket of her dress.

Adella had not expected to hear anything else about her bag, and she had been surprised when the policeman knocked on the door, holding it in his hand. He looked young and eager, eyes full of fun as they moved over her with interest. He said his name was Beresford and she knew that he was Miss Vida's son. If she liked the mother she liked the son even more, thinking how smart he looked in his uniform, how handsome and how good. How was she to know he was already married? That he always had a roving eye? By the time she found out it was too late, and she was already heavy with his second child.

Ten

The room had hung heavy with silent expectation. Green-patterned wallpaper and matching felt squares of carpet did nothing to ease the tension in the air. Adella looked round furtively, feeling awed by the size of it, the wall-to-wall carpet – something she had only seen in magazines. The small square tables littered about the room held neat stacks of magazines. Here and there one of the other waiting women would take one up, flick through it as though the interview did not really matter. Adella felt the usual despair seeping in as the clock on one of the walls showed the slow minutes ticking silently away. She had lost count of the interviews she had attended, the many jobs she had ticked off in the paper, finding precious money to ring before going for the interview. At first it had been factory jobs, people wanting machinists – less demanding jobs than the one she had done before the stroke. She knew that it would mean a drop in pay and that she would have to shift to piecework. There would be no satisfaction in selecting the delicate strands of finely coloured silk and watching patterns form under her hands. But at least it would be something she knew and she could stay working with cloth.

It had not been simple. They had been impressed by her experience and the fact that she had worked at skilled embroidery work. But one look at her crippled side and the face would cloud with embarrassment or rejection. Many of them had been blunt. One even accused her of wasting his time, eyes pinned accusingly on her crippled clawlike hand.

'How do you propose to work the machine?' he had asked sarcastically.

Adella's head bowed under his contempt while the busy sounds of speeding industrial machines caused her fingers to itch with the need to work.

'Give me a chance and a sure a can do it,' she had pleaded. She

84

knew she could do the work; she had practised long and hard, training her left hand on her sewing machine at home using the crippled hand for balance. She knew her movements were a lot better now. Twice a day she had practised, week in, week out, since coming out of hospital, forcing some awareness back into crippled limbs.

'What do you think this is?' the man asked in disgust, his heavy face irritated. 'Some kind of charity for cripples? Labour shortage ain't that bad yet.'

She saw the contempt in his face. The look that mirrored those of all the other people she had seen about a job. It told her they had no use for her; that she was finished as a worker as far as they were concerned.

She had stopped looking for machinist jobs after that. Reluctantly accepting Lisa's words that there was no future for her in the trade. Now she looked around for anything she could find. She was not qualified enough for some jobs; for others she knew it was because she was too black. 'No Experience Needed' the advert would say; but when she got there it was another thing. Always the excuse was that she was a cripple, that she could never hope to keep up the pace and finally, reluctantly, she realised that she had no other choice but to look for work as a cleaner.

Now here she was, come for an interview, sitting in a waiting-room furnished in a way she thought could only happen on the television or in the pages of the magazines she sometimes treated herself to. The company was a big one in the heart of the City of London, a place into which she had never ventured before. It had such big buildings all towering above her, and she had wandered about for what seemed like hours before finding the place. All the streets looked the same, the buildings so impressive – Adella could not believe she could possibly get a job in one of them. She knew from experience what these people thought of West Indians. Better to work for the clothes-makers who needed your skills for their profits.

When she found the building, Adella walked tentatively up to it, bad foot dragging more than ever from the long walk through the narrow streets. She half-expected the man at the door to turn her away, or the woman behind the big reception desk that curved and ran endlessly, its wooden surface gleaming, to ask her to leave. Instead, the woman looked at her disdainfully. 'You must have come for the cleaning job,' she said rudely. 'First floor, second door on the left,' and as Adella started to walk off, 'use the stairs, not the lift.' Adella looked round, feeling suddenly conscious of how shabby she looked. 'It's out of order,' the woman added impatiently before turning back to her work.

Adella clutched her cheap canvas coat defensively, feeling awkward in the plastic shoes already fraying at the toes. She felt a mess in the face of the other woman's well-groomed look and wanted to turn and run out of that imposing building. Only the need for the job kept her there – the knowledge that Stanton was not prepared to take on responsibility for the children or the house.

'Like yu sey, is yu house,' he had said nastily when she had tried to get some extra money out of him. 'A give yu enough fe buy food and look afta me, a doan feel as a owe yu nuting; specially ow yu treat yu cousin when yu fling her out a street.'

It was desperation that had driven her to overcome her disability. Desperation and the certain knowledge that if she did not do something, she would lose Stanton for good. She could see him moving away from her, slipping further and further out of her reach. Adella was sure that if she could get over the stroke, get a job and bring some money in, things would be better. She told herself that he had become used to the little treats she had got into the habit of buying him. The things she would not admit were a form of bribing him, to keep him sweet and off her back. At the same time, money was getting tight. If it were not for her tenants she knew she could not manage. Even so, she hated to think of the times the children went to bed on empty stomachs as she saved the last piece of bread for their morning breakfast. On many days they only ate because Lisa fed them, brushing aside her embarrassment and false pride. Through it all Stanton always ate well, going out at nights to the pub or to a blues party where she knew he spent a lot on drinks and food for himself and other people. All the men she knew kept telling her how generous he was, how fortunate she was to have a husband like him.

Now she was in this well-decorated waiting-room, watching the time slip by. She avoided the eyes of the other waiting women as she cast furtive glances at them. There were only five jobs, and eight women waiting. She saw the way they looked at her, how they dismissed her when they saw her crippled side. Only the desperate need to get a job kept her where she was, the humiliation of her other interviews still alive in her memory. Adella wondered if she

86

would have come if she had known how impressive the place was, how much trouble they were going to to recruit cleaning staff. She had thought that it was a simple matter of turning up, being looked at and told your hours. No healthy person would want a job that meant cleaning other people's floors whatever Lisa said. She could see how wrong she was: everybody else was healthy, looked fit and well and as if they knew exactly what the job entailed.

She was on the point of leaving, having decided that there was no way she could get a job there, when her name was called. Adella's heart sank, a nervous pulse starting up inside her ears. Her legs were unsteady as she heaved herself out of the comfortable chair; her crippled leg suddenly awkward and dragging. She gripped her bag with her good hand, hoping that the shaking she felt was not too obvious. Her eyes accidentally caught those of one of the waiting women, read pity and swerved away. She felt irritation at that pity mingle with her fear and stiffen her back. They knew she could not get the job and they seemed to be wondering why she had even bothered to come for the interview. She was determined not to show them how defeated she really felt.

She got the job! Adella could not believe she had heard the man properly, even when he repeated it patiently. She only half-heard the hours she would work and the day she had to start. Her heart was singing by the time she got out of the big, imposing building. She did not even notice the contempt on the receptionist's face, the way the porter let the door swing back at her. She had got a job and soon she would be earning money again. No longer would she feel guilt at the children's hungry faces or cry silently in the big empty bed, lying awake praying that something good would happen.

Adella could hardly wait for Stanton to return that night. She cooked stew peas for him, using the last of the red peas and the pig's tail he had brought home the day before. She could even forgive him his meanness – the fact that he had forbidden her to give any to the children. She had got a job, and things would be better from now on. He was late coming in that evening. The children had long gone to bed and the stew and rice were cold in the pot. But Adella did not mind. She sat in her favourite chair thinking of all the things she would do now that she had the job. She was used to waiting for him to come, the light left off to save electricity, her mind thinking ahead, calculating their expenses. It had been a long time since she had been able to afford a barrel, and she decided that she must start getting some clothes and gifts together to fill one for her family back home. They would be so surprised to get a shipment from her after so long.

She came awake to the noise of the solid wooden front door crashing shut. Adella sat up with a jerk, realising that she had fallen asleep. Her neck felt stiff from being twisted into an awkward position. She stretched, using her left hand to massage the knotted muscles of her neck as the door opened. She knew it was him, of course. Recently he seemed to need to wake the house whenever he came in late.

Light flooded the room, dazzling her after the soothing moonless darkness, and she blinked owlishly at him. She felt the tightness inside her stomach, the instinctive fear which told her that he was in another foul temper.

'Whe de food?' he asked rudely. 'A waan yu fe run de food gi me.'

'A haffe heat it up again,' she told him, fumbling for her slippers which had somehow dropped off as she slept. Getting awkwardly to her feet, Adella moved slowly towards the door.

She could see by his frown that he had not expected her to have cooked him anything and felt thankful that she had done so. How often had she waited up, leaving the cooking till he came back. It was the only way to save the waste. He would not normally eat food that was not freshly cooked, and when she cooked and he did not come back he would hit her for wastefulness the next day. As far as he was concerned she did it deliberately so she could give her children his food. Of course that wasn't true, but she had learnt to stop protesting, as that only made him more angry. Yet if he came home in a mood like tonight and there was no food, he often became violent.

She waited until he was halfway through the meal. His grunts of appreciation told her the food was good and that he would warm to her as a result.

'A get a jab, Stanton,' she said, watching for his reaction as he ate, head bent over the tray of food balanced expertly on his lap.

Stanton's head jerked up. It was fleshier since he came to England, but still distinguished, with a parting straight down the centre of the greased-back hair.

'A jab?' he repeated, as if he could not quite believe he had heard her right. 'Whe yu get jab fram?'

Adella felt a twinge of disappointment at his response. She knew that he felt she should have gone and begged money from the welfare. Somebody had told him she could claim money from the government now that she was a cripple and he resented her refusal. He thought her pride misplaced. 'Yu doan waan go ask de govament dat have plenty money but yu keep afta me fa de lickle bit a earn,' he would often say in disgust. 'Well if is proud yu proud, yu gwine jus haffe eat pride. When yu wante wante bad enough yu gwine run go beg dem.' Now she saw the near anger in his eyes, the resentment he felt at her announcement.

'Is nuting big,' she said hastily. 'Is jus a cleaning jab in a big office. A start Monday. De pay no good, but it will tek de burden off yu if a working too.'

He seemed to swell visibly under the subtle praise. 'A see dat,' he said more sympathetically. 'Is hard fa me to manage, what wid yu getting sick an all an nobady fe help out.'

'Dat true,' she said hastily, seeing the spectre of Gladys rising between them again. Since she had thrown her cousin out he had never forgiven her. And on the rare nights he still slept in the house, he slept on the settee, refusing to share a bed with her. Adella would not admit that it was because of her cousin, insisted on thinking that it was the pressure of her stroke, the fact that she could no longer work to keep his comforts up. 'Once a get inna de swing a might get some overtime work and tings shouldn't stay so tight no more.'

Stanton nodded, biting appreciatively into the succulent meat before digging his fork into the tender red peas and rice.

'An yu might come back to yu own bed,' she ventured, seeing his pleased absorption with the food in front of him.

The fork stopped moving, poised in mid-air. 'Wha yu mean?' he asked suspiciously. 'A tell yu already – dat part a de marriage done.' He paused, finishing the remnants of the food on his plate before adding, 'Fram yu have de stroke, yu change, Adella. A doan recognise yu de way yu get bitta. Doan tink a can fagive yu fa de way yu treat Gladys an dat afta she give up her room an her work fe come look afta de children.'

Adella bit back her anger, the injustice of it running through her. They both knew why she had thrown her cousin out, and a sudden thought occurred to her. 'Yu still go a blues wid Gladys?' she asked casually.

'Yes, man,' he answered, before realising what he had said. 'Well somebady haffe look out fa her, since is yu mess her up.'

She felt the bitterness like a sour thing on her tongue, tasted the pain before it seeped inside her, spreading everywhere. No wonder he stayed out most nights – no wonder he never had any money though he no longer bought the same amount of clothes. She had heard the rumours on the street, in the market. Everybody was whispering about them carrying on, blaming her because she was losing her husband to her own cousin. 'A know bout yu an Gladys, Stanton,' she said sadly, pushing back the raw pain. The tears threatened to clog her throat and shake her voice.

'Who tell yu someting a go on wid Gladys an me, dat good fanuting Lisa? Why she doan bring her pickney dem ova or go back to fe her husband stead a fasing in ada people business.'

'Lisa know bout it, but is not she tell me.'

'Is nat?' he was surprised now, interest in the plate forgotten as he reached automatically to balance the tray on the arm of the settee. 'So who tell yu?'

'Everybady talking bout it. A even hear some church brethren sey dat yu an she is sinning togeda.'

'Dem people should mind dem own business,' he said sullenly, a little boy caught out in a lie but not ready to admit to guilt. 'A ongly look out fa de chile tru she is blood. Gladys is a good girl, anybady can see dat.'

Adella looked at him sadly. 'Dat where yu sleep a night time when yu doan come home?'

He could see she did not believe him, had not accepted a word he said. 'A haffe sleep somewhere and Gladys grateful fa de way a treat her.'

She looked at his sullen face, the small moustache he had been trying to grow since those long, half-forgotten days when they had been so happy in Kingston. 'Yu doan even gi me money fa yu own children, but yu pay her rent fa her and keep her. A doan believe is jus tru she related to me. If so ow come yu would a mek yu children starve?'

Stanton was looking at her in surprise. His widened eyes told her that he could hardly believe she was throwing those hard words at him.

'She is a she-devil, Stanton,' she continued, past caring about the anger in his face, the likelihood that he would attack her once again, hit and pound her as if she was to blame for all the things gone wrong with him since he had come to England. 'Yu is not strang. Woman can lead yu if dem have a will.'

She had half-expected the blow when he stood up and came to tower menacingly over her. It sent her sprawling back into the chair, her cheekbone aching where the curled fist had landed with all his anger and his strength. Adella sat up shakily, holding her good hand to her cheek, shrinking away from the anger that radiated from him.

'If yu waan de truth, Gladys an me been moving fram way back. She is more woman dan yu an she faithful at dat. Is a shame yu neva learn anyting fram her insteada try mek me feel small all de time.'

She felt sick deep inside, her mind recoiling from an acceptance of what he was saying. He was only trying to hurt her, had to be. He had not forgiven her for her treatment of the other woman and was trying to get back at her for it.

'Yu tink a waan live like dis?' he asked, opening his hands to include the whole house. 'Yu keep tell me is your house, is yu do dis, is yu do dat. Ow yu tink it mek me feel? Gladys diffrent, she mek me know she preciate what a do fa her.'

'But, Stanton, yu know a preciate what yu do fa me,' she said timidly as the back of his hand swept out, and connected with her face again.

'Doan tell lie. Yu was always de same fram way back, always a cuss bout someting, a wante wante an a breed more pickney. Well yu can have yu house cause a leaving right now. A gwine live wid somebady who undastan me.' He turned and stalked out, and she heard him in the bedroom, wrenching open cupboard doors and drawers, cursing above the noise. She sat stunned, unable to believe he was serious, that he intended to abandon her. Panic clawed at her. What would she do without him? How would she manage with him gone? No! he couldn't go, couldn't live with her own cousin right in the same area. She would never get over the shame, the pity of it. Stumbling to her feet, she moved with clumsy haste, bad foot dragging more than ever with her agitation. She could feel shivers of fear coursing through her and she prayed that he would not attack her again. She told herself it was just anger and he did not mean to carry out this threat, would not leave her after their years together. She clutched at the jamb as she opened the bedroom door, mind screaming rejection of what her eyes could see. He had hauled down his grip from the top of the wardrobe and it lay gaping open on the bed. Clothes and shoes were crammed drunkenly inside. He was pulling shirts, vests and socks out of the drawer, flinging them into the case with angry disregard. It was so unlike him. Stanton was always so neat and tidy. Adella couldn't move. Her mind continued to resist the nightmare in front of her.

'Yu caan leave me, Stanton,' she said finally. 'A sorry a vex yu – but yu caan jus up an leave me wid de five children dem.'

He paused to give her an angry look – hissed through his teeth in irritation when he realised that his grip was overflowing. Climbing on the bed, he pushed the clothes down, leaning on the case so he could snap the catch shut.

The bed was still littered with clothes: trousers and jackets strewn on the floor, and hanging in the wardrobe. Without a pause, he pulled down her grip and started to throw clothes in it.

'A will give it back to yu when a come fe look fa de children. A not teking it, jus borrowing it.'

Adella nodded automatically. She didn't care about the grip. He could take Delores and Mikey's cases as well if he wanted. She just could not bear the thought that he was going to leave them, was going to walk out and leave her without a husband, her children without a father.

'Stanton, do a beg yu, doan left me alone. A gwine get betta, a gwine try fe do what yu want.'

She could feel the tears wet on her face, the slight prickling as they traced downwards, the saltiness at the corners of her mouth.

'Yu doan undastan?' he asked cruelly. 'A doan have no use fa yu no more. A caan live up to what yu want, Adella, an a tink is bes a left yu now fore tings get wussa an wussa.'

'But a get a jab now, Stanton,' she pleaded. 'Tings gwine get betta, a know it will.'

He ignored her and continued to toss clothes into the case as if she wasn't there. Adella felt a surge of anger and resentment bubbling over.

'Well go to her den,' she said bitterly. 'Yu tink is yu she want?' She was breathing hard, feeling the injustice inside, her head aching from the force of her emotions. 'Fram she can tek weh her own cousin man, yu tink yu can trus her? Come to dat she not gwine trus yu? Is not she yu want, Stanton, is yu family yu running fram, tru yu caan responsible fa dem.'

He closed the case on an angry snap, hauling it off the bed to join the other one on the floor; giving her a last spiteful look he picked up a case in either hand after making sure he had not forgotten anything. 'Yu should look pan yuself,' he said nastily. 'Yu get ole and ugly. Yu let yuself go so bad a doan tink any man gwine waan look pan yu much less waan move wid yu.' With that he walked to the door, pushing roughly past her.

Eleven

Adella stood where she was even after the finality of the closing door. She could not believe it had actually happened. Her eyes were blank and unseeing as she looked around the room. Inside she felt empty, drained, unable to think, to feel. Finally she moved, stepping jerkily into the room. She acted automatically, picking up discarded items of clothes, smoothing the bed covers, closing cupboard doors and pushing back the drawer that hung open. When the place was straightened, Adella sank down on the bed, hands loose between her legs, staring ahead as if she expected him to come back through the door.

'Ihm haffe come back,' she told herself grimly. 'Ihm caan stay weh. Nobady gwine look out fa him same as me. Ihm haffe come back when tings get tough.'

She felt a little better for the thought. Then, giving herself a mental shake, she got up from the bed. She couldn't leave the sitting-room light burning all night. It cost money and that was something she did not have.

It seemed for ever before Monday morning came. The time between the Wednesday night when Stanton walked out and the Monday after church dragged along. Adella did not tell the children he had gone and none of them seemed to notice. She felt angry with him, realising how little time he had spent at home, how little the children saw of him, even when he had been living there. Only the thought of work sustained her. She told herself she had a job, was not as useless as he said she was. But his words left an open, bleeding wound; the knowledge of her crippled state weighed heavily on her, taking away her spirit. It was nice to be at work again, to get up early in the morning with a solid purpose, knowing that you had a job and still had usefulness.

At first when she donned the overall she had felt awkward,

hating the mop and bulky bucket and the way the office staff ignored her, treating her like she was a part of the furniture. She felt angry with the world. Why should she end up as a cleaner after all the work her grandmother and her parents had done? Why had she become a cripple just when she had been doing so well with her life? It had ruined everything for her.

After a while she got used to the job, even started to look forward to the evening shift when all the office-workers had gone home. It was nice when the long corridors were empty, the airy rooms silent and waiting with all the machinery still. Many of the other women were West Indians. Some worked more than one job to help make ends meet. She had soon got to like the other two who cleaned the floor with her. Cheryl was from Trinidad and had not seen her husband since her last child was born. Adella was surprised at how well the woman took her man's betrayal, the way she shrugged her shoulders when she extended her sympathy. 'Is good riddance,' the woman had said carelessly. 'All he do was sidung on his backside come weekend an go to fete or de gambling place.' Adella had not known what to say. For her Stanton's desertion was too recent to talk about or even mention.

'What about your husband?' Cheryl asked her one day as they were leaving work together. 'He good to yu?'

Adella nodded, feeling bad about the lie, but not able to confide. Only Lisa knew how badly she felt about Stanton's desertion. How ashamed she felt at the gossip it caused. Lisa was always there to help out with the children, or just to keep her company and cheer her up.

The second woman was from Jamaica. She had never lived in a city before she came to England. She had come to join her husband, and Adella envied the way she talked about him. Why couldn't Stanton be like that? They had three children, and they were saving up to go back home and when the woman talked about her family life, the way she and her husband shared things together, worked together, Adella felt her loss more strongly.

She stayed in the City for five years, catching the first bus in the morning. She would walk down to the main road in the cool darkness just as it appeared round a bend in the road. Then she sat listening to the chatter of the early workers as the bus chugged along, stopping to take on more passengers or to let off one or two. Cheryl would get on at Kennington, swaying along the narrow aisle to where Adella sat and dropping in the seat beside her. Adella liked the woman. The way her pleasantly plump brown face was always smooth and untroubled. Cheryl was content to work as a cleaner. She had been at the same place for several years, ever since her husband left her. She was happy with her two children, pushing them along in school and spending as much of her time with them as she could.

'A neva would put dem wid a minder,' she said one morning. 'A tink dat is why Dick did up an lef. He did want me to work full-time. A did come ova to train fa nursing, yu know. He want me to finish de training and den fa us go back dung to Trinidad.'

Adella looked at her in surprise. 'Why yu give it up?' she asked. Nursing was something she had wanted to do, but she had not been able to get into one of the hospitals for the training. She could not believe somebody would give it up. Life was so strange.

'A didn't like de cleaning up,' Cheryl said, leaning her bulk back against the seat and laughing suddenly. 'Dat soun funny, me cleaning an all, but it was diffrent. Deh treat all the West Indian nurse bad, and afta all de training and de studying a fail de exam, an anyway de people dem in de hospital too naasy.'

Adella nodded, the idea of nursing a little less desirable. It was exactly what Lisa had said about the bad treatment and the racism.

'At least dey leave yu alone to do yu work at dis place,' Cheryl said. 'An yu doan haffe put up wid all de name calling fram de white nurses and de patients.' She paused, fishing out the fare as the conductor came down the aisle, exchanging a few words with him before he moved on. 'De truth is dat a neva really wanted to do nursing, and now a lot of de friends a made when a was training is seying tings doan getting no betta.'

Other times they would just sit in silence, watching the elegant houses pass by, or looking out at the river as they crossed the bridge before turning towards the city. She was beginning to like her job, the silence in the evenings and the bus-rides along the empty streets after the evening shift. At least she had the money to feed the children and Lisa was there to take them to school in the morning and take them home at night. Only the house worried her, the way the dampness had turned to seeping waterfalls, running in rivulets down the wall before vanishing into fungus growths. Adella wished she could do something about it, sensing that the house was decaying all around her.

It was after she had been working less than three years that disaster finally struck. Adella had woken to a loud and violent

95

crash. Half-asleep, her heart pounded in alarm. 'De house fall dung,' she told herself, groping for her dressing-gown as she struggled out of bed in the cool dawn air. She heard the confused voices coming from above – shouts and cursing, a little girl crying, and she stumbled out into the passage to a wave of panic and alarm. Mikey was running down the stairs, and she guessed that he had already been to see what was going on.

'The roof come down on Missa Dawson,' he told her breathlessly.

Adella's eyes widened in alarm, heart jumping at the news. God! Suppose something had happened to the man! Suppose she got in trouble for it. She had heard about things like that: people going to court, to prison. She swallowed hard, pushing the panic back. She had to be sensible, keep control. Peering upwards she tried to penetrate the gloom at the bend in the stairs, ears straining to make out what was being said in the confusion. 'Ihm hurt bad?' she asked urgently.

'No but he want his rent money back, and he say he going to move out.'

Adella sighed with relief, mounting the stairs heavily. She couldn't afford to lose a tenant now, but she was glad that at least the man was all right. She knew his wife, a nurse, was on late shift and she wondered what the woman would say when she came back. Mrs Dawson was always complaining that the roof leaked, that it was liable to collapse and kill them in their bed. She had to push past the tenants on the first-floor landing. They were all milling around looking lost.

'Miss Johnson, is true de roof fall dung pan Missa Dawson?' Mrs Weston asked timidly. 'Is true ihm an Miss Dawson dead?'

Adella looked at her impatiently, wondering why none of them had gone up to investigate, why none of the other three tenants on the second floor had come down to tell them.

'A doan know, Miss Weston, a jus gwine look, but Mikey sey ihm all right.'

Adella pushed through the tangle of bewildered people, climbing the last set of stairs. She could hear Mr Dawson clearly now, hear him muttering about crosses. She knew that the others followed her and that they had been waiting for some kind of positive action.

The door to Mr Dawson's room was wide open, and the room seemed full of people, dust and cold air. Adella's eyes went to the gaping hole in the ceiling through which she just glimpsed the lightening dawn sky.

'Lord Jesas Christ! Look pan me house!' she wailed, not able to take it in.

'Ihm dead?' Mrs Weston asked in alarm, voice raised to a high squeal. 'Missa Dawson dead?'

'A doan dead yet,' Mr Dawson roared. 'Though is nat tanks to you, Miss Johnson,' he said glaring at her. 'Look pan de place, look pan me someting dem; is ongly de good Lord know how a doan dead.'

Adella looked round obligingly, seeing the chunk of masonry that had fallen on the wardrobe, and the dust that covered the carpet and the bed. She pulled her robe closer, feeling the damp air pouring through the hole in the ceiling. She was looking around, trying to assess the damage, wondering where she would find money for repairs, when her eyes swung back to the bed in shock.

The woman who was sitting up, huddled under the covers, was certainly not the plump, ageing Mrs Dawson. She had to be at least ten years younger and, from what Adella could see, looking at the exposed arms and the outline under the blanket, she was certainly not plump.

'Yu not gwine sey anyting?' Mr Dawson was asking, voice getting aggressive at her lack of response. He had not noticed her interest in the bed, and seemed to have forgotten his companion.

'Missa Dawson, yu know a doan permit loose woman in dis house,' Adella said indignantly, ignoring the man's words. 'What people gwine sey when dey know bout dis? What yu wife gwine sey when she come fine dat yu put woman inna her bed, minute she go a work?'

Mr Dawson looked suddenly alarmed, as if the predicament he was in had only just reached into his consciousness. Adella knew that he was afraid of his wife, that she ruled him when they were together. How many times had she felt sorry for the man? How many times had she forced herself not to tell his wife to treat him better?

She had really thought that he was different. Big and bluff, he always seemed conscientious, going to work at all hours, handing over his pay packet to his wife at the end of the week. He was always so cheerful, so willing to lend a hand, and on the few occasions that he came back the worse for drink, she overlooked it. After all, she reasoned, everybody needs a little pleasure sometime. But this was something different. A woman in his wife's bed was wrong and she out working all the hours as well. They were saving

97

for a house and she knew Mrs Dawson would probably not get back till well into the morning.

'A hope fa your sake nobady deh ya when yu wife come back,' she told him contemptuously, and he hung his head, seeming to shrink like a deflating balloon.

'A doan tink is any need fe sey anyting to Miss Dawson,' he said pleadingly. 'Miss Johnson, a doan know what come ova me. Yu doan know how shame a shame.'

Adella doubted it. Men! they were all the same, and she almost felt sorry for the woman sitting cowering on the bed – no longer important except as evidence that Dawson had sinned.

'We best clear de room an leave Missa Dawson in peace,' she said on a sudden impulse, ignoring the grateful look the woman cast her from the bed. Her pity was not for her. It was for the unsuspecting hard-working Mrs Dawson.

The others were reluctant to leave, those outside pressing forward to get a glimpse of Mr Dawson's shame. The men inside openly examined the woman on the bed. Adella swallowed hard, feeling disgust move inside her. 'Yu doan hear me sey get out?' she snapped, good hand spreading aggressively on her swelling hip. They moved then, shifting reluctantly, slowly unclogging the door, muttering to each other as they went. The men inside took a last lingering look before joining the others on the landing. Adella closed the door with a final click and stood against it with arms folded, daring anyone to try to get by. Slowly, the excitement taken out of reach, they dispersed and went back to their rooms.

Adella half-expected the other tenants on the top floor to give notice and leave. Rooms were easier to find now that so many West Indians had their own houses. There was no longer any need to stay in a place that had proven so dangerous. Even so she was dismayed when they came, one after the other, to tell her they were leaving. To lose four tenants at one time. What was she going to do? She relied on the rent to help her meet the mortgage payments. She had no illusions that she could manage on the money she got from the cleaning and she felt almost desperate as she put the vacancy sign in the window. The children were growing all the time, needing new clothes, new shoes. It was like an endless nightmare trying to scrape enough to hold together. Sometimes she would come home from work, climb laboriously up the stairs to the top of the house and stand in the empty doorway of the Dawson room just staring at the gaping hole.

98

'At least a have de house,' she told herself grimly. 'Whatever happen a still have dis.'

'Yu haffe try get smaddy fe repair de roof,' Lisa told her when she heard about the tenants' desertion. 'Tings change now yu know, chile. Nobady gwine stay in a place dat can fall roun dem earhole. Not like when we did come a England.'

'Yu doan haffe tell me dat,' Adella sighed. 'A woulda grateful fa anyting when a did come. Now a have three good room empty an nobady want it tru dem hear bout de roof fall.'

'Wha yu need is a man,' Lisa said. 'Is ow long since Stanton leave now? Tree years. Is too long fa a woman fe try manage on fe ihm own, an yu wid de cripple side an five children.'

'Mikey soon ole enough fe get jab,' Adella said evasively. 'Tings gwine betta den.'

Lisa shook her head. 'Cho, man, yu know what a mean already,' she said impatiently. 'If yu did have a man, ihm an ihm fren could even fix de roof and ihm would help yu out. Yu wouldn't need worry bout money so much.'

'Yu know a keeping faith wid Stanton,' Adella said in horror.

'A know ihm come roun fe see de pickney dem every ada Sunday,' her friend countered. 'A know ihm gi dem lickle money now an den, an tek dem fa ride in ihm new car. But look pan yu – is yu fe feed dem and look bout dem, is yu pay fa roof pan dem head. A tell yu, Adella, a see dat goodfanuting cousin a yours an she dress like queen a sheba, an tru she no work; no mus a ihm a pay.'

'Stanton gwine come back,' Adella answered simply. 'Ihm gwine come an a want ihm fe see dat a keep faith.'

'How yu so fool?' Lisa asked angrily. 'Even if ihm come back, de way ihm carry on wid yu cousin ihm caan sey nuting bout yu; an yu haffe tink bout de pickney dem. Dem growing now, yu know.'

Of course she knew, saw the sense in what her friend was saying. She knew plenty of men would move with her, even with the stroke. How many times had they called out to her, men that she knew, some even from church. 'A could show yu a good time, Miss Johnson,' they often said. Or, 'Now dat Missa Johnson gone wid yu cousin yu need a good man fe look afta yu.' It was not that she wasn't tempted. Often she would seriously consider what they could do for her and the children. But she would push the thought away feeling guilty. She felt irritated by her weakness, the ease with which she allowed herself to be tempted. She was married to

Stanton and one day he would come back. She knew that Lisa had been with other men since coming to England. But that was different. Lisa had been on her own for many years. Yet the temptation persisted. She could not pretend that a man would not ease her way, especially since she couldn't do any heavy work or repairs around the house. She remembered times when Lisa would come round wearing a new dress, new shoes, perfume – a present from an admirer. How long was it since anyone had bought her anything, given her money for anything? She needed someone to help her out, someone to look after her for a change and, as Lisa said, it didn't necessarily mean that he would live in the house or anything.

Adella pushed the thought out of her head. She could manage on her own – hadn't she done so since Stanton left? But the idea wouldn't leave. She thought of the empty rooms upstairs, the children having to eat their fill at school because she couldn't give them enough food at home. Often she thought of the difference it would make to her. She would be able to pay Lisa back, get the roof fixed, even get in some more tenants. She had never resented her poverty before, the way her children had to do without; the fact that finding money for new clothes meant doing without something else. But now it preyed on her, mingling with her friend's words about Stanton and Gladys. What would she have to lose? she reasoned. Why should she let her children starve? Stanton was living life with Gladys, and the few visits he made were just as Lisa had said. He would drive up in his new car and toot the horn. He expected them to be waiting dressed in their Sunday clothes, just in case he came. She knew the older ones hated the visits, resented him, his flash clothes and big car. But she insisted on their respect, for he was still their father. Stanton would come in, line them up against a wall, examine them. His mouth would curl at the corner if a skirt or trouser leg was frayed, a shoe too worn. He would send them to the car and then he would curse her, telling her she was good for nothing, allowing his children to walk about in rags. Adella would bow her head in shame, not knowing what to say. She felt guilty when one or the other of the children was denied a ride in the car because their dresses or shoes were too old. It was like a raw wound. She tried so hard to do the best for them, but it was not always easy. Lisa was right, she needed somebody to help her. Working as a cleaner, with her bad side, there was not much she could do – and if she lost her house she would have nowhere for them to stay. Where would she find a place to live with five children and no man? Whatever else happened she would not, could not lose her house. She had to do something before a thing like that happened.

Twelve

It was strange how the pain in her back increased. It had been there for weeks, nagging away like a mild toothache, half-realised, but blending in with the other aches that troubled her. It had worsened, gradually, unnoticed, but now it was almost unbearable. Adella shifted restlessly in the overstuffed chair feeling sudden irritation at the soft tones of Jim Reeves. She had listened to him every Sunday morning since coming to England. But now she wanted to cut him off, finding that he jarred on her nerves. The record-player was on the other side of the room. The small square of carpet separating her chair from the rest of the room seemed too much to cross. She tried to reach behind to rub the small of her back but a lancing pain caused her to wince and give up.

It was many years since Adella had enjoyed a Sunday. The house was quiet as a grave and the hours weighed heavily like any other day. Days ran into each other separated by stretches of night that broke up the monotony of sitting in her lonely room. Still, she went through the motions of Sunday. She got up early as she had done when still active in the church, dragged herself to the bathroom and had her wash. After that she struggled down to the silent, empty kitchen. She would pour out rice into one of the shallow plastic bowls; pick it over with skill born of years of sorting out the bad from good. The chicken placed in a plate in the fridge the day before would be dismembered with ease. As always her mind was somewhere else as she sliced onions and tomatoes over the meat, after singeing off the small hairs over the fire and washing each piece with careful attention. She would often hum to herself as she added the seasoning to the chicken, covering it before putting peas soaked overnight on one of the burners to cook. It was her busiest time since being off work: Sunday mornings when the dog and cat still slept and Carol had gone to practise her netball or one of the other sporting things she did in the evenings and at weekends.

But all that had been hours ago and the sound of the same LP playing over and over got on her nerves. She hoped Carol would hurry up and come back. She would get her to rub her back, fetch a piece a bread and some tea and change the record. Adella felt the pride course through her as she thought of Carol's job. She had got it straight after college and she knew that Audrey, who had been working at the same place, had looked out for her sister and made sure she got the job. But then she always knew that Carol would do well for herself, felt pride when Lisa would tell her, 'A saw Caral at de park; she was teaching sport and plenty people did dere.'

She liked the way people talked about her daughter. The way they had to say how she had respect and didn't let the big job change her. Carol would always talk to the people from the old street, all the other people that she knew and she didn't care what job they did. Yes, her Carol was not like some of the other young people who didn't have respect and brought shame on their parents: even though the self-same parents brought them up and did so much for them.

She sighed heavily, mind wandering back to Stanton, wondering how he was doing now. It was years since he had gone to America and she heard that he had long ago taken out an American passport. He was always telling the children to come and see him, and all of them had gone except Carol. She knew Carol would not go, knew also that he wanted to see her more than any other. Carol was the youngest, the one that hated him the most, and it made Adella sad. She supposed it was since he started sleeping with the young girls in America. From what she heard the latest one was just eighteen when he met her and was now expecting her second child by him. Adella sighed. If only she didn't feel so much pain about the things he did. It was wrong of Stanton to ruin the young girls' lives. She had lost track of how many he had made pregnant in the years they had been apart. In a way she felt sorry for Gladys now. She had gone with him to America, going to stay with his brother who lived there. He had not taken long to dump her, finding young girls there willing to prop up his fading sexuality. Gladys had written her, told her how she had woken up one day to

102

find him gone, a hundred dollars beside her on the pillow and nowhere to go when the rent ran out.

Adella couldn't understand why he had changed so much. He had been so different when she had met him in Jamaica, so responsible and full of plans for them and for the children. She could remember him coming down the dusty lane, the sun in his eyes, his clothes well pressed and sharp, the parting in his hair dead centre and dead straight. It had been soon after she had found out she was pregnant with Beresford's second child.

Adella had been full of fear when her monthly flow did not come. She refused to believe that the one night she had spent with Beresford could cause her so much trouble. At first she told herself that she was wrong. It was guilt at the sin she had committed which made her think that she had missed her monthly period. But weeks had passed and still nothing happened. Instead, her breasts felt sore and tender, and she could swear they looked bigger when she peered into the cracked mirror on her dressing-table. She couldn't believe it. This could not happen, not now, not when she was doing so well with the dressmaking. She had several rich women who came to her from the hill and she knew her cousin's wife was proud of her, that Granny Dee and Aunt Ivy boasted about how well she was doing to the people in the village. Now she had to shame them all by telling them she was pregnant.

Adella remembered the night with bitterness. Beresford had kept in touch after returning her bag. One evening he had persuaded her to come to a dance with him, and she had slipped out without saying anything. She knew that her cousin and his wife would not approve of her going to a dance-hall. They were both devout Seventh Day Baptists, and though she went with them to church she found the five times a week and all day Saturday routine boring. Church was something she attended on a Sunday, and maybe once or twice a week. Adella resented all the devotion she was expected to show. She worked hard all week and looked forward to her Saturdays when she could wander down to the bustling marketplace. But since coming to Kingston she had never got a chance to see the weekend life, and never went to one of the parties Juni had told her about while she was still in Beaumont.

She supposed it was because of her frustration that she had finally decided to go with Beresford. She liked him a lot and often met him on the street when she went to the market. She loved to watch him at crossroads directing the traffic from his booth. He always looked so handsome and dashing in his uniform. She had brought him back to her cousins' house, but though they had been impressed by the fact he was a policeman he had refused to go back again when they had invited him to all-day church the following Saturday. No wonder she sneaked out that fateful Saturday night, bored and fed up after another full day spent at church. Beresford had been waiting for her as he promised. He was standing by the bridge that spanned the concrete gully built to take away the overflow when the heavy rains on the hill caused the rivers to burst their banks.

Adella had felt sick with excitement, the new white frock she had made in her spare time fitting snug and crisp against her slip. She had copied it from one of the magazines a client had brought to have a suit made up from. Never had she dreamt that one day she would get the chance to wear it. Beresford looked different out of his uniform. Ordinary somehow, not so tall and good-looking in his trousers and open-necked shirt. Yet it had not mattered. The moon was big in the sky, the air still full of the day's warmth. The smell of wildflowers drifted to her nose as they crushed them underfoot, while the constant chirping of the crickets barely registered in her ears.

The dance had been every bit as magical as she expected. The hall was full of people dressed in what she thought must be their Sunday best. Women wearing heavy make-up, looking nice and smelling of the perfume counters she often passed in the downtown stores. Adella danced close to Beresford, the music loud and throbbing inside her. Knowledge of her defiance gave her the same heady feeling as the beer he insisted that she drink. It was nice to stand on one side, eating the curried goat and rice he bought. It felt good to press close to him, as one or another person hailed him. She could see the way the women with no men looked at her with envy, and she felt important and happy. It was as if the night was never going to end and there was nothing that was not hers for the asking. She was walking on air, and the feeling had lasted till the music stopped and the dance came to an end.

When he had suggested they go back to his mother's house, she had wanted to say no. The faint lightening of early dawn told her she had been out too long already. She knew there was no fear of discovery. Saturday was the Lord's day in her cousin's house so on a Sunday they lay abed till late, resting after their exertion. But the guilt had started to seep in to her and she did not want the dawn to catch her.

'Is ongly fa a little while,' he told her. 'Mama no deh deh an a haffe keep a eye pan de place.'

Adella had gone reluctantly, though she accepted his story. She would have much preferred to find her own way home, but he had insisted that the night was too dark and it was far too late. On top of that he told her that gangs of men sometimes roamed the streets in cars, falling on lone women or the unwary. She had heard such tales before. Her cousin had even told her how it happened to a woman he knew. She had been attacked while out walking with her sweetheart. They had held him down with a knife to his throat, while doing what he called 'unmentionable things' to the poor woman. Now Beresford was talking about the same thing, bringing back the sick fear her cousin's words had evoked.

After that she had not argued, waiting patiently while he said goodbye to friends, hailed others, or was hailed in turn. The voices were startlingly loud in the quiet silence of early dawn. The sound of her high-heeled shoes had been loud and clipping against the sidewalk; and her feet had ached as she followed Beresford through the tangle of dust tracks, zinc and wooden shacks to the place where his mother had taken her and given her herb tea to drink.

'Come in fa a minute noh,' he had said, as she hovered on the veranda intending to wait for him out there.

She had gone reluctantly, following him into the dark interior, waiting until he lit the kerosene lamp, and hooked it on a peg against one of the walls of the large, sparsely furnished room. She sat gingerly on one of the bamboo chairs as he unbuttoned his shirt further after shrugging off his jacket.

Adella could never remember how they had ended in each others' arms. She had felt uncomfortable sitting there in the yellow light of the lamp. Knowing that the time was ticking away, she moved back to the veranda when he made no move to leave. He had followed her there and afterwards she could never quite remember how a few stolen kisses, sweet to her lips and warming inside, had ended as it did.

When it was all over he had grinned, looking smug. 'Yu neva tell me yu was pure,' he said, making no attempt to hide his satisfaction. 'Girl it was sweet, wasn't it?'

She nodded automatically, not quite sure what she was supposed to have felt. It had been pleasant enough to start with until he had fumbled between her legs. Then there had been pain, stretching into soreness. She had felt slightly irritated at the time it took. Had wondered if she looked as stupid as she felt, skirt wrapped around her waist, panties and suspenders round her feet, while he grunted on between her legs. She didn't have the heart to tell him that it was too much effort for too little, that there had been nothing for her to feel good about. She did not like the stickiness between her legs, the thing she knew was his fluid that ran out and wet her panties before tracing a path down her legs. It was all too messy a business.

He had talked endlessly as he walked her down to the gully, was in high spirits as he led her along its length to the other side where she lived.

'Is a good ting is yu first time,' he told her happily. 'At least now yu will know what yu missing.'

Adella nodded politely, watching her steps, wary of the uneven ground they were walking on. She was hardly listening to him; her mind centred on the need to get home before her cousin and his wife woke up, found her missing and guessed what she had done. She knew she would have to bathe herself, wash her panties. The sticky flow between her legs was irritating; and she fancied that it smelt. It was a relief for her when they finally reached the bridge. There she could part from him, knowing that he watched her still, glad that he was too far away to bore her any longer.

That dance had been weeks ago and now she knew she was pregnant, carrying Beresford's child. She had seen him only once since the night they spent together and she wondered how he would take the news. Adella prayed that he would not be angry. Whatever happened she could not tell her cousin. He would throw her out into the streets which seemed unfriendly, uninviting now that she was in trouble. She worried about telling Beresford for a long time before plucking up the courage to go and see him. He was in his usual booth directing traffic. Adella waited patiently, hour after hour, not caring that her cousin's wife would be wondering where she was. She had slipped out, using the excuse that she had to go downtown to buy material for a special dress she was making for a client. But she had been so long she knew the other woman would realise she was doing something else.

By the time he came off duty her feet ached, the pavement burning through the thin plastic soles of her shoes.

'Adella! What yu doing ya?' he asked, looking around worriedly, as if he was afraid someone would see them together.

'A haffe talk to yu,' she said hastily, clutching her straw bag and trying to steady her voice at the same time.

'What about? A on duty, yu know.'

'Beresford, a carrying a pickney fa yu,' she said desperately, heart sinking as she saw the horror in his face. She knew instinctively that she had chosen the wrong time, had broken the news badly.

'Yu breeding? Yu sure?' he asked sharply, fingers digging into her shoulder.

She nodded. 'A doan see me flow yet an is three week late now.'

He glared at her angrily. 'How yu get pregnant?' he asked sharply.

Adella felt worried and surprised, surely he had not forgotten?

'Yu doan memba de dance?' she asked anxiously, 'when a come to yu mada house?'

'A rememba,' he said impatiently. 'But why yu haffe get pregnant?'

She looked at him, puzzled. She had not known that she could have influenced the outcome, that there was some way she could have prevented what happened. She wondered why he had never mentioned it before.

'It jus happen,' she said now. 'An now a doan know what a gwine do.'

'Yu tell yu cousin?' he asked sharply, as if the thought suddenly occurred to him. 'Yu tell ihm is me?'

'A doan tell ihm nuting yet. Beresford, when dem fine out dem gwine toss me outa street an a doan have nowhere to go.'

He looked relieved. 'A tell yu what,' he said now. 'If yu doan tell dem who did do it, a will fine yu a room fe rent in a yard.'

Adella's heart sank, she had expected more than that. She did not want to admit it, but deep inside she had hoped he would suggest they get married, or that she move out and they get a place together. 'Yu could still sew,' he continued eagerly, 'get money fe pay fa tings fa yuself an a will help yu out of course as much as a can an when a can.'

She nodded, knowing that she had no choice. Sooner or later her cousin or his wife would notice something, guess that she was carrying and tell her she had to leave.

She decided not to tell them, to wait until they found out. Somehow she could not face the disgrace, the shame she would cause Granny Dee. Better to wait until she had no choice.

'Yu want me fe look place fa yu?' he asked her impatiently. 'Sey yes or no cause a haffe leave go back a barracks now.'

She nodded reluctantly, feeling the bitterness inside her; knowing instinctively that he did not intend to live with her.

'A caan live wid yu,' he said in confirmation of her thought. 'But a gwine spend plenty time wid yu an de pickney. Yu doan haffe worry, sweet pea, a not gwine desert yu like some man would.'

She smiled ironically as she watched him walk away. He had been eager enough when he had persuaded her to lie with him. Had enjoyed it loudly enough. Now he was acting like it was all her fault and he the trapped one helping her out just because he was so kind. She had walked away slowly, turning down the dusty unpaved streets of West Kingston, wandering along aimlessly, not knowing what to do. She had looked up at the sound of footfalls, seen the man looking out of place for a weekday afternoon. He was so well-dressed, so neat, his shoes gleaming against the dusty path and she had wondered who he was. He had winked in appreciation as he passed her and she had waited until he was well down the road before turning to look at him. She had not wanted him to know that she was curious but he had turned to look back at her too; and she felt a brief pleasure in the knowledge that he liked her. It was a fleeting feeling, gone almost before it happened. Too many men looked at her like that. Beresford had looked like that and where had it got her? All she had for it was one night in his house and a growing belly. So she had put him from her mind then.

It seemed no time before her belly started to swell, to be noticeable. At first it was just a thickening round the waist and she let her waistband out. She had been able to hide the constant sickness – pass it off as something that she had eaten, or bad water drunk at the house of one of her clients. Even the thought of food made her feel sick; and she would sit at the table, breathing with measured concentration as the food smells wafted to her nose. Her cousin would say grace, making an occasion of the simple phrases, carried away by his new status as an elder in his church. She supposed it was his reward for joining the army, even though he never went further than South Camp Road on the other side of Kingston.

She would sit at the table, wondering how she would get through the long-drawn-out meal, how she would be able to fool them into thinking she was eating when the very thought of food made her

108

want to heave. She knew that she looked ill; she felt washed out most of the time.

'A tink yu sickening fa someting,' her cousin's wife said, noticing her listless face and sudden lack of vitality. 'A tink yu should go see de docta fore it get worst.'

Adella had nodded obligingly, but made no move to do so. She knew what she was suffering from, though no one had told her that she would feel so ill, that the effort of bending over her machine would make head spin. All she wanted to do was lie her head down on the cool sheet of her bed and groan with the sickness that seemed to infect her whole body.

Often she would wish that night had never happened. If only she had not sneaked off to the dance. If only she had taken a chance and made her own way home; and always at the back of her mind was the knowledge of the growing child. The fact that, soon, loose dresses and tight bras would no longer be able to keep her secret.

Thirteen

It was on a Sunday that things had come to a head. She had decided not to go to church on the sabbath, pleading that she was not well and sinking gratefully back between the sheets. They had been silent, almost hostile when they came back that night. They ignored her at dinner, eating the food prepared the day before so they did not have to violate the sabbath; and then going to bed without bidding her good night. But the next day had been different. Sunday had dawned with clouds in the sky, and hissing splatters of rain against the windows. There was a stiff breeze blowing the pink curtains that she had made since coming to Kingston to live, bringing the smell of damp earth into the room. It was the first rain in many months and Adella lay back appreciatively, liking the unaccustomed coolness and the slight haze that hung over the ground. The fresh smell was so much like Beaumont, wet earth and drenched vegetation mingling together with the far-off dripping of water and the lonely echoing cry of a bird.

Her head rested against her arms as she watched the droplets of water on the window pane merging into each other and forming rivulets that traced a path down the clouded glass. There was no need to get up today. Sunday was a day to lie in bed an extra hour, a day to contemplate the world and let her problems swamp her. She was worried about her cousins' behaviour the night before. Had they guessed her secret, did they know she carried a child? She felt weak with fear at the thought, the unknown yawning like a bottomless pit to swallow up her dreams. What was she going to tell them when they asked? The endless questions went round in her head: the fears building as she thought of living on her own.

It had been an effort to get up that day and she had to will herself to move. When she did, her legs trembled as they carried her to the bathroom. Apprehension was like a stone in the pit of her stomach. The swelling mound of her belly was clear to see, protruding forward like the neglected bang-belly children she had often seen begging on the street. The children whose mothers could not feed them after their fathers ran away. Adella had been late for breakfast, coming in after they had already started. Her feet dragged reluctantly as she saw the rigid disapproval on her cousin's face, a look of distaste on his wife's.

'How yu get pregnant Adella?' her cousin asked, coming straight to the point before she could take a seat. He was leaning back in his chair, the fried dumpling in his hand broken in two and half-eaten.

Adella stopped short, eyes shifting away from him, feeling an urge to brush away the crumbs tangled in his short moustache and beard.

'It was a accident,' she said, not knowing what else she could say, how she could explain.

She went to sit in her seat, but he put up a hand to stop her. 'A doan waan yu sitting at de table wid us,' he said mildly and she felt a shock of surprise. 'Yu is a wicked girl,' he continued. 'Sneaking off behind me back and playing aroun wid men. Yu father trus me to look afta yu when yu come a Kingston and look what yu do.'

She bent her head, feeling shame. 'A sorry,' she said, 'a didn't mean it to happen – is accident mek it.'

'If yu did keep yuself pure none a dis would go so now,' his wife chipped in, adding piously, 'de wages of sin is deat, and yu gwine pay dem wages, yu wait an see.'

'She doan haffe tell me dat,' Adella thought bitterly. She was paying already. Look how sick she had been, how worried, and all for what?

'A want yu to leave dis house,' her cousin said coldly. 'A want yu to leave as soon as yu fine somewhere to go. A not gwine trow yu out on de street tru yu is family. But a not gwine have yu disgracing me name by staying here wid dat abomination.' His voice grew louder as he talked and by the end he was shouting at her.

Adella cowered, nodding her head. She could not understand why he was so angry. She had been in Kingston five years and this was her first mistake. She wanted to explain that it had only happened once, that she had not known how easy it was to get pregnant. The anger in his face kept her mouth shut and she nodded mutely instead. She stood there, hovering over the table, not sure whether to stay or go.

'Get outa me sight,' he said in disgust. 'A doan waan haffe see yu. A gwine sen a letter to yu father dis afternoon and a gwine tell ihm, what yu do wid yu time since yu come.'

The injustice of it stung her. 'It ongly happen de one time,' she said, suddenly stubborn, 'an is jus accident ow a get pregnant. Yu going on like a was slack jus tru a mek a mistake.'

The man gave her a bitter look. 'So dat is it,' he said now. 'Yu start get rebellious and now yu dare try mek it seem all right. Yu is a wicked woman, a jezabel, and a gwine mek sure everybady fram here to Beaumont know what yu tun into.'

Adella felt her throat aching, not able to believe the hostility they felt towards her. She couldn't understand it. She had got on so well with her cousin and his wife. Now they were looking at her with hatred as if she had done them personal wrong.

'All a did was get pregnant,' she pleaded. 'A doan tink a is a jezabel; it was a accident.'

The man looked her up and down with scorn. 'So yu doan tink yu do wrang; yu tink is accident, not your fault. Well a can see de devil strang in yu and nuting a can do will change dat. A want yu and your corruption outa dis house come weekend and meantime yu betta keep out a me sight.'

'A tink yu should keep fram roun ya too,' his wife added. 'A doan want de neighba dem to fine out yu breeding fa a man an yu doan married.'

'Yes, mam,' Adella said sullenly, turning and walking out of the room. She felt disappointed in her cousin-in-law. She had thought of her as her friend and felt betrayed. It was obvious that what the neighbours felt mattered more than her. She couldn't understand why. There were so many people living together in the area who everybody knew had not been married. It was always happening, unmarried couples setting up home together, but that did not mean they were no good. She had expected to have to leave, of course. Had expected disappointment and anger; but not this cold hostility, this almost hate that she had got. One thing she knew, she had to get out of that house, get out before the week was out. She did not want to stay where she was not wanted.

Beresford had kept his word about finding her a room, and she had been grateful to him for that. It was not as nice as her cousin's house. It was made of wood, one large room and a veranda and the only furniture was a bed he told her he got cheap. Adella looked at it with distaste, seeing that it was old and discarded. She had to share a pit toilet with several other people and the cooking shack with even more. He told her he had paid the rent for two months to give her a chance to get on her feet. Adella had been grateful. It was nice to get away from the tensions of the past few days, nice to have a place of her own. Small and cramped as it was, it was hers and she could come and go as she liked.

'A can come an see yu when a want now,' Beresford said, loosening the top buttons of his uniform tunic, dropping down on the bed and smoothing the mattress suggestively.

Adella looked at him with sudden distaste. 'A not inna dat, Beresford, a doan believe in living like dat.'

His eyes narrowed. 'Wha yu mean yu not inna dat?' he asked aggressively. 'What yu haffe lose now, yu breed already.'

'It was accident mek dat,' she said. 'All a waan do is mek a way fa meself.'

He looked stunned at that. 'A doan know what get inna yu,' he said indignantly. 'Yu going on like yu doan know wha a go on. A mean a fine yu place fe live, buy yu bed and pay rent wid me money an now yu sey yu naw go gi me de ting.'

Adella felt sick. Was that what he was helping her for? Did he really see her like that?

'Is yu get me like dis,' she said angrily. 'If yu neva trouble me a would neva breed fa yu an none a dis woulda happen.'

'Doan blame me,' he said. 'If yu neva waan de ting a couldn't gi it yu; so doan come tell me bout is my fault. Is me did tell yu to breed?'

112

She could see that he believed what he said, realised the futility of trying to argue any further. Reaching for her handbag, she searched inside for her purse, fumbled about for a wad of notes.

'Ow much yu pay fa de rent an de bed?' she asked angrily. 'Tell me ow much mek me pay yu. Yu tink me is some loose woman yu can jus use?'

He looked taken aback. 'Is all right, a doan want yu fe gi me de money back. A owe yu someting fa de chile; and yu know a like yu fram time.' As he spoke he eased himself off the bed, moved over to her and tried to wrap his arms around her. 'Come on, it not so bad. Yu was always seying how yu doan like living wid yu cousin tru dem so christian. Now yu have yu freedom, an yu have me.'

He had a point about her freedom, but she wasn't so sure she wanted it now. She felt small and lonely in the empty wooden room, light coming from an open shutter in the glassless window. Her precious sewing-machine and bundle of cloth piled up with her grip and the straw basket she had brought up from the country looked out of place and pathetic. 'A not gwine mek yu come ya when yu like, Beresford,' she said with determination. He looked at her, a nasty gleam in his eye.

'Yu tink is up toun yu live now?' he asked spitefully. 'Yu tink yu can jus live by yuself dung ya? Well yu betta learn dis fram now. If yu doan have a man fe proteck yu, yu gwine have plenty trouble. At least yu have me, an tru everybady know me roun ya yu gwine safe long as dem know yu is my woman.'

Adella said nothing, feeling sick. She could see that he was telling the truth, that she really had no choice. The nameless fear he mentioned lapped at her mind, and she clutched her purse, wishing with all her heart that she had not gone to the dance-hall that Saturday night.

'Well, if yu doan want me, a can fine anada woman,' he said now, moving away from her and buttoning up his tunic. 'A doan tink yu gwine fine anada man nice as me, dough.'

She swallowed hard, afraid he might be right, looking down at the dirty wooden floor. 'A neva sey a didn't want yu, Beresford,' she muttered, swallowing her pride.

He smiled contentedly. 'A know yu would see tings my way,' he said, adding, 'A still on duty so a haffe go back dung a barracks. But a gwine come back later an we can do someting togeda.'

Adella nodded, biting back the anger, feeling sickness and distaste mingling. She felt trapped and alone, afraid of living in sin, but more frightened of the nameless thing that he threatened. She had not thought about such a thing when she had made her plans to leave her cousin's house. She had remembered other things that needed to be done; gradually going to her clients' houses rather than have them round, knowing they would desert her if she had to live in the places downtown where the very poor lived. She had saved as much money as she could knowing that she could not stay in her cousin's house when her pregnancy started to be noticed. All those things and yet she had not thought of being trapped. Now she knew she had no choice. She had to believe what Beresford said. She knew nothing about the way Kingston people lived outside of those in her cousin's church. But she could not trust Beresford. Already he had caused her trouble and now she had to pay him for the help he gave.

It was not long before her careful forward planning started to come apart. What upset her most was the customers, people she had sewn for since coming up to town. How many dresses had she made those women, how many times had she walked up the hill, crossing the gully and down by Constant Spring, under the hot sun. She had spent so much time choosing material and copying any dress they wanted. How many of them had said she was the best dressmaker in town, that they would always stand by her if she ever needed help. But that was before she got pregnant. Before they found out she was still unmarried. After that had come the excuses. The 'we can't have you coming here in case it's a bad influence, you know.'

A few of them had stayed, of course, and she had been grateful until they started cutting down the amount they paid. She felt bitter at their hypocrisy, angry at Beresford who still lived with his mother, still enjoyed respect while she had lost everything.

It was after the child had come. One morning early, before the yard was stirring, she heard a knock on her door. She had just settled him down and she felt irritation as he started screaming again at the loud and sudden sound. The door pushed open and Adella looked up, angry words on her lips. She expected Beresford to enter. He had kept away since Danny was born two months before, only dropping by occasionally to press money in her hand. Backing out in embarrassment under the watchful eyes of one or the other women from the yard.

Granny Dee came into the room, eyes critical as she noticed the pile of nappies on the chair, the bucket without its lid in the corner. Adella looked up at her grandmother, shocked. She had written home, telling them where she lived, explaining what had happened. As the months went by and there was no answer she had resigned herself to never seeing them again. It had been a source of constant pain, going to the post office day after day. She would wait impatiently behind the grilled counter while the light-skinned woman checked through the mail, only to shake her head to say there was no letter.

It was no more than she could expect, she told herself, the memory of her cousin's change of attitude still fresh in her mind. She saw his wife in the market sometimes, looking neat and prim as befitted the wife of a working man. But the other woman always looked the other way, hurrying past as if she didn't know her. But now Granny Dee was there, looking as stern as ever, a little greyer but just the same.

'A come to see de baby,' the old woman said, coming over to take the wailing child from Adella's hands, soothing him with practised ease. 'A leave de bag outside in case it was de wrang house. Go bring it in fore smaddy tief it.'

Adella stood looking at her, unable to believe her grandmother was actually there in the dawn cool before the heat rose in the ghetto.

'Gwaan noh,' the woman said impatiently. 'Anybady would tink yu see duppy.'

Adella rushed to comply, heart suddenly light. Granny Dee had come all the way from Beaumont just to visit her. It was as if she had brought the countryside with her.

The old lady stayed with her for a month, taking charge of everything. She looked after Adella and Danny as if they were both the same age. Granny Dee asked no questions about Beresford even when he popped in to give Adella money. Adella was grateful for her grandmother's tact. She knew the old woman was disappointed, could see the sadness in the fading eyes that rested on her whenever the other thought she wasn't looking. She had wanted to explain. Had tried to do so on several occasions; but the old woman cut her off. 'A was young once, Adella. A didn't mek de same mistake, but what's to sey a wouldn't do it if a did get de chance?'

'Yu wouldn't be so fofool,' Adella said, shaking her head, feeling grateful for the love and support the old woman was showing.

'Is always woman who get blame when she breed,' the old woman sighed, 'but it couldn't happen widout de man.'

'A shouldn't a let ihm, dough,' Adella responded.

'Is too late to tink bout dat now,' her grandmother cut in brutally. 'Yu breed now and yu get punish fa de sin. But a want yu fe know nobady gainst yu an we want yu fe come back a Beaumont.'

She had refused, of course. The last thing she wanted to do was go back to Beaumont in disgrace. She knew that her grandmother would look after her child. That everybody would forgive. She would be comfortable in Beaumont, able to find work easily. But she could not go back. Maybe one day. One day when she finally did all the things she wanted to. If she went back now she knew instinctively that she would never leave again.

Her grandmother dropped the subject, concentrating on getting to know the other women in the yard. Adella had been proud of her, the way she fitted in and got their respect. She would sit on a box in the yard or on one of the shaky verandas, skirt lapped between her legs, and talk to them about things Adella hadn't even heard before. She had found out so many new things about her grandmother, could hardly believe that the old lady had indeed come up from country with the market women in the back of one of the high-sided trucks that brought the ground provisions to the big market in town.

It seemed too soon before the old woman was packing up to go. Adella wished she could ask her to stay.

'Why yu doan come back a country wid me,' Granny Dee suggested again, as she drank chocolate tea on the veranda stairs. 'Town is no place fe stay, yu gwine get inna more temptation an yu gwine breed again fore long.'

'No, Granny Dee, a gwine keep meself an go back a church,' Adella said, not wanting to tell the woman that she was forced to rely on Beresford. He had kept away from her – apart from fleeting visits – while the old woman was there, but she knew that he was impatient to take up where they left off before Danny was born.

'Yu caan live in a yard like dis widout a man protecting yu,' Granny Dee said, and Adella looked down in shame. She had forgotten that her grandmother had become close to the other women, know that they must have told her how things were. 'A gwine respeck yu wishes,' the old woman continued, 'but if yu eva

116

waan come back a country we glad fe have yu.'

After Granny Dee had gone, Beresford crept back. He was waiting for her in her room when she got back to the yard after seeing her grandmother off. The sun was hot in the sky, and a breeze stirred up the white dust that seemed to coat everything when she pushed through the gate into the yard. She could hear the little scratching noises of the rats under the stilt-raised houses, the sound of the children playing drifting across from other yards. She had left Danny with the woman next door and now she came out peering over the veranda rails.

'De baby sleeping,' the woman said. 'Yu might as well leave ihm same place till ihm wake.'

Adella nodded, climbing tiredly up the stairs, feeling hot and tired from the walk. Her neighbour had two children of her own and she often looked after Danny when she had to go somewhere.

Beresford was lying on the bed, tunic unbuttoned. 'A was tinking yu Granny was neva gwine leave,' he said, stretching into a sitting position. He shrugged out of his tunic, hands going hastily to the belt of his trousers.

'A have work fe do,' Adella said in irritation, disliking him more than ever.

He looked at her through narrowed eyes. 'A neva see yu complain when a gi yu all de money since de pickney born,' he said coldly. 'A want de ting now Adella, an a gwine tek it if yu waan give it or nat. Yu tek me money so yu can tek me same way.'

She shrugged her shoulders in resignation. What was the use, anyway? The only other place she could go was back to Beaumont and that she could not do. Granny Dee had told her how well Claudia was doing and all the things they expected of her. How could she, Adella, go back with a baby, empty-handed with none of her dreams fulfilled and none of the things she had boasted of getting in the town? So she had said nothing to him, not bothered to resist him. In her mind she knew it was only a matter of time before she had another child and maybe even one more after that. The thought made her feel sick. There were so many other women in the yard who had started out like her. Many of them had come up from the country full of dreams, had fallen to a man and every year another child would burden them. There seemed no escaping from that sort of life.

Often she would wrap the baby up and wander down to the wharf to watch the boats come in. Watch the people with their grips leaving for other countries. She remembered how, when she first came to Kingston, she used to wander down there, spend stolen minutes dreaming of going on one of those ships, sailing away to riches and adventure. Now she could stay down there for hours. There was no one waiting for her to come back, nowhere to hurry to. And inside she was still determined; one day she would get out of the trap that she was in. She had heard of people going off to England, to the Motherland. Heard that country was so rich you could pick money off the street. But first she had to get there, had to find enough money to get away from Beresford and the desperate poverty of the women in her yard.

Fourteen

Adella stared at the letter with furrowed brows, wondering what to make of it. The words were strange, long and hard to understand. All she could make out was that they wanted her house. They were going to take it whether she liked it or not. She sat down in her chair with a bump. All thought of work and the lateness of the hour going out of her head. Half-formed plans chased each other in her mind, scattered flashes of alarm that made her heart race and her palms feel cold and wet. She could never find another place, not one big enough for four of them, the dog and the cat. She thought back to the room she had shared with Stanton in her first year in England. She could never live like that again, and with a grown son and the two youngest so big as well. For the first time she felt almost glad about the disgrace the two older girls had brought down on her head. The fact that they had places of their own now.

'Maybe is a blessing in disguise,' she told herself half-heartedly, not really believing it. She had brought Delores over so that she wouldn't fall into the same trap she herself had stumbled on. How recent it seemed since she had gone to the airport to meet her and Mikey, leaving the other children with Lisa because Stanton had to work late. She could remember them, looking lost and small: Mikey gripping Delores' hand protectively, the two suitcases on either side of them marooning them on their alien island. She had felt proud of the way Granny Dee had plaited Delores' hair, combed Mikey's till it was a short smooth coat across his scalp. Their clothes had been new, a neat contrast to the often-polished shoes. They had looked up at her hopefully. No sign of recognition in the small, anxious faces, only a wistful hope that she was there to meet them. Delores had been, what? Six? She couldn't have been more than that. Which meant Mikey was just gone eight. How different he had been then, straight-backed and proud even in his fear. At least he still protected his sisters, looked out for them. She knew he slipped them pocket-money and bought them new shoes whenever they needed them. He never said a word about it and still gave her half his money every week now that he was working on the tube train. Mikey did get bad treatment from Stanton, she sighed to herself. Stanton had never been able to forgive him for being a boy and not his child. But even though he beat him and took away his pride, leaving him a stuttering awkward child, Stanton had been good to the boy; trying his clumsy best to stop him wetting the bed, and stuttering when he talked.

Delores had been the greatest shame. She had been so pretty when she came; hair long and straight, skin nice and brown. She could remember her. So bright at school, looking after the younger children, combing their hair and cooking. She had grown up too young, Delores, and after the stroke – when Stanton left – she and Mikey had to do so much to bring up the other three. It was no wonder she had gone with that good for nothing Nigel. Poor Delores, with no more luck than her mother. From what the girl had said it had been the first time. Once only and she had been pregnant. Adella had found out, despite her daughter's attempt to hide what she had done. Had found out and for once had approached Stanton for help. He had gone round to see Nigel, who had been denying responsibility, and it had ended with the couple moving into a flat together. Stanton stood up for his daughter then, and he had even forced Nigel to marry Delores. It was no wonder the boy was terrified of him now. She was glad about that, not liking the resentment Nigel felt; knowing that fear of Stanton would stop his beating tendencies, and stop him from leaving Delores as he was always threatening.

Adella sighed. She had scarcely got over Delores when Eena got pregnant. Stanton had blamed her for that, telling her bitterly that it was her slackness that had caused it. Of all the children he loved Eena most. It didn't seem to matter that she was not his, and had been the result of too much moonlight on the long sea crossing from Jamaica so many years before. She supposed it was because of Larry's car. Certainly there was nothing else to recommend the boy. She always thought him shifty, too quick to stray. But Larry had a car, and Eena had sneaked out behind her back. She had not found out all this until it was too late. Until she noticed the girl's fear, the worry in her face and remembered that Eena had not seen her period for that month. How could she have thrown everything away? She had been going to do exams, stay on at school and be a teacher like her aunt Claudia and then she let the good for nothing boy breed her just for the rides in his dilapidated car.

Adella pushed the flood of bitterness back with an effort. It had all worked out in the end and Eena even had a white wedding. The only trouble was people. They had a long memory and never let her forget. Not that she could of course. Hearing other people talk about how well all their children were doing, girl children who had been at school with Eena and Delores, always made her bitter. Somehow all the dreams she had for her children had turned to ashes. At least it meant there were two less to worry about. But there were Audrey and Carol still at school and Mikey who could never manage on his own. He was so thin, Mikey, and all the Irish Moss and Soracee never seemed to do anything for him. She supposed the Irish Moss was for the strength he needed. She knew about him and the white girls, the way he had so many of them coming round slipping up to his room when he thought she wasn't looking. But that was all right, it was good to see that he was 'normal' despite his awkwardness and lack of confidence in most things.

Her mind came back to the letter in her hand. What could she do about it? What was she going to do when they came for her house and put her on the street? She wished Mikey could help her. But with all the schooling he'd had, he hadn't learned anything. She would have to ask Audrey when she came from school, find out if she could stop them. It had to be a bad mistake. She could not believe her normal Wednesday morning could have changed so much. How could she have suspected? She had scooped up the pile of letters from the mat behind the door as she always did, had leafed through the bundle, opening each one, and glancing at its contents without much interest. That was, until she had come across the strange brown envelope.

Adella folded the letter carefully. There was nothing she could do about it now. A look at the clock told her she was already late for work and she hurriedly put the letter on the mantelpiece before struggling into her coat.

She had been an hour late. One hour too much, her supervisor had told her frostily. Adding that they could not tolerate lateness. At first she had not realised what he was saying, too impatient to get started on her floor to really listen. One hour was a lot of time to catch up on. It was not until he had sent her up to accounts to collect her wages that it sank in that she was being sacked. Adella couldn't believe it. She had been working for the company for nine years. Nine years of struggling up at five-thirty and getting the early bus; nine years of riding through the silent streets seeing the landscape change as buildings were pulled down or new ones went up almost overnight. She had seen the big sprawling estate go up, creeping across what had been streets of elegant houses fallen into disrepair like her house. Now she was being sacked. It was the first time she had been late, and she tried to explain, tried to tell the man how things were.

He ignored her, telling her again that she was to collect her cards and go. Adella went reluctantly, not wanting to believe it was happening, all her security suddenly slipping. It was all the fault of the council wanting to take her house away from her. She wondered if they knew how hard she had worked to buy it. How many years of throwing a partner, scraping the money together week after week even when it meant going without a meal here, or a pair of sorely needed shoes there. It was so easy for them. So easy for all of them. All the plans she made, all the work she did, why was she always back in the same place? She felt weary as she walked down the stairs, her bad leg dragging more than ever as she left the building for the last time. The tears pricked at the back of her eyes. The unusual heat of British summer burned around her, lightening the grimness of shaped grey stones that made up the imposing buildings she passed. The tiredness weighed on her heavily and she felt old beyond her time. Why did she keep fighting when it would all end up the same? What was the point? All she had got so far was two daughters who had bred and them still young – just like she had been.

It was Lisa who had come up with the answer. She had lost her job when the factory where she worked as a packer moved out of the City. That was twelve months before and she now worked as a cleaner for the social security office, near Brixton market.

'A know dem looking fa new people fe work dere,' she told her helpfully. Adella was grateful for Lisa's briskness. Trust the other woman to think of a way out, to stop the panic that was spiralling up inside her.

Adella hesitated, remembering the problems she'd had just after the stroke, going from place to place looking for work, getting turned down even for cleaning jobs. She had been so lucky to get the job in the City and she had worked harder than everyone. She had even done extra work without complaint even when she had not always been paid. She knew that the other cleaners were less likely to lose their jobs. They were not crippled like she was. Not that it had all helped in the end. She had still lost the job.

It was after she had been looking for some time that Lisa came up with the suggestion that she try to work for the local council. It had been so hard even to get an interview. There was less work around than nine years before. More people needed jobs as cleaners to make ends meet.

'Dey neva gwine gi me a jab wid me bad side,' she said shaking her head half-defeated. But the thought of having to take welfare money was more than she could bear. It was bad enough that Audrey had to get money from the welfare, that they got school uniform as charity. But to live on it – that was more than she could bear. Especially after the man had come round and told her about something called disability. The same thing they had tried to make her take after she came out of the hospital and Stanton had left her.

'Dem will gi yu a jab, man,' Lisa insisted, scratching her scalp through newly straightened hair. 'A hear sey dat dem waan fe tek on people dat cripple.'

Adella was interested now. She knew that if Lisa said it it had to be true. Though she could not understand why anyone would want to give a job to a cripple.

She had soon found out, of course; soon realised that it was something to do with politics. As Lisa said, she had no trouble getting the job, and she wondered sadly if she would have been so lucky if she had gone for one of the other jobs. One where you could dress nice and sit behind a desk. Adella didn't mind the work too much. At least she could have a gossip with Lisa in the evenings, working side by side with her as they emptied ashtrays, swept and mopped and cleaned the crusted toilet bowl. It was the money that worried her. It was a lot less than she had earned working in the City. A lot less money and a lot more hours. Often she would sit at home, wondering how to stretch it, how to pay the bills and feed the children at the same time. Things had been bad before, even with the money she got from Mikey. Now she started accepting the few pounds she was sometimes offered by an admirer anxious to get to know her better. At first she had resisted them, the humiliation and the hurt of living at Beresford's mercy still fresh after so many years. Hating them even as she smiled, hating herself for what she was tempted to do so that they could have meat on the table sometimes, or money to buy shoes for the children. In the end she had given in, unable to cope. The need of the children more important even than her pride.

She hated the men that used her, hated them while she needed them. Many of them had come, crawled into her bed when the children were asleep. She would watch them bitterly as they tried to buy her children with sweets and toys and promises. She would put up with them; swallow her pride when money got tight. But when they got too close, tried getting comfortable or filling Stanton's shoes, she would drop them, moving on to another, knowing she had no choice. Each year end she prayed that things would be better next year, that she would pay off the bills, get more tenants in. But the house kept getting worse and the tenants didn't come, so she had to entertain the men and work harder; anything to make a better life than the one she had for her children. Still the money was never enough, the bills piled up, red letters from the gas and electric people followed by disconnection. She needed money desperately, even tried to borrow it from the bank. The manager had turned her down flat. She had shrunk from the scorn in his face, feeling the weight of her failure.

It was Mrs Weston who told her about the money-lender. The Westons had stayed with Adella, getting comfortable in their room and then not bothering to move out. Adella knew they could afford to buy somewhere. They had been saving a long time, both working overtime whenever they could. She knew that they had wanted children, and it was disappointment at having none that made them give up their dream of buying a place of their own.

Adella and the Westons had become good friends, they spent most of their Sunday afternoons with her. They would sit across

123

from her on the settee, Mr Weston smoking his pipe while they swopped memories of Jamaica.

One day Mrs Weston came down to speak to her. Adella had been surprised, it was the middle of the day and the woman would usually have been at the factory where she had worked since coming to England.

'A know ow difficult it is now yu working fa de council,' Mrs Weston said, sitting down on the settee. 'A was tinking dat yu was seying de bank wouldn't lend yu de money fe pay de light bill.' Adella had confided in the woman that they were threatening to cut off her electricity and she didn't have the money to pay the bill. 'Dere's a man dung Loughborough dat len out money; a can get yu in touch if yu like. Ihm no cheap and ihm gwine tief yu, but at least ihm will len yu de money.'

Adella digested the information. 'A caan gi ihm no security,' she said cautiously. 'Dat's why de bank sey dem couldn't len me it.'

'Dat all right,' the woman said. 'De way ihm charge fe de money ihm can well do widout it.'

'So ow yu know bout ihm?' Adella asked now. She knew that the Westons had no commitments, that they had managed to save much of what they earned.

'Missa Weston an I did buy a house in Jamaica,' she said. 'Ting was, it did leave us short an we did haffe borrow. Most everybady we know go a de money-lender one time or anada. De bank dem doan like len money to West Indian dem. A surprise yu doan use dem yet, Miss Johnson.'

Adella let that pass, of course she knew about the money-lenders, had vowed never to use them. Right now she was surprised at the news of the Westons' house. Surprised and envious, especially now that she was losing her house. The council had told her they wanted possession in two months when they last wrote. They had sent her a form with long words and many pages. She had not understood it. But Audrey told her it was about housing. They were going to give her a place to rent. Audrey had filled in the form – she did all Adella's writing for her now that Eena had gone to live with Larry – and nothing else had come since then.

'A neva know yu tinking of going back home fa good,' Adella said to Mrs Weston when she had digested the information the other had given her. The Westons had been back to Jamaica several times and they had never mentioned going back for good. Adella had been back, too, scraping the money together in the need to see her son. It had been so different, so strange and she could not see herself returning there to live.

She could remember the disappointment when she had found Danny. He was living in Kingston, in a room very much like the one she had lived in after she got pregnant with him. He had a woman and a job, and she had to admit that although he and Mikey resembled each other, he had remained full of pride and dignity. Danny had been eager to see her, wanting to know if she had come to take him back to England with her. How could she tell him that he was too old? That she had gone to the immigration people and they had refused to listen? There had been other things as well. Claudia had changed, grown thin and looked too much like a schoolmistress. She was very religious and Adella knew from the beginning that she had not forgiven her for Beresford. Granny Dee was gone, a stone out on the hillside surrounded by the breeze-blown grass marking the spot where she lay. Adella had trudged up the hill, feeling the strain on her crippled leg. She had sat there on the tombstone, remembering all the things that Granny Dee had done.

Aunt Ivy was dead too, and like Mada Beck was buried under a tree in her yard. Her mother and father had aged, looked old and tired from the long years of work. She had envied them the respect they had. The fact that their age gave them dignity and privilege. Yet it had not been the same. With Granny Dee gone, much of Adella's acceptance had gone too. She had known then that she could never return. She would never be accepted with the sins she had committed. They had been sure she had driven her husband away, spoken about her life with Beresford. And had even called her name in church. It had been a bitter thing, made worse by the knowledge that she would never have enough money to live well in Jamaica again. Her skill with needlework was gone, destroyed with her stroke. There would be no place to live now that her younger brothers and sisters had grown up and their children lived in her father's house. So she had pretended, like so many others, that she was rich in England, that she had a big house and everything she wanted. 'At least de house true,' she had told herself grimly, glad that she had spent precious money to buy new clothes and presents to take back with her.

She knew from what the Westons told her that they had been disappointed in England. They had come from St Elizabeth, poor hill-people who scratched a living from the soil or worked for the

Busha, the big landowners, when times got hard. Mr Weston had seen England as a chance to escape; a way to make the money they could never earn in Jamaica. They had been hopeful of having children, bringing them up and then retiring back to Jamaica. But the years had passed and they had worked harder and harder and still no children had come. Adella had expected them to split up long ago. Mr Weston liked children and was always talking about them. But later, when the other tenants had moved out and she got to know him, she realised that the man would never leave his wife. They were so good together. Both quiet people who worked hard and went to church. Of all the people she had rented to she liked them the best. They never gossiped and Mr Weston never let his wife down. They told her they were going to return to Jamaica when the council took the house. They saw no reason to stay and find somewhere else since they already had a house and a piece of land to farm.

It rained the day the council took Adella's house, the sound of the water dripping through the ceiling making her want to cry as she moved from room to room making sure that all the things they wanted had been packed. She felt as if the heart was going out of her. Everything she had done gone for nothing. She had put so much into this house, worked so hard to own a place of her own. Now she was back where she had started, paying rent. She had been to see the house, hated it from the first. It was warm, with central heating like they were always advertising on the television. There was no damp there, no constant scurrying of mice and creeping things that the dampness in the old house and the rotten wood had brought. It was an odd house. On three floors like her own house, but one below ground with its own door leading in. There were three rooms down there. Two bedrooms, and a large empty room with a sink and a toilet.

The rest of the rooms were small, the kitchen with fitted units, the dining-room divided from the small square front room by sliding glass doors. On a half-landing was a bathroom with a tiny room and a larger bedroom up the stairs. It was a smaller house and yet it had more stairs. There was less room to stretch herself out, and she wondered where they would put half the things they were bringing from the old house.

They had told her that she would be compensated for the loss of her house, but when the money came it was barely enough to pay

126

the mortgage off, with nothing left for the debt she carried with her. She had expected so much from that house. Now she had nothing. Even the furniture grant they gave her, the money for new carpets and a cooker, was no compensation. She used most of it to pay back the money-lender anyway, finding that she owed him twice as much as she borrowed in the first place. Yet knowing she might need him in the future.

Fifteen

They came to move her things early. The big council van backed up beside the house. Adella watched silently, ignoring the cheerful greetings that the men threw her, the excitement in Carol's face, and her obvious relief that they were going. All she knew was that they were taking her house. Even the fear of homelessness and the relief when they told her they would give her a house could not dim her bitterness. She wondered what she could tell her parents, knew she could never let them know. She would have to find one more lie, to pile on all the other lies that were her life in England.

'Is not so bad,' Lisa said, looking around with appreciation at the radiators on the walls, the lack of growing fungus. 'It betta fa yu healt den de junjo growing pan de wall back a de ole house.'

Adella shrugged. 'But is not my house,' she insisted. 'De ada one neva perfeck but at least it was fe me own.'

'Plenty people loss dem house to de council now,' Lisa said. 'Whole heapa dem did trow pardna like yu an buy it an dem no even see a red cent fa all de money dem spen.'

Adella knew that Lisa was trying to make her feel better. She knew that quite a few West Indians who had bought houses had lost them just like her. But that did not take away her personal failure, the shame of living in a government house.

'A doan tink dem shoulda get weh wid it,' she said flatly. 'When

127

dem come roun fe get yu fe vote fa dem. Yu neva heah dem sey ow dem gwine tek weh yu house. Look ow dis street full up a West Indians dat dem tief house fram. A just doan tink is right.'

'A have sympathy,' Lisa said gently. 'A know how yu suffa fe get de house. De good Lord know it was fa de children dat yu try. A neva tink it was a good idea but yu neva did have a choice. Now me, a save up save up and what wid sending money back home fa me· mada and de pickney a neva coulda trow a pardna and save nuting. Das why is ongly now a can buy house.'

Adella looked at her in surprise. She had never thought of what Lisa had gone through. To her the other woman always seemed so carefree, so full of life. She was always there to help out and the thought of where she was getting the time and money never came into it.

'A suppose de house couda worse,' she said now, feeling ashamed at her selfishness. 'A haffe praise de Lord dat tings neva worser and at least a have a nice warm house now.'

Lisa agreed. 'Yu not getting any younger, an de way yu cough and sneeze mus mean de place did get to yu.'

Adella tried to smile at her good fortune. After all, they had given her money so that she could have wall-to-wall carpet even after she paid the loan. A thing she had always wanted but never been able to afford. Her chair, the over-stuffed one that Stanton had bought, stood nicely in a corner of the room, facing the television, and she even managed to have a phone put in. Or rather Mikey did, with the overtime money he brought home.

Yet despite all that she felt cold inside. Cold and tired like she had lost everything. Evening would find her slumped in her chair, the small room in darkness lighted by the flickering movements from the television screen and the faint penetration of rays from the streetlight directly outside.

Her only consolation was the garden. It was bigger than the one at the old house and with Mikey's help she soon had it looking nice. It was good to stand by the fence, gossiping with the woman next door. Seeing all the familiar faces and shouting out or answering greetings just like life on the old street. Only Audrey of all the children seemed to miss the old house. Adella knew that she often went round there to stand looking at the boarded-up windows and doors or sneak inside through the hole vandals had made in the back door. It was Audrey who told her they had stripped out the lead piping and that she had seen children wearing the old clothes they had left behind.

Winter came suddenly that year. Bleak and cold, forming ice patches on the ground that made walking difficult. Adella felt the icy wind eat into her clothes. It bit through thin tights and plastic shoes so that they felt frozen to her feet. Always there was the howling of the wind. It sounded like a lost and trapped spirit. It was the coldest winter she could remember. But then that was how every winter in England felt. She was glad for the central heating. The way it flooded the place with warmth. It was nice not to feel ever-present dampness, having to soak clothes to try and get the mildew out. She looked forward to coming home, a thing she never did in winter at the old house. She would climb tiredly up the stairs, push her key into the door and struggle in. Most of her time was spent in the small front room, sitting in her chair, worrying about the debts. She could not understand how it was they were asking more money a week than the mortgage to the bank had been, and by the time she had paid it there was little left for anything else. She was about to get another loan from the money-lender when she found out about rent rebate. It was Audrey who found out about the council paying the rent for her, and she had got the paper and forged Adella's signature saying that many of her friends did the same for their parents.

Audrey had got a job, and she now bought her own clothes as well as giving Adella some money for the housekeeping. Adella had insisted on that, feeling guilty after all the child had done but needing the money. She knew how much Audrey wanted to be independent, to get some of the things she had never had. But she had to think of everyone and Mikey already paid his way. She could remember Audrey's bitterness when she had confronted her.

'I buy my own clothes,' she said. 'And I don't even eat much here.'

Adella felt bad. She knew why Audrey was reluctant to eat food at her table, especially when it was meat. It had been okay when she had been younger. None of them had questioned it then, the unexpected treat of mutton or chicken on a Sunday bought with hard work and overtime. As she grew older Audrey started to associate meat with the man friend of the moment. She would look angry and resentful and refuse to eat the food.

'Is not jus food an clothes cost money,' Adella had told the child.

'A haffe pay rent and light bill an fa de gas as well. It all cost money.'

'I only have a Saturday job, mum, and it don't pay much.'

'Whatever it pay will help out in de house,' she had responded. She felt bad about demanding the money, wished she could leave the child with it, but the family needs had to come first.

'It's not fair,' Audrey said angrily. 'You don't buy my clothes and I buy my own food and you want me to give you all the money I get.'

Adella felt guilt and anger mingle. 'Hush up yu mouth an doan back chat me. I is yu mada an yu mus have respeck. Yu tink sey is thin air feed yu and put frock pan yu back all de years dem. Who yu tink look afta yu since yu born?'

'I never asked to be born,' the child muttered sullenly, and Adella felt the pain of the words; the knowledge of the shame the children felt about her.

'A try me bes to do right by all a yu,' she almost pleaded. 'It neva easy, yu know. A know yu tink some a de tings a do not right, but de Lord above know dat it was fa all a oonu.'

She had seen the rejection in the child's eyes, had felt age and defeat weigh on her. How had she lost her child's respect? She had tried so hard to do the best for everybody. Why couldn't Audrey see that? Why did she feel that she was being singled out? She wished she knew what to do. It was so difficult in England. The children wanted to do like their white friends. They resented discipline and responsibility and there was nothing parents could do. What was the use trying to bring them up like in the West Indies when the things you had to do took away their respect? When the white people treated you bad and let the children run wild? She sat in her chair wondering if it had been worth it, if all the sacrifices would end with anything. She had lost her house now. The house she had put everything in.

She did not mention the money to Audrey again, feeling too ashamed of the accusation she had read in the child's eyes.

'At least Caral not like dat,' she consoled herself. 'She an Mikey undastan dat a did what a had was to do.' It was something to hang on to as she struggled through the wind and snow to the bus stop, or walked through the market choosing a piece of yam or sweet potato as a special treat. She was surprised when, at the end of the week, Audrey came down from her room and sat on the settee in the small front room. The child rarely ventured out of her small box-room beside Adella's own. She would come in from school and lock herself in saying that she was studying. Often Adella would struggle up the stairs, anxious in case she was ill and was too proud to admit it. She would find her lying on her back, arms folded behind her head, as she stared sightlessly at the ceiling. Adella would shuffle out quietly, feeling at a loss about what to do, feeling guilty and a failure. She knew that it was disappointment in her that made her daughter so withdrawn. But every time she tried to talk to her, she was greeted with a hostile wall of anger and suspicion.

Adella sat in her chair, feeling tense and awkward as Audrey perched on the settee. She was ashamed of the way her own daughter could make her feel so wary and defensive. Her fingers curled in her good palm; all thoughts of the Western on the television wiped out by worry. What was Audrey going to confront her about now? She had tried so hard to make ends meet, even going to the money-lender when things were really tight rather than asking her manfriend to help her out. But it was so hard when you had to pay so much for the little that you borrowed. Even the shopkeepers were charging interest for the things she had on trust; and she had finally gone back on her resolution. But how had Audrey found out? She had been so careful, inviting her friend round only when the children were at school, between coming in from the morning shift and going out for the evening one. She sat there, tension mounting, worsening with the girl's continued silence.

'Mum, I . . . a . . . well, I brought my wages like we agreed.'

Adella looked round in surprise and the child shifted uncomfortably, looking awkward.

'I'm sorry about the other day,' she said now. 'I know how difficult things are for you, and I want to help.' She held out the money wrapped up in the brown paper wage-packet, and Adella felt a sudden stab of shame. Hesitated, wanting to tell her to keep her money. 'Take it, mum,' Audrey said urgently, thrusting it at her. 'It's not much but it will help out a little bit.'

Adella took the brown paper, feeling embarrassed, not knowing what to say. The awkward silence stretched between them, unbridgeable with any words and Audrey got abruptly to her feet, muttering that she had to go, and leaving the room hastily.

Adella looked at the small brown envelope with loathing. All the things she had thought of her daughter, making her feel uncomfortable. Audrey looked so much like Stanton. She could never forget him with the child around. It was not that she did not love her, but her critical attitude brought so many bitter things to mind. Stanton had always liked that one best after Eena, liking to see himself in her. The way she criticised was so much like him, the way she pretended that the family was not her business. Adella smiled wryly. No that wasn't exactly true. All the children born in England were like that. All of them thinking that they only had to look out for themselves. Her heart ached when she thought about Eena and Delores' children. What kind of life was here for them? Children didn't grow up with the proper respect any more. She had tried so hard; but she had to work all hours to find money for so many things; and now Stanton was gone to America, after telling her how badly she let him down. He felt that she set a bad example and led his children astray. Adella had wanted to tell him that she had tried her best and that it was he who had deserted her for her own cousin, but experience had taught her not to talk to him like that. How many times had he hit her in anger since they parted, brought down his fist with all the weight of his body on her unprotected head?

She told herself it was Gladys' fault, that he would never treat her like that if they were still together.

'Yu neva treat me bad like dis when yu live wid me,' she would say reproachfully, cowering against a wall; trying to hide her good side, knowing that her crippled side would feel less pain.

'A doan know why a bada wid yu,' he would reply aggressively. 'A neva so happy as since a lef yu gwaan go live wid Gladys.'

'But is me still haffe respansible fa yu children,' she flung at him. 'An look ow yu mek de pickney dem run wild. If it was me, yu tink it coulda happen?'

She had wanted to tell him to take them, to do a better job. It was so unfair. He spent all his money on that woman, on other people and on clothes. In fact, on everything except to help her with his children.

It was the children who rejected him, getting more aware as they grew older. They had long stopped cluttering around the front-room window watching for him to pull up and soon they were taking turns to go with him, none wanting to be the one to have to endure a day with him. She often heard the fighting, the arguments, and she felt sad and angry that they should have so little respect for their father. Adella could remember trying to warn him

132

about how the children felt; how much they disliked and resented him.

'Is yu trying to tun dem gainst me,' he had said, looking at her with contempt.

'Yu know dat not true, Stanton,' she had said pleadingly. 'Is jus dat dem know is me haffe fine money fa everyting and den come Sunday when yu come, yu a beat dem like is yu bring dem up.'

'Yu telling me a caan beat me own pickney?' he asked aggressively.

'Is not dat, Stanton, is jus dat all yu do is beat dem an gi dem lickle money now and den.'

The look he gave her made her shrink, flinching automatically from the blow she thought was coming. He always did that when he felt frustrated or in the wrong and she had long got used to it. But the children were different. They had got infected with white people's ideas. They just did not respect him.

'A look out fa my children,' he said now. 'Yu try sey a doan love dem?'

'A neva sey dat,' she denied, shaking her head. 'A jus sey dat to dem it seem so. Tru dem know yu live wid me cousin an ow yu spen so much money on everybady save dem.'

He grabbed the front of her dress, shaking her. 'So yu start talk me in front a de children now, ee?' he said angrily. 'Yu doan content wid driving me weh; now yu waan fe tun de children gainst me.'

She had looked at him in surprise. How could he believe that? Everybody knew that he treated his children badly. How could he blame her for what he was doing?

'A neva tell de children nuting bad bout yu. A try tell dem fe respeck yu; but dem growing an dem jus doan listen no more.'

He looked angrily down at her. 'Jus tru yu caan get me back yu get spiteful,' he said bitterly. 'But yu gwine sarry fa what yu do, Adella. God gwine punish yu, yu wait an see.'

She had looked at him in amazement, seeing that he really believed what he was saying. She supposed it was that woman's fault. How could Stanton not hear the talk about him and Gladys? Often the children would come back from the market, the tumbling of the trolley alerting her to their presence before they reached the gate. They would come in angry and embarrassed. The other black women from the street had stopped them in the market, talked about their father and how well he was doing. They would always pity them, tell them what a shame he didn't care about them. Adella hated and resented that, feeling angry for the children; hating to see the embarrassment they were feeling. The shame that the other children on the street and in their school knew their father had run off with their mother's cousin.

Stanton had gone after her revelations about the children and had not come round for many weeks. Then one day she had received a letter with an American postmark on it. Adella had looked at it in surprise, turning it over and over in her hand, she could not believe the familiar handwriting would be on a letter from America and her heart raced as she tore it open. It was only a short note, hastily scrawled. 'Gladys and I decide to come over here after what you did. Send and tell me how the children are getting on and get them to write me.'

She had read it and re-read it; not able to believe what she was reading. It was the second letter he ever sent her, apart from the things about the divorce. The first one had been when he came to England. The letter sending for her to join him. In her mind she knew it was because of the children that he had gone. He never even noticed that things were changing, cushioned by his vanity and his world without responsibility. It had taken her words for him to see the sullen expressions; the dragging feet and resentment in their faces. He had been unable to take the loss of adoration. It was the only thing he wanted from them. To be able to show them off, to be an occasional father dazzling them with presents and his car.

Adella wished she had not spoken to him. Maybe he would have stayed. As long as he was there, near her, within reach, she could see him sometimes; dream of the day he would knock on the door with his grip and tell her he was coming back. Even so, she refused to admit that he was gone for good. She had to believe that he would come back. Wasn't that what she had worked for? Waited for? She had heard rumours that he was seeing other women, that he was getting tired of Gladys. She had hoped then, expected that he would return to her and the children. How she had cleaned the place. Every week washing and airing, wanting things to be just so. Now he was gone. But still she clung to the hope: Stanton would come back. After all, this was not the first time he had left her to go abroad. He had left her in Kingston; boarded the boat to come to England. She had stood on the wharf, waving and waving until her arm ached and the spot that was the ship had long disappeared over the horizon. She had not been sure of him; had doubted if he really meant to send for her. But the letter had come with the money. Just like he had said. She had boarded one of the ships she had dreamt so much of sailing in. Her mind shied away from what she had found in England: the small dingy room, Stanton with many friends but no money because he spent it all on drinks and fancy clothes. That had not been important, she told herself. No, he would come back. She knew he would. He loved her like she loved him and when he got rid of Gladys he would be back with his grip and the one he borrowed from her when he left and they would all be a family again.

She had not told the children that he had gone to America, and she was hurt that they did not ask for him. As the months stretched on, they never once asked why he never came round any more. It was only after a woman in the market asked after him, that Audrey came back and mentioned it.

'Is Dad really gone to America?' she asked, as Adella tried to watch a Western on the television.

'Yes, ihm leave nearly one year now,' Adella said, stiffening, expecting the girl to say something nasty because she had not told them.

'Good. That mean he won't keep coming round any more.' She seemed pleased, indifferent that her father had left her for another country.

'Yu should have respeck fa yu fada,' Adella said wearily, not remembering how many times she had repeated the same thing.

'He's no father to us,' the girl said sullenly. 'He can stay there as far as I'm concerned.'

'Ihm gwine come back,' Adella told her, automatically. 'Ihm love me still an is ongly yu Auntie Gladys dat did cause trouble between us.'

Audrey looked at her impatiently. 'He's never coming back, mum. Can't you see that he don't care about anybody but himself?'

'Yu should have respeck,' was all she could respond.

Sixteen

'There doesn't seem to be anything obviously wrong with you, Mrs Johnson. However, to be on the safe side I'm going to send you down to casualty so they can do a series of X-rays on your chest.'

Adella had been sitting on the edge of her chair, leaving the talking to her daughter. She had insisted that Audrey came with her to the specialist. Audrey was the most practical and she had gone to university.

'Why does she keep having the pains?' her daughter asked as she got up from her chair.

'Let's wait and see what the X-ray shows, Miss Johnson,' the man said kindly. 'Time enough to worry after that.'

They spent nearly an hour in casualty. Adella was surprised at how long the X-rays took. She was doubtful about lying on the narrow length of the hospital couch. She was sure that the thing would collapse, that she would roll off at the very least, and she lay stiff and unmoving, hardly daring to breathe. She was glad when it was all over, when the woman helped her to struggle to a sitting position and she could slide gingerly on to the step leading to the floor.

'A did like dat special docta, but a not gwine to no more,' she told her daughter as they crossed the road to where the car was parked on a sidestreet away from the hospital. 'A tell yu nuting no wrang wid me. A jus need fe go back a work.'

'Mum, you know the doctor said that was out of the question, and anyway remember what happened the last time you tried to go back.'

She remembered all right. She had not been able to go back for the afternoon, too tired and worn from the morning. Even walking across the big main road to the hospital today left her joints aching; and already she was wishing she could just sit on one of the stained wooden benches on the piece of open land they were passing. 'A gwine betta soon,' she said without too much conviction.

'Mum, why don't you let us send you home to live with Aunt Claudia?' Audrey asked gently. 'I'm sure you would be a lot happier in Jamaica.'

Adella hissed through closed teeth. 'Yu waan rid a me, eeh?' she said grumpily, knowing that she was being unreasonable yet needing to take out her frustration on someone. 'Ow much time a haffe tell yu, a waan stay wid all a yu children.'

Audrey sighed. 'You know we would come to see you a lot if you were in Jamaica. I mean, you'd still be our mum.'

Adella shrugged, she knew all of that. The children would look out for her, make sure she was comfortable, but that wasn't all that mattered. There were still the same reasons why she could not return. 'We talk bout dis already,' she said in dismissal. 'Me children deh ya, so me a go stay ya.'

It was two weeks later that she had woken with the pain, coming to awareness with Carol shaking her urgently. She had called the doctor, overruling Adella's protest. Adella was furious, listening in tight-lipped anger as the man warned Carol to get her to take things easy. She was burning with anger by the time he picked up his bag and she had to force back the insult ready on her tongue, as she watched Carol show him to the door. What did he know anyway? she thought angrily. She had always trusted doctors but this one was different. She felt a sudden resentment against her daughter. She had told Carol not to call the man. She didn't need a doctor. All she wanted was to go back to work. She would feel better then.

'If ongly a neva so tired,' she told herself heavily. 'If ongly de bone dem inna me body would stop hurt.'

The doctor had poked at her, looking down at her. 'You should go out in the fresh air, Mrs Johnson, the change will do you good,' he said, swinging his stethoscope absently in his hand. He was acting just like the doctors in the films, the actors who she knew had no training. Of all the doctors to call! She had heard about Dr Sam. He was new at the practice but already the word was that he was no good.

'Is jus de ada day Audrey was telling me bout her friend pickney,' she muttered angrily, feeling a fresh irritation as she thought of the man's visit. 'Caral!' she shouted as it burned inside her, her voice a dying echo in the silent house. 'Caral, yu no hear me a call yu? . . . Caral!' She was wrapped up in her anger, hardly hearing the sounds of movements made by the suddenly restless dog. 'Caral!'

'I'm here, mum.'

Adella looked at her daughter with annoyance. 'Why yu haffe creep bout de place? Why yu neva ansa steada mek me bawl dung de place?' She knew it was unfair, that only her preoccupation with the doctor's visit made her fail to hear the other's footstep. Nobody could say Carol crept anywhere. With her wide flat feet, she often made enough noise to rouse the cat.

'I did answer you,' her daughter was unmoved by the criticism. 'But I can only get here so fast.'

Adella sniffed, not wanting to lose face. 'Well next time yu betta ansa fasta,' she said now.

Carol shrugged her shoulders, slumping into the settee good-naturedly. 'What do you want, mum?' she asked.

'Why bring dat goodfanuting docta come see me?' Adella asked, the anger bubbling up again with fresh thoughts of Dr Sam.

'I told you, mum – I had to get the doctor on call, and he was on call.'

'So why yu couldn't get me own docta, yu coulda get ihm still?'

Her daughter sighed. 'Mum, I told you how they work. One of the doctors at the practice is on call outside of normal hours, and you have to make do.'

'So why yu did haffe call dat one? Is jus de ada day yu sista did tell us bout dat man; how ihm tell her fren fe tek her baby outa de cold street fe bring dung ihm temperature.'

'I know, mum, and I wouldn't have called him if you hadn't been so sick,' Carol answered, anxiety in her voice and shadowing her eyes.

Adella felt disgruntled. 'Wha yu mean so sick?' she asked angrily. 'A did tell yu a neva need no docta, no true?'

'Yes, mum,' Carol said heavily, voice flat with resignation.

'A did warn yu dat dem would sen out some fofool man dat no know nuting.' She paused and Carol continued to look at her, a slight frown creasing her wide forehead. 'A neva warn yu?' Adella prompted, feeling the rage building up again.

'Yes, mum,' Carol said in the same voice, and Adella wanted to hit out at her, knowing she was humouring her. She could see the

138

worry in her daughter's face, knew the girl was concerned and felt guilty for it.

'A doan dead yet,' she said defensively. 'A still living and a still yu mada. When a was your age an my mada did sey someting a use fe haffe obey her. Yu doan hear yu mus obey yu parents?'

'Yes, mum.'

'Yu tink me is fofool, bout yu yes mum. Well a tell yu when a was growing up we use to learn fe obey. We did haffe learn tings like eem, mek me see, yes a memba it "Children obey your parents". ' She racked her brains suddenly unable to remember the rest, adding after the silence stretched for some minutes, 'It go on fe sey, "Hona dy fada an dy mada so dy days may be lang pan de earth dat de Lord dy god has given dee." '

Carol had one elbow on her knee, her head lying on her outstretched palm as she listened.

'I think you told me that one before,' she said now, not even pretending to be ashamed. Adella felt impatient again. How could the child be so good-tempered all the time? Even when she was warned.

'Yu pickney jus doan have no respeck,' Adella said heavily. 'Yu doan fear de Lord an yu doan hona yu mada.'

Carol shrugged, trying to hide the smile creeping on her face. 'Come off it, mum,' she said mildly. 'You know that's not true. You're just grumpy because the doctor said you can't go back to work.'

'If a doan go back a might as well dead,' Adella said now. 'An dat's not why a vex; is true yu no listen when a talk an yu bring dat fofool man come ya.'

Carol flinched, her smile replaced by worry once again. 'Look, mum, can I get you anything?' she asked, changing the subject abruptly. 'I have practice this evening and I have to take Shela for a walk.' Adella felt ashamed suddenly, regretted her attempt to hurt the girl.

'Yu get green banana an plantain?' she asked, changing the subject.

'I did that yesterday. You know I always do the shopping on Fridays.'

Adella nodded, suddenly wanting to hold on to the company. 'Why yu doan sit wid me lickle bit?' she suggested placatingly.

'Mum, you know I have to go. I'm working later.'

'Yu neva have no time fa me,' Adella complained. 'All a oonu

139

pickney doan have no time. Oonu always too busy doing dis an dat.' She knew it was unfair, but suddenly the endless stretch of lonely hours filled only by the flickering lights of the television was too much to bear. Since she became sick all she ever did was fill the hours with memories, uncomfortable, half-buried memories; some good, some bad. All left her lonely and bitter, weighed down with the feeling that she had wasted her life.

'All right, but mek me lickle tea, and two slice a bread fore yu go,' she said finally. She did not really want the food; but at least it would keep Carol a little longer. It was nice to hear the sounds of movement and activity coming from the kitchen. The impatient voice raised in anger as cat or dog got in the way. If she closed her eyes she could almost pretend it was long ago when all her children lived at home. Now they were all gone. Even Mikey only came round now and then, sleeping the night with one of the white women he always hung around with.

Adella looked at the thick slices of buttered hardough bread and the steaming enamel mug of tea without enthusiasm. Her eyes wandered to the flickering movements on the screen in front of her and she wondered who would be down the market today. It was so long since she had braved the icy winds and walked along the wrong-way paving through the yellow brick estate. There the mortar crumbled from the cracks and showered her as she cut through towards the market. The only outings she took now were when one of her daughters came by to take her out. They would tuck her into the car as though she was sick, and take her visiting or to their homes. She shook her head at the thought, reaching absently for the cigarettes which had joined the rum underneath the chair. Visiting was all right but the gossip was never as sweet when she had to pick it up second-hand. She had nothing to contribute to the talk, she had seen nothing, could dispute nothing. No, the market was the place to be. Everything happened there.

She could remember when Miss Vi and Sister Campbell from down the road had a fight. Adella had been hesitating between a piece of yam and the rare treat of a breadfruit. The breadfruit wasn't fit, but she was thinking of leaving it to ripen and roasting it for Sunday dinner. She was weighing the two in her hands, comparing the price of the large yellowheart and the soft white yam. She wondered if she could get a piece of dasheen as well and then she heard the crash. Adella had swung round, mouth dropping in surprise as she saw Sister Campbell with her wig askew, all her dignity gone. She was holding off Miss Vi, twice her size, with desperation. Everybody had been frozen with shock, unable to intervene, or even believe what they were seeing. Miss Vi and Sister Campbell. Two long-time friends pounding at each other in broad daylight in the middle of the market. They had struggled for a while locked together, crashing into stalls. They were calling each other vile names, revealing secrets that Adella stored avidly in her memory, eager to pass on when she was next in company. Finally Miss Vi gave Sister Campbell a hefty push, sending her crashing to the ground. The woman seized a bottle from a nearby watcher's startled hand and started to hammer Sister Campbell's defenceless head.

It was only then that people had started to react; everybody talked at once as two men from Sister Campbell's church moved in to separate the warring women. Adella could remember her shock when Miss Vi smoothed down her brown coat and appealed to the market at large for understanding. 'Yu see how de devil strang?' the woman asked the bewildered shoppers. She looked round, eyes lighting on Adella. 'Yu see how de devil strang, Miss Johnson?'

Adella was at a loss, not quite sure of the devil's role in the fracas. She agreed quickly, the way Miss Vi had reduced Sister Campbell to a shivering wreck was vivid in her mind. At that point it was as well not to upset Miss Vi.

'A tell yu, Miss Johnson,' the woman went on, encouraged by the agreement of a familiar face. 'A get up dis morning praising de Lord.'

Adella doubted that, but knew better than to voice it. As far as she knew, Miss Vi didn't even know who the Lord was.

'Yes indeed a was,' Miss Vi continued. 'Den dis woman come a me yard sey is me tek her man.'

Adella's ears pricked up. Sister Campbell's husband had left! Now this was news. She wondered why she had never heard about it, why the women had kept it such a secret. From the corner of her eyes she could see Sister Campbell's head bow in shame, and she felt sudden fellow-feeling. Adella wished Miss Vi would keep her revelations to herself. She wanted to shut the woman up – she had been in the same position once. She could remember the heads gathered round gossiping, breaking up when she came near. But Miss Vi was not going to stop and the truth was that Adella burned with curiosity to find out why Sister Campbell had acted in the way she had. It was such a foolish thing to do. Everybody had heard the rumours about Miss Vi. How she used to fight with bad women down by the wharf and lived in the Dungle before she met a well-off man and got him to pay her fare to England.

'A tell yu, Miss Johnson,' Miss Vi was saying now. 'A try warn her dat a doan have endless patience. She even come inna yard an search de place. A tell yu, Miss Johnson, de devil strang.' She paused, giving Sister Campbell a nasty look. The defeated woman quailed and backed away. Only the crowd pressing in on her prevented her from making an escape. 'A get me tings,' Miss Vi continued, 'and de woman falla me all de way dung ya, a ask me fa her husband an tell me what an what gwine happen to me. De truth is a ongly see de man two times, Miss Johnson. A tell yu, as God is my witness, it was ongly two times.'

Strands of memory curled about in her head and she felt sympathy for Sister Campbell. How she had wanted to confront Gladys, to attack her, beat her – demand her husband back. She had been exposed as well, naked to the world. She remembered seeing the eagerness on faces as people digested how she looked, what she said. Yes, she had fed the gossip for a long time. It had really hurt her for she knew what they were saying. After all, didn't she do it as well? How many times had she picked up some piece of information too hot to keep to herself?

Adella walked away from the market, remembering. She had got Lisa to find out where Gladys and her Stanton lived, had even gone round there. Walking up and down outside the house. But she had not had the courage to be like Sister Campbell or the woman who had stopped all the people going into the house to tell them how a woman there had stolen her husband. She smiled as she remembered that the hounded woman had been forced to leave the house, and her man returned to his wife.

Adella sighed, moving slightly in her chair. She felt older and older as the pain in her bones increased. She was always lonely now, cut off from the life outside. The sights and smells, the milling people and the market. It didn't matter how many people came to visit her, how long they stayed and how much gossip they passed on; she was still locked in her room, her tiny world, and they just came to visit. She envied them. How many of them had lived in her house, roomed with her when they first came to England. She had charged so little – just enough to keep the roof, or what there was of it, over the heads of her children and herself. Now all those people had their own houses. Most of them had returned to Jamaica. Often, she only found out when they no longer came round to see her. She had nothing to go back to. Nothing to take back to show for thirty years of pain in England. She had provided a place for so many people to start out. A cheap place while they saved a deposit on a property. Now she had nothing, and her bones were too old, her back too painful to enjoy her life again. It all went wrong after five years in Kingston. All those plans she made, all the things she wanted to do. All that gone because of one mistake. Even God had been against her, punished her by visiting her sin on her children. Adella thought back, mind groping through the clutter of her memories, feeling again the first real disappointment in her life.

Looking back she realised that even after Danny things had still been possible. Beresford had not been good, but she had learnt to accept that. To live each day as it came. The dressmaking had fallen off after she moved down to Denham town, but at least he gave her money so she did not starve or worse ... Adella knew she was one of the better-off people in her yard. Most of the other women scratched a living as best they could, cleaning floors and taking in the dirty washing from the houses on the hill. She would see them leave, large wash baskets balanced on their heads – her mother had carried a basket like that, hips swaying for balance as she carried the ground provisions up the steep road to the market in Highgate. She had watched them age, sicken, bellies swelling regularly with child, in the time that she was there. And yet they shared together, helped each other out with a piece of saltfish here, rice there; or just by minding the children. Adella admired their cooperation yet feared the idea of turning into one of them. She knew that all that stood between herself, and those dead-eyed, hopeless women was Beresford's interest in her body. She often listened to him talking about the other women, how faded and washed out they were. How he would hate his woman to look like them. He would squeeze her waist admiringly, and Adella would force back the anger and contempt she felt for him. One day she would get away, and in the meantime she slipped out weekly to the obeah man in the gully, buying quatty-worth of herb, and drinking it to stop the swelling that would herald another child. As soon as Danny was old enough, she was going to leave. Every time Beresford brought money, she put a little aside. She would tie it carefully in a piece of cloth and push it right under the clothes in the small drawer, for which she had never been able to afford a dressing-table.

It seemed like things were going so well, when everything went wrong. She had noticed straight away when her monthly flow did not come. Every month the same anxiety clutched at her, the same calculation to see if dates were wrong, if she was overdue. She marked off the days on a piece of slate that she had picked up at some long-forgotten market stall. Every day she would make a stroke, and when the flow came for the month, she wiped them off and started over again. She had done it month after month, two years of worrying. Afraid of the trap of pregnancy. She had fallen so far the first time and she was terrified of falling to the level the other women in the yard had reached. But it had all been for nothing, now it had happened. She counted the strokes on the slate, again and again. Tried to tell herself that she was only late. It would not be the first time. But this time she knew it had really happened. The knowledge of her pregnancy pushed at her, however much she tried to deny it.

In the end she was forced to face the problem and tried all the remedies the women in the yard had told her about. None of them had worked and she finally had to admit there was nothing she could do. She was two months pregnant by the time she got the courage to tell Beresford. He still came only three or four times a week, claiming he was working overtime, or that his mother was sick. Adella knew he was lying – but what could she do about it? He knew the power he had, the fact that she needed the money he provided. He would come in on a Friday and force her to do whatever he wanted. 'Yu waan money?' he would ask when she argued, or tried to stand up for herself. 'Yu waan feed yu pickney dis week, eeh?'

'Beresford, is your pickney too,' she once said in exasperation. 'Is not jus me did mek it.'

'But is yu breed and drap it,' he answered callously. 'And is jus fram de kindness of me heart dat a giving yu money.' He rubbed his chest through his unbuttoned tunic as he always did. 'Now yu betta show lickle preciation fore a decide yu not worth me money, afta all.'

She pushed the bitterness and resentment down, swallowed her pride as she tried to coax the money out of him. Now she had to tell him another child was on the way and she dreaded the confrontation and his reaction to her news.

'Wha yu mean yu carrying again?' Beresford asked, looking at her in stunned disbelief. 'Wha wrang wid yu, mek yu breed so?'

She bit down on the angry words, wanting to tell him that it was not all her fault. How many times had she told him no, pleaded with him, told him of her fear of another pregnancy? Always he would laugh. 'Dat was accident,' he would say airily. 'Yu jus worry worry too much. If it was gwine happen it woulda happen lang time. But de pickney reach two an yu doan breed again.'

She had still been worried. It was all right for him, as far as she could see nothing much had changed in his life. He still had his job, and his freedom. She did not believe he was working all the time he did not come to see her.

'Is not my fault mek a get pregnant,' she said wearily.

'Den is whose fault, mine? Is me have yu body? Is me can get someting fe stap yu breeding?'

'A did tell yu bout getting pregnant,' she replied, worry lacing her voice. 'A did go dung a de obeah man dung de gully, an try everyting a could. Is not dat a waan breed again.'

'Dat's what yu sey now de ting happen,' he snapped.

Adella swallowed hard, wondering if this was the time to broach the subject on her mind since she found out she was pregnant. He seemed so angry, so sure she was trying to trap him. Yet she had to say something, make some plan. Soon her belly would swell. And when she was heavy and awkward she would get nothing out of him. No favours meant no money. He was unyielding on that point and had been since her work fell off and he realised her dependence on him.

'We could get married,' she suggested hopefully. 'A know dis place too lickle and yu mada place not much bigga. But if we married yu could get one a de policeman house dat dem building, an tings would betta. A could work fa de big house dem again an we could do all right.'

'Wha yu talking bout? Who tell yu bout de police house dem?'

'Everybady talking bout dem. A know dey building dem up Stonygate.'

'But ow people know bout dem?' he persisted, looking suddenly scared.

'Dat doan matter,' she said, swallowing pride even further. 'A mean, once we married it woulda betta, tru a could carry me weight again.'

145

He had laughed nervously. 'A caan married yu,' he said moving shiftily.

'Why not?' she asked, puzzled.

'A married already.'

Adella looked at him, shock vibrating inside her. She was not sure she had heard right. The words sank into her head, one by one, big heavy stones weighing her down. He was already married, had a wife somewhere. All that overtime. All those special assignments, it had all been time spent with his wife.

'Why yu neva tell me?' she asked numbly, 'why yu mek me get inna trouble when yu have a wife?'

'It wasn't yu business,' he said dismissively. 'My wife is a good woman; an is her father did help me get in de police. A woulda neva get nowhere if a neva meet her.'

'A was a good woman once,' Adella said quietly. 'A was good and God-fearing till yu trouble me. Now a caan even go a church tru a backslide an a living a life of sin.'

'Is yu mek it,' he said with indifference. 'If yu was a good gal yu would neva did let me. Yu should tankful dat a stay wid yu an help yu out. Is not a lot a man would do dat.'

She had looked at him stunned, not wanting to believe what he was saying to her. She couldn't listen to him as he went on and on, justifying himself. That was always the way with Beresford. When he was wrong, or hurt someone, he always spent a lot of time trying to convince them and himself that he was in the right. Adella felt sick with worry. What was she going to do now? She could not continue to see him, let him use her in return for the money that she needed. Yet what was the alternative? How could she watch her dreams die in the grey dust of the ghetto, her body sagging and worn out from misuse and grinding poverty? She thought about the other woman – Beresford's wife. Wondered what she was like. She had heard so often of men who had a wife at home, a woman somewhere else. She had always hated the idea, thought how she would feel if that ever happened to her. How was she to know that one day she would be the other woman? She felt guilt mingling with her anger. How could he do that? She thought of his wife at home. Did she have any children? Did she know what her husband was like? She hoped suddenly that the other woman did not, and she hated him the more for that unknown woman's sake.

146

Seventeen

Somewhere in the distance a door slammed, and Adella shifted heavily. Her bottom felt sore from too much sitting, too little movement. She reached for the remote control switch and depressed the button that lighted up the television, flooding the room with sound.

'Caral?' she shouted automatically.

The dog bounded in, smelling of raw winter streets, tail wagging with the excitement of the walk and the sound of her voice.

'Move, Shela,' Adella had said impatiently, pushing the small energetic bundle aside as the dog tried to jump into her lap.

'Caral, yu no hear me a call yu?'

Her daugher's head popped round the dining-room door. 'I can't stop, mum, I have to get ready to play volleyball.'

'Yu neva have time fe listen to me. What a suppose to do, stay ya an starve?'

'I got you something to eat before I took Shela out,' Carol said, coming to the sliding doors. Her eyes spotted the untouched food, the tea gathering scum now that it had cooled. 'You haven't even touched the bread and tea,' she said accusingly. 'Honestly, mum, sometimes I just don't know what to do with you.'

'A did fall asleep,' Adella said defensively. She had totally forgotten about the bread, had just wanted a little company. 'Jus get me some fresh tea and a will eat it.'

Carol sighed, walking into the room and picking up the cold tea with reluctance. 'Okay, but I can't stay. I'm going to be late as it is.' She hesitated, a half-impatient look on her face. 'I'll come back as soon as I can,' she said finally. 'We can spend the evening together.'

Silence descended after Carol had gone and the dog soon wandered into the garden too full of excitement to settle in one place. The new mug of tea stood on the drying stain of the old one; and Adella

147

picked it up half-heartedly, taking a sip before putting it down again. There was nothing good on the television, her eyes looked at the boxers circling each other on the screen without interest. She wished there was somewhere she could go, that she could get her coat, and escape the prison of her room. Adella sighed, feeling the ache deep in her back, the burning pain in her legs that got worse as the days slipped by. 'If ongly Stanton was here,' she thought sadly, eyes going to the faded brown picture. He had always known how to cheer her up. She pushed the despair aside. 'Stanton gwine come back,' she told herself with conviction. 'Is a long time a wait fa ihm and a know ihm not gwine let me dung.'

She wriggled her bottom, trying to find a comfortable spot for it. Eyes going back to the faded brown picture, lingering with sudden longing and regret.

'Ihm always was too sharp fe stay wid a cripple and five pickney,' she told herself sadly. 'Ihm did haffe go live life, till ihm get ole.' She could remember when he gave her that picture. The day she had gone with him down to the wharf and watched him climb on the boat with the other passengers. He stood out against the drab suits of the other men, so handsome in his new suit. The picture had been new then, his suit black and sharp against the studio background of painted coconut palms, and a calm flat sea. It was strange how all the pictures from back home had the same background. She wondered if the same man had painted all of them or if they all stole a copy from him. 'It woulda jus like dem,' she thought with a smile. 'Dem smaddy is all de same, one get it an everybady wante wante.'

Yes, Stanton had always been a handsome man. He was not very tall, but the way he wore his clothes had style. The parting in his hair was always so straight, and his shirt was always crisp and clean. Even now that the picture had grown old, had lost most of its definition, he still looked handsome, still stood sharp and proud. She could still see the humour in his eyes, the ready smile playing around his mouth. 'England tek ihm pride,' she said sadly. 'It mek ihm did haffe run weh fram ihm wife an pickney dem.'

He had been so different back in Jamaica, coming into her life and picking her up after Beresford. She had decided not to hold on to Beresford. She knew how she would have felt if she had been his wife and there was another woman. It had been a hard decision. The child was growing and moving inside her and every day there was less work to find. The bitterness of his words ate into her.

And she knew that she had to let him go for the sake of her pride. He did not think she was decent, did not think she was as good as his wife. She wondered if it was because she could not give him anything, get him a better job. He told her that his wife had light skin. Father had a good position in the police and had only got him the job because of her.

'If a did lef her, a sure a woulda haffe leave de police,' he had pleaded, realising that his words had hurt. 'But a need de jab. A haffe help out mama and a have yu and de pickney dem.'

She had felt the contempt inside her again. This time it refused to be suppressed after allowing him the use of her body for so long, of humbling herself for the money she needed. She could not do it again.

'A not gwine sleep wid yu again,' she told him stubbornly, ignoring his anger and his threats. 'A neva know yu tink so bad bout me; an a doan waan see yu again.'

Beresford had looked at her in stunned disbelief. Had tried to persuade, pleaded; then threatened. 'Yu see ow yu gwine feel when yu have two hungry pickney an no man fe support yu,' he said savagely. 'Yu tink a gwine gi yu money fa nuting? Yu tink me is idiot?'

Adella said nothing, arms folded, mouth grim as she listened to him. She knew it was going to be hard. She felt the spirals of panic and almost forced herself to beg him not to go. Instead she thought of the bitter years she had spent waiting for him, forcing herself to smile at him, be nice to him; while she hated and despised him.

But it had been hard when he had not returned. 'If yu change yu mind, yu know whe a work,' he said, stalking through the flimsy wooden door. The words were to haunt her after Mikey was born, dog her steps as she tramped the streets, knocking on doors looking for any job that would feed her children. How many times had she crawled into bed, defeated by the day, hunger gnawing at her stomach, burning inside her, Danny's crying in her ears? He had been so thin when she met Stanton, his belly swollen and distended like the other children in the yard. She worried about the baby suckling at her breast. What would happen when he was weaned? Already she was behind in the rent; and how many times had she sat down holding the baby, the little mouth tugging with desperate hunger at the dwindling milk from her shrinking breasts. She often walked down to the crossroads and stood looking out at Beresford isolated in his island, directing traffic. She had been angry seeing him looking fit and healthy. Why did she have to starve? Why did her children have to suffer? She would watch him standing there, knew that the money she needed was in those white-gloved hands moving about in complicated gestures, as the tangle of vehicles sorted themselves out and moved sluggishly in different directions.

Stanton had taken her from all that, coming into her little room, lifting Danny on his knees and listening with sympathy as she told him about Beresford and how he had a wife already.

'A doan have no wife,' he told her with a grin. 'But a gwine help yu out cause a like yu.'

She had been on the point of giving up, her dreams crumbling around her. She would go back to the country. Back to Granny Dee. What did it matter that she would be going back in disgrace? She had not told Granny Dee about Mikey; too ashamed that she was again pregnant and still not married. But she could live with all the shame and the talk if it meant the children could run about and be happy, that Danny could lose that haunted look, the skinny arms and bang-belly. She had never been hungry as a child and she resented the pain her children suffered.

Stanton changed all that, coming just when she was giving up hope. He had helped her with the children. Giving her money, and taking her out dancing; and she had filled out, got pretty again. It had been good, the two years they spent together, and when she got pregnant for the third time he had been full of pride. He insisted that they got married and took her to see his family. It had been good to move out of her one room, to move into a little house so like her cousin's; even to have a girl come in and help her with the work. She got work now. She was respectably married and the rich ladies in the big houses came back to her for clothes. Stanton was a carpenter working for the corporation and she loved the way he dressed and looked sharp. She remembered seeing him walking down the dusty road when she had been pregnant with Mikey. Who would believe that one day she would be his wife, have a wedding ring with both their names on it? Only his family made her uneasy.

She knew they did not like her from the start, had hated the way they crowded around – so many of them that she couldn't count. He had told her that two of his brothers were in England, but he never said how many were left behind. They were littered all over the cool brick room, flowing off the settee, wedged into every corner. It was as if everybody connected with him had tried to cram into that room. Stanton told her later that they were worried about the fact that she was two years older than him. She had not thought about age before. Stanton was always so kind and responsible. Look at how Beresford had treated her and his own children. He was seven years older than her and yet he couldn't be responsible. Adella had looked at Stanton anxiously as he told her what his family said. 'Dem right, yu know. A is two years older dan yu an a have two pickney.'

Stanton had laughed, lines creasing at the corners of his eyes. She always loved the way he laughed, the way his head went back and his eyes gleamed with the pleasure he felt.

'Is not my family yu gwine married,' he said airily. 'An a doan tink yu is ole fowl yet. Yu tell me how yu come fe get pregnant an a doan have no reason to disbelieve yu.'

She had been frightened that he would leave her. That he would seize the excuse of her age to leave her with her swelling belly and push her back down into the despair he had dragged her from. She had almost decided to go back to the country, try to salvage something from her life before her journey into town. But his eyes had been so steady she found that she trusted him.

Yes, they had been happy in Kingston. Stanton used to work hard then. He would come home in the evening, sit at the table in the outhouse kitchen and watch her as she prepared his dinner. He had been good with the children, taking them for walks and bringing them unexpected treats.

'Yu too good to de pickney dem,' she told him one day when he came back from the beach, carrying a sleeping Mikey in his arms, Danny trotting beside him looking happy and content. 'Yu really spoile dem bad.'

'A haffe get inna practice,' he told her, patting her swollen belly. 'A gwine have a son soon an a waan fe help out wid ihm and do tings wid ihm.'

'It might be a girl chile,' she had told him teasingly. 'A mean is two son a have already an bwoy chile no plentiful in eida fe we family.'

The smile had gone from his face and his eyes had narrowed. 'A doan want no girl chile. A want a son fe carry me name,' he had said coldly.

She should have guessed his obsession then: his burning need to have a boy of his own. But she had only felt a slight uneasiness and then the frown had gone, the smile coming back. It disarmed her as it always did. 'We won't bad-mouth de pickney,' he said now. 'A tink we should wait till it born. But a did sey a prayer fa de birth.'

It was when Delores was born, when he finally realised that the boy child he wanted was just a dream, that things had changed.

'A didn't want no girl chile,' he said angrily, looking indifferently down at the small sleeping bundle in the cradle he had carved. 'How come yu have girl chile now?'

Adella could hardly believe that he was acting like that. He had been so nice before.

'We can have anada bwoy chile next time,' she said hopefully.

'Anada bwoy chile?' he asked heatedly. 'What yu mean anada bwoy chile, dem two is fe yu. I don't have none yet.'

She told herself that it was the disappointment he was feeling, the shock of not getting what he wanted after he had pinned all his hopes on a boy. He had refused to allow the possibility of a girl, preparing for a boy as if he knew for certain that was what they would have.

After Delores was born, he still treated her well, still treated the two boys as if they were his own. He taught them to play cricket. He often took them to the wide green common land across the white stone road with its covering of marl; and gathered other children who were there flying kites or playing marbles. He was good with children. He would organise them into teams and act as referee. Often Adella would go down to the blue-painted wooden gate or lean against the neatly staked fence, watching them playing in the cool shade of gently swaying trees. She would stay there until the heat of the noonday sun took the shadows away. It made a vivid contrast between the white marl and the deep, deep green of the tall grassland and gave a strange echo to the voices at play. Then she would shift, walk along the mud path back to the house where the woman who worked for her would have Delores in her arms.

Yet despite the time he spent with the children, things had changed. It took her a while to pinpoint what it was. He still smiled and joked and planned all the things they would do. But now he talked about going to England, making money and coming back rich. She had long given up that dream, content with her house and the fact that she now had a maid. But he was so full of life, so sure of what

152

they could achieve, that she had gone along with it. Yet she felt uneasy with the change in him. The restlessness she saw, the bitterness in the eyes that rested on the boys, dismissed the baby, and seemed to look accusingly at her. At first she thought she imagined it, made sensitive by his reaction to his daughter. But the eyes would linger a moment too long, the look unmistakable; and the restlessness soon became concrete plans to leave Jamaica. Adella told herself she was as full of excitement as he. After all, she had always wanted to board the long cargo ship and sail over the seas. But now it had a hollow ring. She saw the future looming, uncertain, full of pitfalls. On her shoulder, haunting her, the spectre of the yard that she had lived in; the children crying and hungry. A man like Beresford dragging her down, exchanging money for favours. Deep in her heart she did not want to start again, not now that she had achieved what she most wanted out of life. She was respectable, could go to church again. Now she could invite people up from the country, feeling happy as they marvelled about the coolness and the space in her brick house. Yes, Stanton was her man. He had taken her in and made life good for her. The fact that she could work and earn good money was all due to him. Whatever he wanted she would accept. She loved him and she trusted him.

They had talked about the move, long talks going way into the night. Sometimes the faint greyness of the new day would find them still talking, planning what they would do. He would go to England first, stay with one of his brothers who had been there since the war ended. He would work hard and save enough to prepare a place for her. Then she would join him, leaving the children with Granny Dee or with Claudia who always wanted Delores to come and stay with her. They would stay two years in all, saving all they could, and after that they would come back, buy land and a little shop. It was going to be so easy. Stanton had a trade. 'A well-respected man,' she often heard people say of him. They would be able to buy a house way up on the hill or in the bay at St Ann's where she had always wanted to live.

Adella had discussed the plans with Granny Dee and Claudia, and they had agreed to take the children.

'But what yu gwine do while Stanton gone a England?' Granny Dee asked worriedly. 'Is three children yu have now; and plenty money on de house.'

'A have some money put by, an Stanton will send money fram

what ihm earn,' she said simply.

'They say you can earn a lot of money in England, more than in the islands,' Claudia said now. 'Stanton is a skilled man and he is earning well; so if he goes to England he should do very well.'

Claudia, quiet as ever, supported her all the way. She had trained to be a teacher and now taught at the village school and Adella couldn't suppress her pride in how well her sister talked.

'Why yu doan go a England, Claudia?' she asked her sister. 'Yu could get rich real quick, seeing as ow yu have book learning and yu bright.'

Claudia smiled. 'You know I don't like to travel,' she said gravely. 'And anyway, I don't mind just taking Delores while you go. I don't need to get rich and I manage all right down here.'

Claudia had never changed. She had studied in town, sharing the cramped room at their cousin's house with Adella for two years while she went to the training college. Adella knew she could have got a job in Kingston but Claudia hated the city and had gone back to the country as soon as she could. Yes, Claudia hated travel, or anything that disturbed the routine of her existence.

Stanton had boarded the ship on a Wednesday, looking full of life and expectation. She had watched him go, feeling the pain of losing him, wondering how long it would be before she saw him again. But she had trusted him. He would send for her and together they would make a better life for the children.

Adella sighed, eyes focusing on the darkening window, the sound of the television penetrating her memories. She shifted heavily in her chair, feeling a sudden need for a cigarette. Fumbling awkwardly underneath the cushion of the chair she withdrew the packet she kept there. They thought she had cut down on smoking. She had heard Carol telling Eena triumphantly that she had stopped; but at times like these she needed a cigarette. It was the only thing that kept her sane. She lit the tip clumsily, inhaled deeply, dissolving into a fit of coughing before settling to watch the smoke drift up towards the ceiling. She had expected so much from England, so much in return for the two hard years of her life they planned to stay. Her eyes moved around the tiny room, resting on the yellow-patterned council wallpaper. Yes, she had expected a lot, all the dreams of a better future for her children. 'Stanton let me dung,' she thought sadly, remembering the disappointment of arrival, of finding that there was no place to stay. He had not kept his promise then, and she had suffered for it. 'But ihm did sen fa me, like we plan.' She held on to the thought, inhaled it with the next draw on the cigarette..It was a comforting thing, persuading herself that he would come back. He had sent for her. This was not the first time she had waited for him. Twenty years, thirty, what did it matter how long she had to wait? Stanton would come back and that was all that mattered.

Eighteen

Strange harsh lights penetrated her closed lids, stabbing at the pupils. They seemed to swell in her head, aching against her temples. It was hard to breathe, the sound of her labouring lungs was loud and ugly in her ears. She tried to move her arm, but it was heavy, aching with pain. Her whole body felt heavy, and something was pressing down on her chest. She struggled to lift her lids. Where was she?

'Lie still, mum. It's all right, you're going to be all right.' Was that strained voice Carol's? What was happening? She tried to think, forced the clogging mist from her mind. The effort made her head ache, but she had to remember this couldn't be a dream, not with so much pain. She could remember being in bed. Yes, that was it. She was in bed, she had had a stroke. Was that where she was? Where was Stanton? Her mind strained, head swimming from the effort. 'Stanton neva come back last night,' she thought finally, 'but ihm wasn't to know.'

A sudden thought occurred to her, and she tried to force her lids apart. She had to call out to the Westons, but why were they making so much noise? It was all around her, and why was the light so bright? She tried to move again, tried to throw off the suffocating thing binding her chest.

'Don't move, mum.' Carol's voice came again, full of worry and tears. 'The doctor will come back soon, they are trying to get you a bed. It won't be long to wait.'

Adella's brow furrowed, that was what was nagging at her mind.

Why was Carol's voice like a big woman's, and where were Mikey and Delores to take care of her? She couldn't stay here, not with the children to get ready and all that extra overtime at work this week. She had to get up; somehow she had to move. She tried again, concentrating all her effort on forcing reluctant lids apart. Light stabbed at her eyes, causing her to blink, and narrow them for protection. She peered around cautiously, not able to move anything but her eyes. She was in a blue-curtained cell. A strip light stabbed down from a white ceiling, and the smell of hospital penetrated the fog in her brain. She could just see the machine, the tubes around her, feel the thing on her face, on her chest that pinned her down.

Tendrils of memory stirred, forced their way into her consciousness. She had been in bed. Had woken to the sound of strangled breathing, a hand shaking her roughly. Her eyes shifted, found her daughter's anxious face as it peered down at her. 'So much like me when a was young,' she thought sadly. 'Caral neva let me dung, not like de rest.'

It was Carol who had found her, she remembered that. Coming awake to the commotion and the fear in her daughter's eyes. 'Lie still, mum, don't move, please don't move,' Carol had said, as she struggled in the tangle of the bedclothes. 'I phoned the ambulance and they are coming.'

She wondered how long they had waited for the ambulance to come. She knew the hospital was just down the road and she had waited patiently; hearing Carol on the other side of the room, dialling, talking rapidly, dialling again. She lost count of the phone calls. But she waited, mind unable to stay too long in one place. She was used to waiting in dim half-lights. This was just another wait.

Adella had finally wondered if she was losing track. It seemed an endless wait. She had been in the ambulance before. Five minutes it took from her house to the hospital. She supposed it just seemed long, time stretching out with her pain and the noisy, laboured breathing in the room. Carol was walking up and down, muttering under her breath; and Adella tried to concentrate on her movement, counting the footsteps in her head. It was comforting somehow, the regular rhythm of the steps, the pause as she turned before going back the other way. It soothed her, listening to the even tread. She must have drifted off to sleep, because when she lifted her lids again the footsteps no longer sounded. Adella could hear Audrey's voice and realised that they thought she was still asleep.

156

'How long since you called the ambulance?' Audrey was asking worriedly.

'Nearly an hour.'

'Are you sure?' the older daughter persisted.

'Of course I'm sure,' Carol said impatiently. 'I even rang them again; she's going to lie here and die five minutes from the hospital,' she said in frustration.

'Let's give them another five minutes and then we'll just have to take her in the car.' Audrey tried to soothe. Adella felt a slight smile. Trust Audrey to be practical.

'We can't,' Carol wailed, 'supposing we cause her more harm; supposing we killed her?' She dissolved into helpless sobbing; the sound loud and distressed, trapped in the room despite her attempts to muffle it.

'Look, calm down,' Audrey said impatiently. 'Listen, we can't leave her here. At the rate they're going, mum'll die waiting for that ambulance.'

Carol only cried harder, and Adella felt sorry for her. Despite her bulk and her tough appearance, Carol was soft. She wished she could say something to comfort her; but her tongue lay heavily in her mouth, and the fog was filling her head again.

She drifted in and out of consciousness, the waiting endless, the pain in her back and in her head increasing. She could not feel anything on her good side and she wondered if that had been crippled too. It had gone on like that, half-formed thoughts, sounds intruding into her cotton-wool world. There had been movement at one point, a tilting like when she had ridden on the Ferris wheel and thought she was going to fall off. Then had come the bumpy feel of driving along bad roads. And now she was in a little curtained cell with the stabbing light hurting her eyes; and her daughter's anxious face, leaning over.

'What . . . a . . . doing . . . ya?' she asked, after several attempts, spacing the words carefully. Her throat ached when she spoke, but she was glad that the sound came out all right. She did not want another set of endless lessons. She was too old to learn to speak again.

'You had another stroke, mum,' Carol said gently. 'But the doctor said your condition has stabilised and they are going to find a bed for you in intensive care.'

She wanted to nod, but her head was held rigidly by the thing that pressed into her face. She wasn't sure what intensive care was, but if Carol thought it was okay she wouldn't worry. She closed her eyes again, trying to block out the light, seeing images that jumbled together. A man with a middle parting, looking sharp. Ships pulling away from Kingston harbour. The house, her house with the tenants and the leaking roof. Where was Stanton now, she wondered vaguely. She had heard something about him breeding a little girl. Or had she dreamt it? Her mind felt muddled, and she clung desperately to the image of him, so full of hope and pride, walking up the long ridged plank to the ship. Stanton would come back, and all she had to do was wait. She would keep faith with him.

Her head was clearer when she opened her eyes again, and she looked around, searching anxiously for Carol. She felt herself relax as she found the familiar face, right where it had been all along.

'Whe Audrey gone?' she asked faintly.

'I'm here, mum,' Audrey said, face appearing over the bed. 'I just went out to find out how much longer you'd be here.'

She could tell by the tightness of the voice that she had been there a long time. 'What de time?' she asked, trying to establish how long.

Audrey's head disappeared, came back again. 'It's just past one.'

She was surprised how late it was. She must have been lying in her little, over-bright cell for the whole morning. Her lips felt dry and she licked them. 'Yu can gi me some wata?'

'The doctor said you're not to drink anything,' Carol said reluctantly. 'They said it's in case they have to give you treatment.'

'Whe Eena and Delores?' she asked now. 'Ow come dem not ya fe see me?'

She saw the uneasy look in Carol's eyes; the way her gaze shifted. And she knew the answer. They would be too busy to come to see her. Delores wouldn't want to take the day off work in case she needed a day later in the year. Eena, who had gone back to school, would be at home studying. It was like that when she had the gout. She could remember waiting for them to visit and listening wordlessly to the excuses when they phoned to say they were not coming. She felt a tightness in her throat and swallowed painfully. At least Carol and Audrey were there with her, so she was not alone.

She heard footsteps moving about, heard them enter the room.

'The doctor would like to examine your mother now.' The voice

158

was crisp and full of authority, 'If you would like to wait outside, I'll call you as soon as he's finished.'

'When is she going to the ward?' Audrey asked coldly.

'We're doing our best to find her a bed, but I'm sure she's quite comfortable here,' the voice replied.

'Quite comfortable? I've been here for three hours and in that time a nurse has looked in on her twice.'

'I'm sorry, Miss Johnson, but we are rather busy at the moment and your mother is not in any danger, I can assure you. Now, if you would like to wait outside . . .'

Carol's head appeared briefly, her eyes red and puffy, and Adella wondered how she hadn't noticed the tears before.

'Is all right, man,' Adella croaked, squeezing her hand. 'A not gwine die yet, do what de nurse tell yu.'

The room seemed over-crowded all of a sudden, white-coated figures peering down at her, poking at her. It was like having a baby. They talked as if she couldn't hear them, as if she was not there.

'How are you feeling, Mrs Johnson?' the doctor asked finally.

'A feel all right,' she said, wondering why doctors always asked such stupid questions. If she was feeling all right, she wouldn't be lying there with tubes in her arms, and all the things pressing her down in the bed under the harsh lights.

'These a little uncomfortable?' he asked, pointing to the thing on her chest.

'Is all right,' she said, not wanting to cause any trouble.

'Not to worry, we'll soon have them off,' he assured her, not even listening to what she had said. He stood up, and she heard him talking with the other white-coated people – long impressive words that she could barely understand. She felt safe with them. They knew so many big words, they had to be very bright. Not that she knew what they all meant, but none of that really mattered. They knew what they were talking about, and they looked so professional as well.

Her chest felt lighter, now that the thing was no longer pressing down on it; but why did it hurt to breathe? The pain was like a fire and she wished they would give her something for it. She could hear the harshness of her breathing, loud in her ears. She tried to call out, to move her head. It was no use, the effort was too much for her. It had been like that before, she remembered, when she had been sick. She tried to concentrate on the memory, felt it slipping away, let it go. She could wait for it to come back. Time slipped past, dragging and hanging heavily, but moving on and on. She heard Carol and Audrey come back, but her lids were too heavy to open. Somebody took her good hand. 'Mum, are you all right?' Carol's voice asked anxiously. Adella squeezed the hand feebly. She felt weak all over and couldn't understand the sudden draining. Her mind seemed out of control, veering from subject to subject. She wondered how long she had been there now. Her mouth seemed to be sinking in on itself, gums coming close together; and she realised that somebody had taken her teeth out. It made her feel naked, and she wondered if she looked as mash-mouthed as she felt. She could remember other people dying, the struggle to get their teeth back in, so that they would look right for the lying in state in the coffin. Adella pushed the thought away uneasily, concentrating on the warm firm grip of her youngest daughter. She could not go yet. Stanton had not come back, and he would never know she had kept faith.

How long was it since she had been in England? She tried to remember, brow furrowing with concentration. How old was Eena? She had been pregnant with her when she came over on the ship. She remembered the ship sailing to Trinidad; the strong raw smell of salt and the fresh wind. They had arrived at night and the coastline had been a surprise, it had been so much like Jamaica, coconut palms had waved in the breeze and the wharf had been full of noise and bustle. People had got off in Port of Spain, and she had felt a strong urge to do so. Suddenly she wanted to turn back before they headed out to sea and it was too late. Her mind moved backwards to the last days before she had left home. She could remember the letter coming, the English postmark. She had seen one before. Stanton's brothers used to write to him, a long exchange of letters in the years it took him to make his preparations to leave the island. She had looked at the flimsy blue envelope, turned it over and over in her hand, almost reluctant to see the contents. He had been in England for eighteen months and had not sent a single letter. Adella had been disappointed, not wanting to believe that he had abandoned her; not able to believe anything else. 'Dere's no disgrace inna it if de man good fa nuting,' Granny Dee had said, comforting her when she had come up to town and heard the news. But Granny Dee had been wrong, like her friends and children were wrong. Stanton was a good man and he would never abandon her.

The letter had money – enough to pay her passage – and he had told her how much he was missing her and looking forward to seeing her again. She had been so full of joy, packing and taking the first bus back to Beaumont, loving the importance as her news went round the village like wildfire. All the people who had pitied her, talked about her husband's desertion – they all had to eat their words, admire her because she was going abroad, and her husband had made it rich enough to send money for her passage and for new clothes.

She tried to open her eyes, feeling the pressure of the harsh light against her lids. There was a drumming in her ears and she tried concentrating her mind on it.

It had been raining the day she left Jamaica. The water hissing and pounding against the zinc roof. Adella had slept badly the night before, dreams peopled with nightmare figures, Mada Beck rising from her grave under the spreading branches of the old tamarind tree, and she had woken up cold inside; scared of leaving the familiar smells and things. Granny Dee had come up to see her leave, crowding into the little house with Aunt Ivy, Aunt Vi and her parents. Aunt May and Juni had come, too, using the excuse to visit their beloved town. Yet the house seemed empty and echoing, without the familiar noise of children playing, fighting and just moving around with their usual cheerful disregard. Everything had been dripping, sounds muffled by the cloak of rain. The swishing of wet leaves on the trees across the road was the only sound penetrating the rain noises.

'Is a bad omen,' Aunt May said solemnly, standing at the door and allowing the rain to splash against her feet as it drove on to the concrete doorstep.

Adella felt the fear bubbling up inside her; the harbour water suddenly sharp in her memory. Mada Beck once told her about going on a boat: days and days of water and always the fear of drowning. Like all the other members of her family she could not swim, and sea-water fascinated and terrified her. 'May, doan bad mouth de chile jus when she going a fareign,' Granny Dee said disapprovingly. 'Yu should a pray fa her and gi her yu blessing.'

Aunt May muttered under her breath, making no attempt to hide her envy. 'If me husband did live, is we woulda go a fareign. We woulda rich by now an could live in town all de time.'

Adella felt sorry for Aunt May. How close she had come to being

161

like her. Bitter and unforgiving, her dreams trampled in the dust of Kingston; no alternative but to go back to the country – defeated. Instead, she was going to England, going to join her husband. He had obviously done well to be able to send her so much money and he talked about England as if it was the promised land. How many times had she read his letter in the weeks she waited for her papers to be ready? But now she was going and it seemed that all of Jamaica was weeping, shrouded in rain clouds and silence.

She wished they would put the tubes back; even that weight would be better than the pain in her chest. The way she could count every breath she took because it was such hard work. There was a thin mist in front of her eyes and everything seemed to waver through it. She wanted her children, all of them.

'Whe Mikey and Delores?' she croaked, adding, 'Eena come yet?'

'We're trying to find Mikey,' Carol's voice said, coming from a long way away, sounding faint and distressed. 'We left a message with the London underground people, and they said they would tell him as soon as his train came back into the depot.'

She felt disappointed, brows furrowing. Mikey would want to know she was sick. She knew that he would come, that he would drop everything to be with her. Mikey was a good boy, he always looked out for her. It was not his fault Stanton wanted a boy child of his own. Stanton took away his confidence, all because she had failed. It weighed heavily on her: the fact that she produced four girls. Not that she didn't love them; but her failure to give him a boy had driven Stanton away. She clung to that thought, dissected it. 'Anyway it doan matta now,' she told herself, 'Stanton love me still and we bot getting ole. Is long time since ihm dump Gladys. Stanton gwine come back and a did keep faith wid ihm.'

'Whe Eena?' she persisted, needing the children around, needing their strength. The one blessing was that they never deserted her. So many children did that nowadays. They all followed fashion and did what the white children did to their parents.

'I think she's coming later,' Carol said evasively. 'She just has a few things to do and then she will come.'

She knew she was lying, Eena wasn't coming. But she could wait anyhow. 'De way de chile resemble Stanton, she could almost be ihm chile,' she mused. The thought pleased her, shifted a little of her guilt, and a fleeting smile appeared on her lips. Stanton could

162

never abide sickness. Always avoided it. It didn't mean he didn't care; just that he could never abide it.

She was dying. The thought came to her stark and raw, making her heart jump. She was going to lie here and die, waiting for a bed. 'A caan die here,' she told herself, 'not here, not yet. If a die Stanton not gwine have nobody fe come back to; and de children not gwine respeck ihm.'

She forced the panic down, concentrated on clearing her head. 'What de time?' she asked painfully. Her throat ached all the time now, her head heavy with the cotton wool inside, her mouth raw with thirst, her throat dried out and scraping.

'Ten to three,' Carol said, adding, 'I'm going to see why they haven't moved you yet.'

Adella's fingers tightened on her hand. 'Mek Audrey go,' she said, not wanting her to leave. She felt she was drawing strength from Carol and she was afraid to let the hand go. It didn't matter anyway, they were not going to move her. Not that she minded. She was used to being still.

She closed her eyes, tired out by the effort of talking, of keeping her mind pinned on one thing. She felt tired, her bones aching with all the years of struggle and pain. All she wanted to do was rest. It would be a long time yet. Why did the young have to be so impatient? She wondered if she had been like that; realised she had. How much she had wanted to do, to see. She had left the countryside, impatient to go somewhere and make something of herself. But no, it had been earlier than that. Waiting for the ackee season, standing tall against the measuring wall as Granny Dee measured, year in year out, seeing if she was tall enough to carry the ackee stick. She had been too impatient to wait. Then the day had arrived, and soon she had hated ackee picking, waiting for the day when she no longer had to take her turn. Then there had been school. She had been so impatient to leave. Claudia had stayed, had become a teacher and kept her pride and dignity. Yes, she had been impatient; leaving for Kingston before she was fully grown. That was where her failure started. She had let everybody down, sleeping with Beresford when he already had a wife. She had wanted so much for her children. Wanted them to have a better life. Wanted to protect them from the life she had had. Yet all of them had suffered hardship, gone hungry, as she never had as a child.

'Adella.' She blinked, straining her ears, widening her eyes to clear

163

the gathering mist. It couldn't be, she must be hearing things.

'Adella.'

She moved her head around, saw him through the mist, a faded brown picture, with the painting of coconut palms and a calm sea behind him.

'A seeing black an white,' she told herself, blinking her eyes again as the image wavered.

'Stanton?' she asked hesitantly.

'Yes, mum, what is it?'

She heard Audrey's voice in the background and ignored it. 'Is yu, Stanton? Is yu come back?'

'We tried to phone him,' Audrey said, worry in her voice. 'We couldn't get him, he was still at work. We tried to phone and tell him.'

What was the child on about? There was Stanton looking at her, wearing the same suit as in the picture. He had not aged at all, he was still the same and he was smiling the same smile she had always loved.

'A did sey yu would come back,' she said triumphantly. 'A did sey yu wasn't goodfanuting.'

He stayed there, smiling, just smiling, and her mouth moved in a painful smile. It was hard to focus: but that was okay. Stanton was here now and nothing mattered. She knew she was dying, that was why he was at her bedside, smiling encouragingly at her. He always hated sickness, so she had to be really bad for him to be there. She shifted her head slightly, seeing shapes behind him, behind the picture of the coconut tree and the calm brown sea.

Mada Beck and Granny Dee, Aunt Ivy, Aunt May and Juni – who she could swear somebody had written and said was shot dead somewhere in town – all of them were there smiling. Granny Dee was still the same, looking sad and brave, just like the day she had boarded the ship. Aunt Ivy was just the same, Aunt Vi stern as when she sat in the yard teaching dressmaking.

'They're not going to move her.' Adella heard the words penetrating her happy state, the bitterness eating into her consciousness.

'Well they can't just leave her here,' Carol said panicking. 'She's getting worse, even I can see that.'

'We'll have to wait till the doctor comes back,' Audrey responded grimly. 'She's been lying here all day, and they haven't even bothered to give her something to make her feel better.'

She wanted to tell them that she was all right now, that she had not felt better in a long time. Everybody was there and they were not condemning her. They knew she had done her best.

She heard him call her name again. Softly, in the secret way that was just between the two of them. Adella forced her lids apart, feeling apprehensive. But he was there, fainter now, more faded. Everyone was there. All the children smiling at her. Loyal now. They had never blamed her, kept telling her how great she was, how much she did for them. Everyone was there, and it didn't matter that the doctor didn't come, and the bed they promised would be too late. Stanton had come back, just like she knew he would. He had come back and she had kept faith; and now he knew she had waited. The images flickered, faded slowly as her eyes dimmed. But it didn't matter now, nothing mattered. She had fulfilled her promise to herself and she knew in her bones that they would keep a Binkie for her like Mada Beck and Granny Dee.

'All dat respeck,' she murmured to herself, and this time her eyes smiled as they closed.

Also of interest:

Joan Riley
The Unbelonging

'*The Unbelonging* is a small book but not a slight one. Riley writes economically and with a fine ear for arguments.'

The Times

'There was no oil to rub in her scalp, and she was too afraid to tell them that twice a week was too often to wash her hair . . .'

'Our families have been fragmented, and many girls came here to fathers or stepfathers who were strangers . . .'

Joan Riley

Summoned to Britain by a father she has never known, eleven-year-old Hyacinth finds that she has exchanged the warmth and exuberance of the backstreets of Kingston, Jamaica for the gloom of British inner-city life, finding herself in a land of strangers with hers the only black face in a sea of white.

But Hyacinth is not a victim as, through academic achievement and dreams of her homeland, she survives and triumphs against the hostility of her classmates and threatened violence at home from her father, sustained forever by the sure knowledge that her dreams hold the truth.

This is a moving story of self-discovery and survival from the popular author of *Romance, Waiting In the Twilight* and *A Kindness To The Children*.

Fiction £5.99
ISBN: 0 7043 3959 5

Joan Riley
A Kindness to the Children

Jean has 'returned home' to Jamaica for a holiday – yet is
unable to find the support and help she desperately needs.
Seeking comfort in alcohol and casual affairs, her life
deteriorates inexorably. And, as relatives and friends refuse
to face the reality of her decline, her despair threatens to
destroy, not only herself, but the lives of her children.

With powerful narrative, Joan Riley, in her most
accomplished work todate, exposes corruption, sexism and
poverty, unveiling the dangers that haunt many black
women. This uncompromising novel reveals with sympathy
and understanding the horrific consequences of cultural
distortion.

'Joan Riley has an extraordinary ability to portray pain and
loneliness . . . her novels become powerful parables of the
creation and destruction of illusions . . . It is this quality
which steels Joan Riley's work and the lives of her
characters.'   Chris Searle

'Joan Riley handles her material with great skill.'
                                                   British Book News

Fiction   £6.99
ISBN: 0 7043 4319 3

Joan Riley
Romance

'The way Riley writes can be simple and beautiful. She is one of the most unaffected writers we have in Britain.'   *Chic*

'Should appeal to any woman who has fought to assert her own identity.'   *Everywoman*

At twenty-seven, Verona is bright and capable, but confused. Defiantly fat, she seeks refuge by imagining herself the blonde, blue-eyed heroine of the latest Mills & Boon romance; where the heroes are tall, dark, handsome . . . and white.

Her sister Desiree is a housewife who spends her life looking after John and the children. Her friend Mara has rid herself of her husband, got a good education and found a job – which she manages along with a home and two children – but Desiree believes that, for her, change is impossible.

Then Grandpa Clifford and Granny Ruby arrive from Jamaica with a radical new approach to life – and both sisters start to rethink their lives, with unexpected results . . .

Fiction   £4.95
ISBN: 0 7043 4101 8